To the Creator who by design has made it all possible.
Mom & Dad, I thank you for everything.
To my mother in law Irene for her support during the writing of this book.
And finally to my dearest wife of nineteen years, love you always...

"Woe to the inhabitors of the earth and of the sea!
For the devil is come down unto you, having great wrath,
knowing that he has but a short time."
Revelations 12:12

PROLOGUE

The young doctor drove quickly through the endless fields of wheat. He was unfamiliar with the area and the dusty farmland roads were difficult to navigate. He knew, with the sun setting, he had to find the house before dark. There was little time to get there and Martha was already thirteen hours into labour.

At the end of a long track stood the old wooden house. It was just about dark and there was hardly a light on. He let himself in and made his way following the voices. Martha lay in the bed surrounded by a gathering of women. It was clear that after fourteen hours in labour she was drifting in and out of consciousness. Despite her contorted face, Dr Brockman was immediately struck by how young Martha was.

"How can we help you?" asked one of the women.

"Who are you?" asked Dr Brockman.

"I'm Annamae. Martha's sister."

Immediately the doctor saw the resemblance.

"Annamae, you will help me deliver this baby."

Turning to the other women, he said, "I need some more light in here and get me some clean towels and bowls of hot water."

Two hours passed and the unmistakable sound of a baby's cry filled the air.

"It's a boy!" said Annamae.

Dr Brockman then glanced up at the unconscious mother, before giving Annamae a knowing look.

CHAPTER 1

08 APRIL 1969

Martha laid her son in the small bed, took his hand and made the sign of the cross over him. With a gentle kiss to the forehead, she closed her eyes and said a silent prayer. It was hard to believe that tomorrow would be Simon's first birthday, so much had happened.

Martha lit the fire and made herself a cup of coffee. She sat back and reflected on the last year, the joy of her first child followed by the sadness of losing her husband in the war, and the thought that Simon would grow up to never know his father. So many sleepless nights staring into the darkness, the loneliness and the tears that ran down her face onto the pillow. *Why did you take my husband, Lord?* Her faith at times was unable to overcome her anger at God. She clung to her sanity by thinking of Simon; it was all she had and he gave her a reason to live.

Annamae did not need reminding that it was a special day. She wrapped the gift, got dressed, and drove the short journey over to her sister's home. From childhood it had always been a difficult relationship. Despite the obvious resemblance, Martha was always the prettier one, the one that got all the attention, the one who all the boys spoke about. It was impossible for Annamae not to harbour a deep jealousy of her sister. However, from childhood she had mastered the art of never letting her true feelings show.

For the first time Annamae witnessed her sister suffering and somehow felt it was justified; after all, her own life had not been easy and Martha had seemingly gone through life without a care in the world. Suddenly, it was the first time Martha had to face real pain and it made Annamae feel better.

The events of the last year had done much to bring the sisters closer to each other. In the weeks after the death of Martha's husband, John, Annamae visited more often and spent an increasing amount of time with Martha and Simon, who became the centre of their lives.

"Come on in," said Martha, "the birthday boy is just finishing his breakfast in the kitchen."

Martha and Annamae sat at the table, lit the solitary candle on the cake, sang happy birthday and together blew it out.

Annamae opened her handbag and handed Simon a gift. Martha took Simon's small hands and together they opened it. Inside the silver box was a small white cross.

"It's for above his bed," said Annamae.

"It is perfect," said Martha. "Thank you so much. Now, how does a cup of coffee and a slice of birthday cake sound?"

"That would be great thanks."

"How are you doing, Martha?"

"Oh, I'm fine, keeping myself busy."

"No, I mean really how are you doing? I'm referring to your faith."

Martha paused for a moment to collect her thoughts; Annamae had never asked her this before and the gift of the cross was also so out of character.

"It is hard but I'm slowly coming to terms with losing John." She looked over at Simon, "I have a lot to live for."

The sisters' conversation was stopped by a knock at the door.

"You expecting visitors?" asked Annamae.

"No, I'm not – I'm not sure who that could be."

Martha went to the door, stopping briefly to look in the mirror and fix her hair. She opened the door and in front of her was an attractive young man.

"Hello, Martha. My name is Dr William Brockman. You may not remember me – I delivered your son."

Martha stared at the young man's face, searching her memory. There was something definitely familiar about him. She remembered Annamae telling her about a doctor that arrived that night and she promised herself that she must pay him a visit to say thank you. However, with the death of John, she had completely forgotten about him. She composed herself.

"Please, come in. My sister is here and would love to see you. Dr Brockman, you remember Annamae, don't you?"

"Of course I do. How are you, Annamae?"

"Oh, I'm very well, Dr Brockman. Can I offer you a coffee?"

"Sure I'd love that."

As Annamae poured the coffee, the young doctor passed his hand through Simon's hair.

"Let me take a look at you," he said.

With that he picked Simon up out of his high chair and looked intensely into his eyes. Martha noticed that her baby did not cry but returned the intense look. Martha broke the moment's silence.

"Dr Brockman, do you know it's Simon's birthday?"

"Yes, I do. In fact, I have a gift for him in my car."

"You must have a really good memory to remember his birthday."

"Well, in general, I'd say its average but you never forget your first birth so it was easy for me, and I've become familiar with the area so finding your home was not too difficult."

"Oh, that is so nice of you. There is still some cake left; would you like to try a piece?"

"Ah no, thank you. This coffee alone is great and I can't stay too long as I need to get back for an appointment. In fact, I really should get going, Martha. Why don't we take a walk out to my car?"

"Annamae, can you stay with Simon? I won't be long."

"Sure, Martha. Have a safe journey, Dr Brockman."

"Thanks, Annamae. It's been great to see you again."

And with that Dr Brockman and Martha went out to the car.

Doctor Brockman opened the passenger door and picked up the immaculately wrapped gift and handed it to Martha. "This is the most important gift you can give to your son."

"Thank you so much, doctor. Not only for this but, more importantly, I never got the chance to thank you for delivering Simon. I'm forever grateful to you."

"I will see you again, Martha." With a hint of a smile, the young doctor got into his car and sped off, leaving a slow moving cloud of dust behind him.

Martha picked up the half-drunk cup of coffee and put it in the sink. *He really did not stay very long*, she thought, *but it was so nice to see him.*

"What have we got here?" she said as she excitedly showed Simon the present. She put it on the table in front of him and sat down. "Annamae, you know I've just realised that I've not even asked Dr Brockman for his number. I don't even know where he works, do you?"

"I've no idea. I'd imagine it would be at the main hospital in town. Anyway, I'm interested in seeing what he got Simon so, come on, let's open it."

Martha took her son's small hands and together they removed the paper to reveal a book wrapped in brown cloth. Martha read the cover to her son, "My First Bible."

Simon's small hand flicked at the pages with the colourful pictures.

"Wow," said Annamae "I was actually thinking of getting that for him. I'm so glad that I chose the cross instead."

"I know things have been difficult, Martha, but what about baptising Simon? I can have a chat with the parish priest to see when would be best. We don't need to invite anyone but we really need to have it done."

Martha knew Annamae was right. *Church*, she thought, *I've not been to church since John's funeral and that was over seven months ago. In fact, I used to be able to count on one hand the number of times I'd missed Sunday Mass since I was a little girl, yet I've not gone for so long now.*

"You know, Annamae, you are right. I'd appreciate that, please have a word with Fr. Mark, we need to get this done."

★

The church was empty, except for the front pew, which actually fitted the small group: Martha, baby Simon, Annamae, and a few of their neighbours (who Martha had chosen to act as Simon's godparents). After the short service, they all stood and gathered around the baptismal font. Fr. Mark had only recently been ordained. His voice was strong and it echoed through the empty church.

"Almighty and ever-living God, you sent your only son

into the world to cast out the power of Satan, spirit of evil, to rescue man from the kingdom of darkness, and bring him into the splendour of your Kingdom of Light. We pray for this child: set him free from Original Sin, make him a temple of your glory, and send your Holy Spirit to dwell with him. We ask this through Christ our Lord.

"Simon John Holman, I baptise you in the name of the Father," he poured water upon him, "and of the Son," he poured water upon him for a second time, "and of the Holy Spirit," he poured water upon him a third time and the baptism was complete. The small gathering then sang a short hymn that Martha had chosen.

"That was lovely," said Fr. Mark. "I'm just off to get changed and then I'm going for lunch. You are all welcome to join me. In fact, one of our parishioners has opened a café nearby. I can definitely recommend the home-made soup."

"Thanks," said Annamae. "But I have an appointment I really must get going."

"What about you, Martha?" asked Fr. Mark.

"Well, I can't promise Simon will be on his best behaviour but, if you're willing to take the chance, I'd love to join you."

Martha turned to Simon's God Parents. "What about you guys?"

"Thanks, Martha, but we really need to get going as well but we'll come round to visit you this week coming."

"Sounds good," said Martha. She strapped Simon into his pushchair and, turning to Fr. Mark, she motioned up at the sky. "I hope we don't regret it. Perhaps we should have taken the car."

"Don't worry, Martha; the rain should hold off. It's not too far and I need to make the effort to walk more rather than drive. Well, truth be told, what actually happened is I asked the bishop for a running machine and he told me I should just walk more."

"So, in other words Father, there's cut backs at the church as well, huh?"

Fr. Mark smiled.

The waitress put the two bowls of soup on the table and handed Martha the milk she had warmed up for Simon.

"You know it's great to see you again, Martha. Every Sunday Mass I look over to where you used to sit and wonder if I'm going to see you again. How have you been?"

"Well, I won't say it has been easy. In fact, it's been the hardest time of my life, but I am coping better than I was and Annamae has given me great support. We are closer now than we have ever been."

"I'm happy to hear that, Martha. Actually, I was a bit surprised when Annamae called to ask about arranging the baptism, I thought it was you. Both of you sound identical on the phone I knew you had a sister but I was under the impression that, ah, how should I say it? You were the spiritual one and she was less so?"

Martha smiled. "Yes, you are correct, Father. I got a bit of a surprise also when she suggested baptising Simon a couple of weeks ago. As kids, when I think back to the arguments she had with Mom every Sunday about going to Mass, it's so unlike her to encourage anything that involves religion."

"It's never too late, Martha."

"You're right. I'm really happy for her and, to be honest, being in the church today, it felt like coming home. I forgot how much it had been a part of me before John died."

"That is wonderful to hear. Perhaps I'll see you in church a bit more often?" Martha did not want to commit, so she just smiled, but she thought to herself: *yes, I think I am ready to make peace with God.*

"How is the soup?" asked the waitress.

"It's fantastic," said Martha.

"Can I get you anything else?"

"Do you have some more napkins? Simon's made a bit of a mess."

"Sure no problem, anything else?"

"Just the bill please," said Fr. Mark.

CHAPTER 2

Over the next nine years Martha dedicated herself to raising Simon. It was not easy. Times were hard, and living on a VA Pension meant she had to be frugal, but Simon wanted for nothing. Annamae continued to visit Martha and the bond between the two sisters continued to grow. Despite the fact that Martha took Simon to church every Sunday, the only time she got Annamae to go was when Simon made his First Communion.

*

"Well done," said Martha. She handed the exam results to Annamae to look at.

"I'm so proud of you," said Martha, "those are your best results yet. I told you that you can do anything you set your mind to."

"Yes, Mom," Simon replied, "but I've no idea what exactly I want to do."

"Don't worry. You will be guided. Right now, all you can do is keep working hard at school and continue to build your relationship with God. Would you like me to make you something to eat?"

"No, thanks, Mom, my stomach has not been good. I did not even eat lunch at school today, I think I'm just going to lie down."

Annamae put her hand on Simon's forehead. "It feels a bit warm. If you need anything, don't hesitate to give me a call. Otherwise, I'll be over to see how he is in the morning."

Martha was up all night. Simon's abdominal pain steadily got worse and at 5am she picked up the phone. "Annamae, can you come over? Simon is not well. He has started vomiting and the pain in his stomach has gotten worse. I'm really worried."

"I'll be there right away."

Not long after, Martha heard a knock on the door. Thinking it was Annamae, she shouted out from Simon's bedroom, "Come on in." But Martha looked up from Simon's bedside to see a man in a white coat standing in the doorway.

"We got an emergency radio call to come here. What's wrong with him?"

"It's his stomach. The pain started yesterday and it just got worse."

"The medic turned to Simon. "Can you put my hand on the spot where the pain is worst?"

Simon moved the medic's hand to the left side of his abdomen. The medic turned Simon onto his left side and hyperextended his right thigh. Simon cried out in pain and the medic looked at Martha.

"I suspect its appendicitis. We need to get him straight to the hospital."

Within minutes, Martha was in the back of the ambulance with Simon. The screaming siren shattered the still of the morning as it sped towards the town.

★

Martha and Annamae were seated in the waiting room when the door opened and the doctor came out of the operating

10

theatre. They both stood up together as soon as they saw him.

"He's going to be okay. You got him here just in time – it was acute appendicitis and it was about to burst."

As he was speaking, Martha observed over his shoulder another doctor coming out of the operating theatre. She made the briefest of eye contact with him and, despite the green surgical mask and head cap, she knew she had seen him before.

"Simon will have to spend two to three days here under observation. I doubt you got much sleep last night, Mrs Holman. Why don't you go home and get some rest? You can come back in the morning. Would you like me to arrange a lift for you?"

"No, thanks, doctor. Annamae has her car outside."

"Well, you may as well head home now; it will be a while before Simon wakes up. I'll see you tomorrow."

The sisters got in the car and left the hospital. It had been a long day. They were both tired and neither of them felt like talking much. Thinking about Simon, Martha said a silent prayer of thanks that he was going to be okay. Still, she could not get the image of that doctor out of her head. Suddenly the silence in the car was broken.

"I know who he was," said Martha.

Annamae took her eyes off the road and looked at Martha. "Who are your speaking about?"

"The doctor that delivered Simon – I saw him today at the hospital, coming out of the operating room. What was his name?"

"Oh, I don't remember, that was so long ago, Martha."

"Don't you remember? He gave Simon that Bible…"

"Yes, of course, I remember that, but I don't remember his name and, besides, I doubt it was him you saw today. I think you're just tired."

The following morning, Martha woke early. She took a shower, changed the sheets on Simon's bed and tidied his room. Looking out his window, she saw Annamae's car approaching.

"So, Martha, did you get some sleep last night?"

"Actually, yes I did. I must have been really tired, but I feel great today. I can't wait to see Simon."

"Do you mind if I just drop you off, Martha? I've a few things to do in town and then I will see you back here in a couple of hours."

"No problem and thanks once again for the lift. The mechanic says my car will be ready soon so you won't have to drive me everywhere."

"Not a problem, sis'. Give Simon my love."

★

"Good morning, Ma'am."

"My name is Martha Holman. I'm here to visit my son, Simon."

"Sure," said the receptionist, "let me see… it shows he is out of the operating room and in Ward D. In fact, you can have a seat over there and I'll let the nurse know you're here. She will come and take you through."

Martha walked towards the seating area, passing the staff photos displayed on the wall. They reminded her about that doctor but she still could not remember his name. Martha sat down and picked up a magazine from the table, when suddenly it came to her. She got up and walked back over to reception.

"Sorry to trouble you again, but does a Dr Brockman work here?"

"The name is not familiar – let me have a look... no, definitely. His name does not appear on our records."

"That's strange. Are you sure?"

"Pretty sure, perhaps he has his own practice. Why do you ask?"

"I thought I saw him working here yesterday."

"Excuse me for interrupting, but are you Martha Holman?"

"Yes I am."

"My name is Lindsey, I'm the head nurse. Simon is looking forward to seeing you. Would you like to follow me?"

"Sure," said Martha." Turning to the receptionist, she said, "Thanks anyway for your help."

★

Martha approached the hospital bed. *My baby*, she thought. She closed her eyes and kissed him on his forehead. "How are you feeling?" she whispered.

Simon did not reply but just stared at her without expression.

"The doctor told me yesterday you will have to stay here for a few days until you heal. I put a few things in this bag for you: a tooth brush, some clothes, underwear and, oh, I stopped off and bought you a new book as I know—"

Before Martha could complete the sentence Simon interrupted her. "It's good to be back with you, Mom."

Martha took her eyes off the book she was holding and looked at him. "What do you mean it's good to be back?"

"When I woke up this morning, I realised I had been taken away – away to somewhere I'd not been before. I was alone, drifting in space. The loneliness was frightening and I knew I was going to be there for a very long time. It was cold. I wanted to come back; I wanted a hug to feel human contact. I could see you. I called out but you were so far away, it felt like I would stay there forever, but I was given this chance to return."

"They would have given you an anaesthetic son. You would have been completely out of it. I'm sure it was just a bad dream you had." Martha tried to change the subject. "Annamae sends her love. She had a few things to do in town but she should be here in about—"

"You saw him, didn't you, Mom?"

"Saw who?"

"The doctor that came out the operating theatre."

"Yes… I spoke to him after the operation. He said you were going to be okay."

"No, Mom, the other doctor. You looked at him. You know the one I mean."

A chill ran down Martha's spine.

"You know him, don't you, Mom?"

"Ah yes, I thought I recognised one of the doctors coming out of the theatre."

"You do know he's not a doctor, Mom. Don't you?"

"You're scaring me, Simon. Why do you say he is not a doctor? And how do you know any of this?"

Simon did not reply. Martha leaned over the bed and hugged her son; she felt her whole body shaking. "I love you, son."

"Can I come in?"

She looked up from the bed to see a nurse standing at the door. "Sure," said Martha.

"The doctor will be here in a couple of minutes. He wants to see how Simon is doing."

Martha's heart started racing. She looked at Simon and knew what he was thinking.

"Is everything alright?" asked the nurse.

"Yes, everything's fine. It's okay if I stay, isn't it? I'd like to see the doctor when he arrives."

"I'm sure that will be fine."

Martha sat in the chair next to the bed. She held Simon's hand, her heart still racing as she waited to see the doctor come in.

"Good morning, Martha. I take it you got some rest last night?" The doctor observed a clearly shaken Martha. "Sorry, I did not mean to startle you, Mrs Holman. I told the nurse to let you know I was on my way."

"Ah yes, she did tell us. Sorry, I was just in a different world when you walked in."

"So, how's our patient doing?"

Simon looked at the doctor and smiled. The doctor picked up the clipboard next to his bed and reviewed it. "Well, everything looks good here; you are on your way to a full recovery. I'll ask the nurse to come in after lunch to put on a fresh bandage and then I'll come back and see you before I finish today. Mrs Holman, I'll need you to fill out a few forms for us – just formalities, nothing really. With it being an emergency, we did not get the chance to do it yesterday. If you follow me, I'll take you to reception – the nurse will assist you."

"Simon, I'll be back in a few minutes, okay?"

As they walked down the corridor, Martha turned to the doctor.

"May I speak with you for a minute?"

"Sure, my office is just coming up on the left. We can chat in there."

"Can I ask you, doctor, who assisted you with Simon's operation?"

"I had a couple of nurses with me; Miss Thompson and one or our most experienced nurses, Mrs Stevens. I assure you your son was in the best of hands."

"Were there any complications during the operation?"

"Why do you ask, Mrs Holman?"

"I'm just curious to understand how it went. So, were there any complications?"

"Simon had a bad reaction to the anaesthetic; his blood pressure became elevated and his heart rhythm erratic. However, his condition stabilised. It's rare, but it happens with some patients from time to time. However, there are no lasting effects."

"How exactly did you stabilise his condition?"

"Honestly speaking, we did not do anything. It seemed to just stabilise on its own. A bit unusual, I might add, but the human body is an amazing thing."

"Doctor, do you know a Dr Brockman by any chance?"

"No, can't say that I do."

"I'd really like to see him again. Is there a list of registered doctors in the area I can look up?"

"You can always call the AMA."

"Sorry, but what's the AMA?"

The doctor smiled. "American Medical Association. They will help you find him."

"Thank you, doctor. You have been really helpful, and don't worry; I'll go by reception on my way out and fill out those forms before I leave today."

★

"It was great to see Simon today," said Annamae. "I wish I could have stayed longer with him. I was not expecting to be so late getting back to the hospital. Half the problem is the traffic; I mean, just look at the number of cars in front of us, it is just getting worse and worse."

"You know, Annamae, I remembered his name but the hospital has no record of a Dr Brockman working there."

Annamae was caught out by the sudden change in the conversation but she recovered quickly. "Well exactly, that proves my point: it was not him you saw. Now, I really think you should just forget it, you're becoming obsessed."

Martha wanted to discuss it more. However, she sensed Annamae was going to dismiss everything she said so she decided to leave it at that. "You're probably right, Annamae. I should forget him. I really need to just get home, take a shower and have an early night."

Martha got home, dropped her handbag on the kitchen table, and picked up the phone. "Good afternoon, operator, do you have a number for the American Medical Association?"

"Sure, would you like me to connect you?"

"Yes, please."

"AMA, how can I direct your call?"

"Good afternoon, I'm trying to find out where my previous doctor is now working, I've lost touch with him over the years. His name was Dr Brockman, he definitely worked in Sidon up to ten years ago, however I can't remember his first name."

"Is this all the information you have, Ma'am?"

"Sorry, but yes."

"Can I call you back on this tomorrow? It will take me a while to look into it thoroughly and we are about to close for the day."

"Sure. That would be great, thank you."

Martha was awakened by the sound of the phone. She jumped out of bed and ran to answer it.

"I'm sorry, Ma'am, but I've gone back over ten years and we have no record of a Dr Brockman registered in Sidon. I even expanded the search to cover your entire state and nothing is showing up."

"Are you sure?"

"Oh, I'm very sure, Ma'am. Is there anything else I can help you with?"

"No, that is all, but thanks again for your help."

The days passed slowly, but finally the day neared when Martha would bring Simon home from the hospital. She could hardly contain her excitement. She spent most of the day cleaning the house from top to bottom. She went into Simon's bedroom determined to finally clear out all the clothes he had outgrown.

At the back of the drawer, in the side table next to his bed, the title caught her eye; My First Bible. Martha paused briefly. She picked it up and the memories of those years came flooding back, those special nights lying in bed reading the stories to Simon, and Martha was filled with nostalgia. She looked further into the drawer and saw the brown cloth it came wrapped in. She took it out and unfolded it. Suddenly she realised there was something written on it. She held it up to the light. It certainly looked like writing but not writing that she had ever seen.

CHAPTER 3

"Make a wish, " said Martha.

Simon blew out the sixteen candles. Martha thought to herself, *what a handsome young man,* and she knew she was not just seeing him through a mother's eyes.

"Happy Birthday, Simon," said Julia.

And with that she kissed him on the lips.

Martha looked at Annamae and both women felt their blood pressure rise. From the first time Simon brought Julia home, neither of the sisters had taken to her. Martha had tried her best to like Julia. She did not even know why she disliked her. She just knew how she felt and, as the weeks passed, Simon spent less time with her and more time with Julia. *He's getting older*, she told herself. *I have to accept he does not need me like before. I must learn to let go.* It did not help that Annamae took every opportunity to criticise Julia.

It was an overcast day but the rain was holding off. Martha and Annamae were sitting out enjoying a glass of iced tea.

"You know she is no good for him," said Annamae. "You need to stop making excuses for her and put an end to it."

"I'm not making excuses. I feel exactly the same as you do. They are both young and I just think if we gave it time it would just come to an end and we won't have to do anything."

"I don't agree, Martha. Either you have a talk with him or I will and, believe me, I'll put an end to it."

"Annamae, think about what you are saying. We can't let Simon know how we feel and I'm certainly not going to make him choose between me and her; there are other ways."

Annamae took a sip of her drink. "Oh believe me, Martha, I know there are other ways, lots of other ways…"

★

I must do it, he told himself. *I have no choice*. And, with that, he held her down on the bed. She reached up and grabbed his hair. Placing one hand over her mouth he plunged the knife deep into her heart. He kept his hand over her mouth as her head moved violently from side to side, her eyes filled with terror. It did not take long. He watched as the life quickly drained from her. There was no more movement – *it is done*.

"No!" he screamed.

With that, Simon awoke, shaking. He looked at his right hand; he could feel the knife. He held the side of his head; the pain was real from where his hair was pulled. Turning on the bedside light, he looked at the clock 3:05am. He took another look at his hand: he could still feel the knife; he could see the black handle but there was nothing there.

★

Summer was coming to an end and the following morning was chilly. Pulling up his collar, Simon kissed Martha and said goodbye.

"You really should be wearing a scarf!" she shouted out.

"I'll be fine, Mom."

Simon walked to the top of the road and waited on the school bus; it felt like time stood still. In the distance he saw the dust rising and his heart started pounding. As the yellow bus approached, he strained his eyes looking for Julia. She always sat in the same place but today her seat was empty.

"You getting in or not?" shouted the bus driver.

Simon composed himself and stepped into the bus. He stared at the empty seat as he walked down the aisle. Someone said, "good morning, Simon", but he did not respond.

★

Sherriff Joe immediately jumped in his car and raced from the police station. With a couple of miles to go before he got to the house, he slowed down, his eyes scanning the fields to the left and right. As he got out of his car, a senior officer approached him.

"What have we got?" asked the sherriff.

The officer took the black book out of his top pocket. "Victim's name is Julia Marie Osbourne, sixteen years old, daughter of Robert and Beth Osbourne. Her mother is too distraught to speak but her father told me they said good night to her and she went to her room about 8:30pm She never showed for breakfast this morning. Her mother found her in bed about 6:45am covered in blood. Her bedroom window was open."

"Your initial impression of the parents?" asked the sherriff.

"I don't think so, sir. I think we are looking for someone else."

"What is happening in the house right now?"

"The team is processing the crime scene. They will be a while yet, sir.

Sherriff Joe made his way through the house, taking in as much as possible. *These are wealthy people,* he thought. In the living room, Beth and Robert were sobbing uncontrollably. There was a young lady in a white coat with her arm around Beth trying to console her. He went upstairs, passing the forensic team that was waiting to enter the bedroom. He nodded at them and entered the room.

"I'm just about finished, Sheriff. I'll have them on your desk by this evening," said the police photographer.

On the bed lay the body of a young girl on her back, a knife protruding from her chest. In her right hand there were a few dark-coloured hairs. The bedside light had not even been knocked off the table. *This happened quickly*, he thought. Walking over to the open window, he looked out onto the ground and saw footprints.

★

Simon went through that school day in a trance; his mind not there but his body, as if programmed, went from classroom to classroom. He got onto the bus with one thing in mind: he was going to get off at Julia's house.

Simon stared out the window of the bus as they approached the farmhouse. Despite it being set back some distance from the road he could see flashing lights, a number of cars and people standing outside. He got out of the bus and walked towards the house.

There was a small study room at the end of the hallway that was away from everyone in the house. Sheriff Joe thought this would be the ideal place to ask the boy some questions.

"Come on in, Simon. Have a seat."

Simon sat down nervously. He struggled to make eye contact with the old sheriff.

"What made you stop off at this house today, son?"

"Well, I didn't see Julia in school today and I was worried about her. We have been friends for a few months now and it is not like her to miss school."

"When was the last time you were with Julia?"

Simon tried his best to stay composed. "I was here yesterday evening, but I left and got home just after dark."

"I'm sorry to tell you this, but Julia was found dead in her bed this morning."

Simon tried to speak but the words did not come out of his body. He started shaking uncontrollably – his nightmare had come true.

The sheriff observed his reaction closely. He then reached over, switched on the desk light and adjusted it. "I need you to bring your chair round to the side of the desk here and sit still for a minute."

"What for?" Simon asked nervously.

"You just do what I tell you, boy!"

Remembering the strands of hair that were in Julia's right hand, the sheriff looked closely at the left side of Simon's head. Simon felt the sheriff's fingers immediately move to the exact spot where he had felt the pain when he woke up – he tried to stay calm.

"What size shoes do you wear?"

"Nine and a half, sir," he replied hesitantly.

"Young man, you were among the last people to see Julia alive."

The sherriff was interrupted by a knock on the door. "Come in!" he shouted.

"Sorry to interrupt, Sheriff, but I am the medical examiner you requested."

"Where's Bob?" asked the sheriff.

"Unfortunately, he could not make it today so they asked me to help out."

"Fair enough then. I am Sheriff Joe."

"Good to meet you, Sheriff. I'm Dr Brockman."

Simon turned instantly and looked up from his chair, terror written all over his face.

★

Robert Osbourne walked into the Sheriff's Department and passed by the front desk. The receptionist tried to stop him but he was an imposing man with broad shoulders. He had no interest in making an appointment. He stormed into Sheriff Joe's office.

"Look, Sheriff, it's been over one month now. Beth and I have waited long enough. I think we both know who killed my daughter."

"Please have a seat," said the sheriff. "Believe me, Robert. I want to arrest him but the District Attorney said we've not got a strong enough case. Unfortunately, the prints on the knife were not a match."

"And what about the hair? It's his. I know it is."

"Same colour, same length, I agree," said the sheriff. "However, it's not enough. Black hair that length is too common and when the medical examiner looked at his scalp, he could not confirm they were pulled from his head."

"And the shoe prints, nine and a half, they are his size feet, no?"

"Yes, same size, but we have turned his house upside down and we can't find the shoes. I've brought the boy in twice for questioning, but he is sticking to his story, that he left your house that evening and walked home."

"Bullshit, Sherriff! You and I both know it is him, my daughter had no enemies. That boy left my house and returned later through her window. He tried to have his way with her but she resisted and he killed her, it's that simple."

"Look Robert, between you and me, I think that is what happened and so does just about every other officer in here. However, I'm sorry, unless there is more evidence I can't move forward with it."

"You might give up but, believe me, Beth and I won't. We are going to get the little bastard one way or another."

Since Julia's death, Simon had not been to school. He was not eating and he had lost a lot of weight. Martha was struggling to cope. The screams coming from his bedroom were taking a toll on her.

Simon's nightmares frightened her. She would find him shaking in bed, the sheets covered in sweat, and there was little she could do to comfort him. She wanted desperately to speak to him but he seldom responded. Her husband's death was one thing but nothing could compare to witnessing what her son was going through; still Annamae was always around to try and comfort her.

Sidon was an expanding town and there were many new families moving to the area. The murder had been front-page news in the Sidon Daily Express and there was no shortage of photos of everyone involved. Martha's biggest fear was running into Robert or Beth Osbourne. How could she even face them?

As the months passed, there were fewer questions to answer. The police did not come round as often and Simon's nightmares gradually subsided. Martha finally mustered the courage to go into town with Annamae. She did not care what people said or how they looked at her, she was still young and her responsibility was to Simon, and he needed her more than ever.

"Here you go, son. Just the way you like it; four spoons of chocolate." Martha placed the cup next to his bed and kissed him good night.

"Mom, please stay with me."

Simon moved over and Martha sat on the bed.

"I saw when Julia was killed."

"What do you mean?"

"The night she was killed, I saw how it happened. I saw everything. She tried desperately to scream but her mouth was covered when the knife went into her chest."

Martha observed her son. His tone was unchanged throughout and there was no expression on his face.

"Did you see who was in the room with her?"

"Yes, Mom. I saw him."

"Who did you see?"

Simon's eyes filled with tears. "It was me, Mom. I did it."

Martha looked into her son's eyes and took a deep breath. "You could not have done it, son. You were here with me all along."

"No. I went there. I loved Julia, I don't know why I did it. Who am I, Mom?"

CHAPTER 4

For fourteen months, Robert and Beth Osbourne had gotten nowhere in their pursuit of justice for their daughter. Sheriff Joe had gradually lost interest in the case and Robert felt the Sherriff had just been counting down his days to retirement.

Robert got his break when his lifelong friend, Amos Johnson, was elected as the new sheriff of Sidon. The following morning Robert and Beth were in his office.

"It's good to see you, Robert, and how have you been keeping, Beth?"

"I'm managing as best I can, Amos."

"Amos, you and I go back a long way," said Robert. "I want access to everything you have on Julia's death."

Sheriff Amos was taken aback by the unexpected request.

"Look Amos, I know what I'm asking you to do, but this is Julia we are speaking about. You have known her since the day she was born."

The sheriff looked at Beth; he could see the pain in her face.

"Amos, you guys have done everything you could have for fourteen months now. So please, all I'm asking is for you to give me what you have and let me look into it."

"You know, Robert. I'm not supposed to do this. I'll tell you what. Why don't you leave it with me and I'll see what I can do for you."

"Thank you, Amos. We owe you for this."

"Remember, Robert. I want no trouble. You turn up something we missed, I want to know about it. There is a lot of raw emotion involved here, so I don't want you going after that kid on your own."

"You have my word, Amos."

"Thank you, Amos. You're a good friend. This means a lot to us," said Beth.

Simon was still reluctant to leave the house but with Martha's help, he finally got the confidence to return to school. The friends he had before Julia's death, for the most part, alienated him and he always felt people viewed him with suspicion. After school, he would come straight home and study. There was a lot for him to catch up on. At weekends he attended Mass with Martha. Fr. Mark was still the parish priest and Simon volunteered to do odd jobs in the church.

Martha was happy to see the relationship that was being built between Fr. Mark and Simon. She felt he really needed more people to interact with. She began seeing Fr. Mark as a man Simon could confide in, someone who could fill the role of a real father. One day at a time, things started to look a little brighter for Simon and Martha.

"Do you remember the last time we were in here, Father?" asked Martha.

"Of course I remember. I picked up the tab."

Martha laughed out loud. "We came here for lunch after Simon's baptism. In fact, I remember we sat at the table over by that window."

28

"I'm very impressed, Father!"

"So, I'm curious, Martha, what is it you wanted to show me?"

"Well, to cut a long story short, Simon was given this Bible for his first birthday."

Fr. Mark took the book and examined it. With a smile, he said, "Yes, I can see it's been well used; a few torn pages and he's even practiced his colouring in a few places."

Martha smiled.

"Well Father, it's not so much the Bible itself that I wanted to ask you about but it came wrapped in this cloth. I noticed a few years ago that there was some writing on it. I was hoping you could tell me what it meant."

Fr. Mark took the cloth from Martha. He held it up to the light and studied it for a long time.

"What does it say Father.?"

"It is written in Aramaic."

"What language is that?"

"It is an ancient language, along with Greek and Latin. It is one of the languages priests study and it dates all the way back to the Phoenicians."

"Who are they?"

"A civilisation that existed a thousand or so years before Christ on the eastern shores of the Mediterranean Sea. Amazingly, the language is still spoken today in parts of Syria, be it in a slightly newer version. What I find curious is that what is written here looks like a very ancient version of it."

Martha paused and looked at Fr. Mark. "Can you make any of it out?"

"There are two parts to it. I can only read the first part."

"So what does it say, Father?"

"I'd rather not say, as it is incomplete without the second part."

"I'd like to know, Father. Even if it's incomplete."

Fr. Mark looked intently at Martha. "I HAVE CHOSEN YOU."

Martha paused for a moment and looked down at the cloth. "So what does that mean?" she asked warily.

"Who gave this to you, Martha?"

"It was the doctor that delivered Simon, Dr Brockman. He came over a bit unexpectedly for Simon's first birthday."

"Why don't you just ask him?"

"I've tried tracking him down, but without success."

"And you've not seen him since?"

Martha hesitated. "No, not exactly…"

"Do you mind if I keep this, Martha? In fact, can I also have the Bible as well?"

★

"Have you got a camera?" asked Sheriff Amos.

"Yes, I do," replied Robert.

"Bring it with you and meet me at the police station tonight at 11pm. The guy at the desk will let you in, and one other thing: I don't think you should bring Beth along."

"I understand, Amos."

"We don't have much time before the night shift guys come on duty. Robert, we need to move quickly," said Amos.

Amos handed Robert a pair of black gloves.

"Put these on and they don't come off until we are back inside this office, understood?"

Robert nodded.

"Good. Now, follow me. The Evidence Room is in the basement."

The two men made their way downstairs, along the corridor, and through the metal doors that led into the Evidence Room. There were rows of brown cabinets labelled in alphabetical order.

"Should be coming up here on the left," said Amos. "Here we are."

Robert looked at the name written in red, OSBOURNE / JULIA. MARIE. He reached out and touched the label gently with his finger tips as if he was reunited with his daughter.

"You sure you want to do this, Robert?"

Robert nodded.

Amos pulled opened the drawer. Robert's eyes were drawn immediately to the blood-stained knife in the clear plastic bag, "Remember the gloves stay on, Robert."

Robert slowly reached into the drawer and picked up the knife. He placed it on the table behind him. He stared at it for a few moments before photographing it.

He then broke down at the sight of the gold pendant; he had given it to Julia on her tenth birthday. He stood there seeing his little girl when she wore it for the first time.

Amos held up the cream-coloured envelope.

"Do you want these?"

"I want everything, Amos."

Written on the envelope were the words: "OSBOURNE / JULIA MARIA, CRIME SCENE PHOTOS."

Robert opened the envelope and removed the photos. His knees buckled, his back slid down the cabinet and he sat on the floor sobbing. Amos squatted down and put his hand on Robert's shoulder. His eyes were filled with tears for his friend.

"I'm sorry, brother. I should not have agreed to do this."

"No, we have to, Amos."

"Just stay there, I'll do them for you."

Amos gently took the envelope and camera from Robert's hand and proceeded to photograph the remaining evidence. A few minutes later, the two were back upstairs.

"Thank you so much, Amos. I'll be sure to let you know if I turn up anything you guys missed on Julia."

Robert motioned to head out the door.

"You can take the camera, Robert, but the film stays with me."

Robert looked at him quizzically.

"I have someone that will develop the pictures. I can't let you take what's on there into a high street photo shop."

"Good point, Amos. I'd not even thought about that."

"I'll bring them to you at home in a few days time. Robert, go home and try and get some rest."

★

"Fr. Mark, how are you?" asked Bishop Connor.

"I'm very well. It is good to see you, Your Grace."

"How are things in Sidon? You know I am scheduled to visit your area in the coming weeks. I wanted to stop by and see you; I have heard glowing reports regarding your work in the community."

"That is very nice of you, Your Grace. Of course you are welcome to visit any time."

"So what can I help you with?"

"I came to see you as it is well known that you read the Holy Scriptures in their ancient Aramaic form."

"Yes, Father I believe it gives a better understanding."

"I have a parishioner, Mrs Holman. She has been through some difficult times of late. She came to see me recently and gave me these two items."

Fr. Mark handed the Bible, and the brown cloth it was wrapped in, to the Bishop. He examined them closely. He looked up at the priest.

"I HAVE CHOSEN YOU

THE APOCALYPSE IS WRITTEN IN THE BACK"

The Bishop opened the drawer of his desk and took out a note pad. "Tell me more about Mrs Holman."

Fr. Mark told the Bishop what he knew about Martha and the doctor that gave her the cloth.

"You mentioned her son, Simon. Why is that name, Simon Holman, familiar to me?"

"Your Grace, just over a year ago a young girl was murdered in the area. The police named Simon Holman as the main suspect but, to date, they have not moved to arrest him."

"I remember it, and they are saying a sixteen year old boy committed a murder like that?"

"It's what the police believe, Your Grace."

"How well do you know Simon Holman, Father?"

"I baptised him. He has also done his First Communion and Confirmation. In the last few months he has been helping out in the church. I have spent a considerable amount of time with him."

"Initially, I wanted to dismiss this, Father. However, based on what you have told me, regarding the boy and the brutality of that murder, I'd like to look into it a bit further. I also want to speak with Dr Brockman. He can't be hard to track down."

CHAPTER 5

Sheriff Amos had spent his entire career in law enforcement. He knew that emotion gets the better of sound judgement. Over the years he had seen, on more than one occasion, officers being taken off cases where their families were involved.

"Now, here I am," he said to himself. "Without authorisation, I've accessed the Evidence Room and I'm giving someone state evidence in the unsolved murder of their daughter. I'm less than two weeks into my new job, so much for keeping my nose clean."

"Come on in, Amos. Beth's just made a fresh pot of coffee."

"Thanks, Robert, but I won't stay long. I just want to have a word with you guys and then I'll be out of here."

Beth came through from the kitchen.

"I've got your coffee poured, Amos, so you have to stay."

The sheriff smiled.

"Fair enough, Beth. You win."

"You know," Robert said, "before we get started, I just want to apologise. Beth and I were speaking the other night and we feel terrible about what we have asked you to do. We had not considered it from your point of view. You are putting a lot on the line to help us. When we heard you got the job, all we thought about at the time was Julia."

"Don't feel bad, Robert. You are like a brother. We grew up together and Julia was the closest thing I've had to a daughter. I'll do anything I can. Unfortunately though, even as sheriff now, it is difficult for me to allocate resources to this when the State has just cut our budget for the second time in three years."

"We really appreciate what you're doing, Amos," said Beth.

"What I do want to highlight to you both is that, emotionally, this is going to be as difficult as the day Julia died. What I have here is very disturbing to look at. You are going to have to find the strength to see it as evidence and not Julia."

"We understand what you are saying. I told Beth about some of the evidence I looked at. I had tried to prepare myself beforehand but I still broke down."

"It's completely understandable, as I say, I can't put my guys onto this, there are too many other priorities, but if you and Beth do the footwork and come up with something then let me know. I have people in departments that I can call on for a favour."

"You'll be the first to know if we come up with something or if we need your help."

"Remember, Robert, you can look into this but you are not allowed to break the law and you can't go after the kid on your own. Now I'll leave this envelope on the table and I'll see myself out. You need anything, you know where I am."

Sheriff Amos was right. It was the hardest night Robert and Beth had experienced since Julia's death. The photos of Julia covered in blood; with the knife sticking out of her chest were graphic and harrowing to view. They knew that, emotionally, they were in no position to start following up on any evidence. They agreed to look at the photos every night for the next week, make written notes and try and build up some immunity to viewing them. They had the rest of their lives to find who did this to their daughter.

★

"I told you, Father I was coming to see you in the coming weeks."

"It's wonderful to have you visit Sidon, Your Grace."

"I am happy to be here. I have to say, before I came in I had a walk around and you have done an excellent job. The church and the grounds look fantastic."

"Thank you. I have a lot of people helping me, I can't take all the credit."

The Bishop took a large red book from his bag. "I have a number of items I wish to discuss with you. The first on my list is Simon Holman. I have some of the clergy looking into his background. They are due to report back to me by the end of the month. In the mean time, I would like you to keep close to him. He trusts you, I take it?"

"I believe so, Your Grace."

"Good. And his mother?"

"Yes, I have known her a long time. Can I ask what is it you have seen that has made you look into this?"

"There are three main things that trouble me about it, Father Firstly, that form of Aramaic is particularly ancient. There are a limited number of people in the world that would be aware of it. I am very surprised someone in Sidon would have this knowledge.

"Secondly, I had the cloth sent for testing. All the results are not back yet. However, I am told that there is no ink, dye or pigment on the cloth. The letters are burnt into it. Of course, this is not difficult to do but it is difficult to do well.

"And thirdly, as you are aware, it is only when held up to the light can you see there is anything actually on it. Most unusual is the way it has been done. The dark shade of brown chosen for the cloth cleverly disguised it. Someone went to great effort to create it.

"If you don't mind I would like to keep the cloth for a few more weeks; we have not finished all of the tests. However, I can return this children's Bible to you now. We have reviewed it over the past few weeks, it is certainly only just as the title says 'My First Bible'. We particularly focused on The Book of Revelations but nothing has been added or removed. It is as it should be."

"I'm sure keeping the cloth will be fine, Your Grace. I'll let Mrs Holman know."

★

"Sorry I'm late, Father The stupid car wouldn't start again. The battery was dead so Annamae drove over and gave me a jump start."

"That's okay. I just arrived a few minutes ago myself. I ordered a coffee and the soup of the day for you."

"You realise it's a small town, Father. People are going to start talking if they see us here having lunch again."

Fr. Mark smiled. "Believe me, Martha, my cooking skills are non-existent. Unless one of my parishioners invites me over to dinner, I'm pretty much going to be eating out, either with someone or on my own."

"So, should I feel guilty for not having you over for dinner?"

"You should," he smiled.

"I'll keep it in mind. I may surprise you one day. So how is Simon doing? He seems a bit happier now he is helping you out at the church."

"He's doing great. He was weeding the flowerbed at the front yesterday. People don't realise it's just constant upkeep. With more and more paperwork, finding the time for jobs like that is getting really difficult. It's great when people offer to help."

"So, did you get anywhere with the Bible and cloth?"

"Actually, that is what I wanted to chat with you about. I went to see the Bishop a few weeks ago and showed both the items to him." Fr. Mark leaned forward and lowered his voice. "He confirmed that the words on the cloth are indeed an ancient form of Aramaic. He is quite knowledgeable on the language and his best interpretation of it reads: '*I have chosen you. The Apocalypse is written in the back.*'"

Martha looked at the priest, gathering her thoughts. "Why would someone write that on a cloth and give it to a child on his first birthday?"

"I don't know, Martha."

"What does it mean anyway? The Apocalypse is written in the back? I've seen the word 'Apocalypse' in the Bible, what is that all about?"

"Apocalypse comes from the Greek word Apokalupsis. In a religious context, it means revelation, like lifting a veil or revealing something hidden. Apocalypse is mentioned in The Book of Revelations, which as you know is the last book in the Bible."

"Then 'The Apocalypse is written in the back' would

imply something is written somewhere in the back of the Bible. So that means it's in The Book of Revelations, right?"

"I don't know Martha. I have put a lot of thought into it. The Bishop and I have both looked closely at The Book of Revelations, in this particular Bible, but the words are as they should be. I don't even know if it means anything at all. It may be, as I told you a few weeks ago, nothing to be concerned about."

"I'm going home tonight to read Revelations, Father. To be honest, I have tried in the past. All I know is that it's about the end of the world and the signs to look for – but how it's written makes it difficult to understand."

"Good luck with it, Martha. I hope you don't mind. I can give you back your Bible, but the Bishop would like to keep the cloth for a few more weeks."

"That concerns me. Why does he want to keep the cloth?"

"I'm guessing he is well read in Aramaic, so it is of some interest to him."

"I have a small confession to make, Father I told you I had not seen Dr Brockman since he gave Simon this Bible. However, I believe, in fact, I know I saw him again. Simon went into the hospital. It was an emergency and he ended up having his appendix removed. I am sure I saw Dr Brockman at the surgery."

"I wish you had told me this before, Martha. How sure are you that it was him?"

"I'm just about positive. We looked at each other. I recognised him and I'm sure he knew I did. He tried to turn away quickly and that is what made me try to track him down. I've asked at the hospital. I've even called the AMA, but there is no record of him."

"It's a bit odd they would have no record of him. Leave it with me. I'll let you know if Bishop Connor comes back to me with anything further, but don't worry yourself now."

★

"They really have to do something about the price of food," said Martha. "We won't be able to afford to eat if this continues. I've just spent a small fortune in there and look on the back seat. There is hardly anything in those bags."

"I know, Mom. You say that every time we go, but let's just get home before the car breaks down again."

"I wish you'd stop talking down our car. It's all we have, and it's been taking you everywhere since you were born."

"You mean it's been breaking down everywhere since I've been born."

"Funny guy."

"You really should get a new one, Mom."

"Haven't you heard? I'm planning to buy a Mercedes at the end of the month, when my next VA pension cheque comes."

"Yeah, if only, huh?"

There was a moment of silence and Martha thought to herself, this is the most light-hearted conversation I've had with him since that dreadful day. My son is coming back, thank God. I am so happy.

"So, I hear you were weeding the church garden. I've been asking you to cut the grass out back for ages."

"I'll get around to it, Mom, but I really need to study these days."

"When do your exams start?"

"Six weeks time and then…"

"And then you cut the grass?" Martha said quickly.

"Actually, I'm not sure what I will do then, but maybe I'll cut the grass. Seriously, Mom, when am I going to know what I want to do with my life? I've prayed. I've asked people for advice. I've researched different fields and I still don't know."

"Who have you asked for advice?"

"Most recently, I asked Aunt Annamae."

"You asked her for advice? What did she advise you?"

"You won't believe me if I told you. She said I should ask Fr. Mark."

"Are you serious? That was her advice? What did you say?"

"I told her she must be joking. Fr. Mark will probably advise me to join the clergy."

"What did she say?"

"That would not be so bad. I would get to help a lot of people, which is the only thing that makes me happy."

"She is right in that regard, but I can't believe Annamae, of all people, told you to ask Fr. Mark.

"Your aunt surprises me sometimes. She is always bad-mouthing the church. She came over the other day and read out some article she found in the newspaper about corruption at the Vatican. Now, here she is telling you the clergy is not so bad."

"Could you imagine it, Mom? With the name I have in Sidon, what people would say if they hear I'm joining the clergy?"

"You worry too much, Simon. There are so many career opportunities these days, with computers and all the new technology; I saw a video player in the shop the other day. The man was showing it to me. You just put a movie tape into it and watch it on your TV. You can stop it, or start it, when you want. Imagine being able to watch a movie like that?"

"Some of the kids in school already have video players, Mom. Actually, at school they have started putting in computers. They won't be ready for a while yet, but I want to learn about them."

Martha tapped the dashboard. "See, got us home safe and sound."

Simon just shook his head.

★

Martha kissed Simon good night, put the Bible next to her bed, and brushed her teeth. She lay in bed and said a prayer of thanks. She could not remember the last time she had felt so happy. My First Bible, she looked at the title and remembered lying in bed with Simon and reading the stories to him. Now, in a couple of months, he would be graduating from college.

As she lay in bed, the words were going around and around in her head: *'I have chose, you, The Apocalypse is written in the back.'* She went to the last chapter of the Bible, The Book of Revelations. *Right,* she thought, *I need to put the 'I have chosen you' part out of my head. It gives me the creeps. I need to focus. There must be something in here that the Apocalypse refers to and I'm going to figure it out.*

CHAPTER 6

The trauma of reviewing the photos every night proved too much for Robert and Beth Osbourne. They would close their eyes and were haunted by the images of their only child's murder. After three weeks of nightmares, sleepless nights, arguments and tears, they were emotional wrecks. Their marriage was suffering and they both knew it could not go on. Sheriff Amos stopped by to see how they were doing.

"Come on in, Amos," said Beth. "Robert should be on his way home. He went to collect a prescription for me."

Sheriff Amos was stunned at how Beth looked. Her hair was a mess her cheeks were sunken. There were bags under her eyes. *She looks terrible*, he thought.

"Can I get you something, Amos?"

"I'd love a beer, but a glass of water will have to do as I'm on duty now."

"You're the sherriff, aren't you?"

"If only it worked like that, Beth."

"Here you go, have you had lunch? I can fix you a sandwich."

"I'm fine, Beth. I'm trying to cut back a bit."

"That is Robert just pulling into the drive. He'll be happy to see you're here."

"Hi, Amos, I saw your new car outside. At last they gave you something decent to drive."

The sheriff looked at Robert. *Wow,* he thought, *you actually look worse than Beth.*

"Don't be fooled, Robert. It's the same piece of junk car I've always had. They just repainted it and put the star and 'sheriff' on the doors. Can we go through to the living room and talk?"

"I'll be honest, both of you look like hell. I'm sure neither of you are getting any quality sleep and you have probably taken no notes, or have any plan for what evidence you want to look into."

Beth and Robert knew there was no point pretending, Amos knew them too well.

"This stops today. Both of you are going to stop looking at the photos, or even speaking about Julia. You're retired, Robert. Take Beth and book into a hotel out of town. I don't want to see either of you back home for at least a week."

"I think your right, Amos. I actually have somewhere in mind that Beth and I can go."

"I'm gathering up these photos and taking them away now. Remember, no talk of Julia. Go do some adventure stuff. Walk the hills, take a spa and enjoy the outdoors. When you return, I will give you back the photos. However, only look at them between 9am and 5pm. Take your notes and do research then. After 5pm that is it for the day. Switch off, have dinner, go to a movie, whatever, but clear you mind before you go to bed."

Amos left with the photographs. Robert and Beth sat in the living room with the realisation of the toll these last few weeks had taken on them.

"Come on in, Father I'm sorry to summon you over here at such short notice."

"It is not a problem Your Grace. How can I help?"

"Again, it is regarding Simon Holman and his family. As you know, my contacts are not limited to members of the clergy. There are many officials and government departments I call on from time to time. I have the report on Simon Holman in front of me. We are continuing our enquiries. However, there is no Dr Brockman registered with any medical practice. If Dr Brockman existed, my people would have found him. We decided to review the murder case against Simon and we got access to the evidence. The murder weapon used was not an ordinary knife, as reported, but an Athame."

"What's an Athame?"

"It's a sacrificial knife, used by those practicing pagan witchcraft. Unfortunately, the police viewed it as a regular knife and only lifted the fingerprints, which did not match Simon's. The origin of this knife should have been looked into at the time. Now let's assume, Father, that Simon is the killer. How would a sixteen year old, living in a place like Sidon, get his hands on an Athame?"

"This leads me to think he is innocent, Your Grace."

"I would tend to agree with you. However, let us suppose he did commit the murder using a knife that he knew he could not be associated with, just to add to the element of doubt."

"I know Simon quite well. I will tell you now, he did not commit that murder."

Bishop Connor gave the priest a stern look. "You

misunderstand me, Fr. Mark. I am not interested in the innocence or guilt of Simon Holman. If this is just another murder then it is a job for the police. However, if there is some element of evil connected to it, then it is very much my responsibility to look into it. When I look at the writing on that cloth, at the brutality of the murder and now the murder weapon, I have no choice in this.

"Father, you are well aware that demons enter this portal from time to time. They can exist both outside of us, as well as within us. If allowed to, they can take full control of an individual."

"Your Grace, I have thought about this and I have looked into his eyes, as I have held up the bread and wine before him. There is no demon in Simon Holman."

"We have two other members of his family." Bishop Connor looked down at the notes on his desk. "His mother, Martha, and her sister, Annamae. What do you know about them?"

"Martha I know quite well. However Annamae less so, as she comes to church only on special occasions, like Simon's baptism. Otherwise, I only see her in town occasionally."

"Fr. Mark, I will need to establish if there is an infestation in the house. There may be a demon, or even some disembodied entities, that have attached themselves to that house. I want you to visit Simon's home. Look around for any unusual objects; statues, idols, books on witchcraft, sacrifice, anything disturbing. Find somewhere quiet, close your eyes and say a prayer for guidance." Bishop Connor then opened the drawer of his desk and held up a small black book. "Do you recognise this, Father?"

"Yes, I do. I got it during my training. However, I have never used it."

"Everything you need is within this book. Take it and

study it carefully. When you use this book, you will quickly know if there is an entity in the house. Be warned, it will react violently. You will have no doubt regarding its presence."

"It may take some time to arrange to get into the house, Your Grace. I will get back to you when I do."

★

Martha, Annamae and Fr. Mark took their seats at the graduation ceremony. Martha could not be prouder of her son. In her eyes he had overcome so much and still managed to graduate with honours. At the end of the ceremony, Fr. Mark excused himself and apologised for not being able to attend the after-graduation party. Martha ran over, threw her arms around Simon and hugged him.

"I'm so proud of you, I love you so much."

"Mom, not in front of everyone."

"I don't care what they think. You are my only son and I could not be happier for you. You should be so proud of yourself. Not one of these kids here has had to deal with what you have been through. You have come out the other side of it, with your whole life ahead of you to look forward to."

"I think you and Aunt Annamae have had a few too many cocktails, Mom."

"Trust me, son, it is not the alcohol talking. Your Aunt and I are so proud of you. Now, tell me who is the girl I saw you dancing with?"

"Just a friend, Mom."

"Just a friend, huh?"

"Yes, Mom. If you must know her name, it's Linda Bernstein."

"Her dad isn't Martin Bernstein, by any chance, is he?"

47

"Yes, you know him?"

"Well, he is the Manager at Horizon Bank. He turned down my last application for a loan."

"What did you want a loan for?"

"Do you really need to ask?"

"Oh… are we getting a new car, Mom?"

"Well, we would have been but for Mr Bank Manager. Is he here? I'll go give him a piece of my mind."

"No, Mom."

"Just joking, son. I would not embarrass you like that. Well, not without at least a few more cocktails. Anyway, how long have you and Linda been together?"

"We're not together, Mom, just friends."

"Friends that want to be together or just friends?"

"I've got to go, Mom. Hope you and Aunt Annamae enjoy the rest of the party."

"We're actually leaving soon. How are you getting home?"

"I'll get a lift with someone. No problem, Mom. I'll see you later."

"So, did you find out who she is?" asked Annamae.

"Her name is Linda Bernstein. Her dad is the Manager at Horizon Bank."

"I did not like how they were getting so close, Martha. Did you see that dress she was wearing? She looked like a tart. He can do so much better that that."

"I quite liked her dress and Simon looks happy, happier than I've see him in a long time and that is all that matters to me. Two years ago, I would have given anything to see him like I see him tonight. Don't ruin it for me, Annamae."

"Well, we need to keep an eye on her, that's for sure."

★

Robert and Beth Osbourne enjoyed their holiday so much that they stayed on a few extra days. Sheriff Amos had given them the best advice they have ever received. Of course, individually, they thought of Julia but they never discussed her. They were both determined to make the most of every day of the holiday. They returned home feeling refreshed and with a completely new mindset. The following day, Sheriff Amos came to see them.

"Well, I don't even need to ask how the holiday was. What a difference! Both of you look fantastic."

"We really enjoyed it, and thanks again for all the help and advice."

"Don't mention it."

The sheriff reached into his case. "I'll leave this on the table here for you. Remember what we discussed before you left. Try and stick to it. Julia would not want to see you the way you were."

"Thanks, Amos, and you take care."

Over the next week, Robert and Beth stuck to Sheriff Amos's advice. There were still the tears and some sleepless nights, but they were slowly building up an inner-strength. They were determined that, whatever the outcome of their efforts, they would do everything possible to find Julia's killer.

"Ok, Beth, between the police report and evidence, what have we got so far?" asked Robert.

"The size nine and a half footprints have never been matched to a particular brand of shoe. The Holman home was searched numerous times, but no shoe matched despite the fact that he is the same size.

"The hair length and colour matches Simon Holman. It would be nice if we had a sample of the hair from the crime scene. These photographs of the sample in Julia's right hand and later here next to the ruler, shows the exact length. We also have photos of Simon Holman's hair, taken by the medical examiner the following day.

"This photo here is of the report done by the medical examiner. Dr Brockman's report states that he examined Simon Holman's scalp the day after the murder and it cannot be determined with any certainty that the hair came from his head. His report also goes on to state that he did not find any sign of blood or cuts on Simon Holman.

"The knife used was examined for fingerprints and compared to Simon Holman. They were not a match. These are the photos of both the prints on the knife and Simon's Holman's prints." The knife handle was a dark colour with a symbol of some sort on the handle.

"The police report states that, based on the footprints, the killer came from the field west of the house. He came across the ground to outside the bedroom window. The same set of footprints was then traced from the bedroom window and headed west back across the ground and into the field. So he came and left from almost the exact same point. The killer entered through the bedroom window and left the same way. Prints on the knife matched prints on the window and the victim's blood was found on the window. The report also states that the field is in the direction of the Holman home.

"Simon Holman lives with his mother, Martha. His father, John A Holman, died in Vietnam. Simon Holman has no brothers or sisters, just one Aunt. He lives approximately 2.5 miles from the victims home. He is sixteen years old and fit. Running, it is estimated he would take approximately thirty minutes, presuming he knew the fields. An almost full moon would have aided navigation that night.

"The report states that the victim was last seen alive by parents at 8:30pm and discovered the following morning by her mother at 6:45am.

"No clothes with blood have been found at any of the searches conducted at Holman's residence.

"Fingerprints from the knife were checked against the data base, within the county and state wide, and no matches were found. Finally, Sheriff Joe Cabral has signed off the police report.

"So, Robert, what do we want to start with?"

"I think a trip to the library. Let's take the photo of the footprints. We need to try and match it to a brand of shoe. Perhaps we can see where he purchased them. And the knife, it would be a good if we could trace it. I'd also like to know a bit about his father, John A Holman. We may as well look into him while we are there."

★

Martha lay in bed reading *My First Bible.* She had just about completed reading The Book of Revelations. *This is so difficult to understand*, she thought, *I'm getting nowhere.* Martha had underlined everywhere she saw the word "Apocalypse." She had read and re-read the paragraphs. The frustration was getting to her.

CHAPTER 7

At the end of Mass, during the singing of the final hymn, Fr. Mark always walked to the back of the church and stood just outside the door. It was his way of greeting everyone as they left the church and welcoming any new faces.

"It's great to see you again, Martha, and how are you doing young man?"

"I'm doing great, Father I'm really enjoying just relaxing; the last eight months was so much studying."

"That is wonderful to hear, Simon. You deserve a well-earned break."

"Yes," said Martha, "but it does not mean sit around all day."

Fr. Mark laughed.

"You know, Father, I've been reading Revelations, I've nearly finished and I have not a clue how to interpret it. What exactly is the author talking about?"

Fr. Mark saw his opportunity. "Why don't we make a deal, Martha?"

"What do you have in mind, Father?"

"A meal!"

Martha smiled.

"What if I help you with The Book of Revelations and you make dinner?"

"That sounds like a fair enough deal."

"What would you like?"

"Roast beef and macaroni is my favourite with lots of gravy."

"When do you have in mind, Father?"

"What about Wednesday this week?"

"Yes, I can do Wednesday. How does 7pm sound?"

"I'll see you then, Martha."

"But Mom, I'm not going to be home on Wednesday. I've made plans that night, so I'm going to miss it."

"Going to see Linda, are we?"

"Maybe, but the point is you never make roast beef and macaroni for me."

"If you cut the grass more often, perhaps I would. Anyway, I'll make extra and you can have it for lunch the next day."

Fr. Mark smiled. "I'll see you Wednesday, Martha. Bye, Simon."

"Okay, Father"

★

"Good morning, Ma'am. My name is Robert Osbourne, this is my wife, Beth."

"My name is Irene, I'm the head librarian, how can I help?"

"We have some items that we are trying to research. We have a photo of some footprints and I'd like to find out who manufactured the shoes that made them. Where would be the best place to look for books on that? We also have a knife with an unusual—"

Irene cut Robert off before he could finish the sentence.

"Sir, we have a dozen newly installed computers against the wall over there. Type in what you want and it will direct you to the relevant section. The books are in alphabetical order, based on the author's surname and the rows of books are numbered from one starting here all the way to the far end, with row number seventy-eight."

"Thank you, Ma'am."

Robert and Beth walked towards the bank of computers. Beth turned to Robert and said, "Wow, it's like she is from the military, the way she cut you off and then rattled on about the layout in here. Did you get the alphabetical numbers thing? I'm not going to ask her again."

"Don't worry, Beth. At least with the computer we won't have to deal with the old woman."

Robert and Beth pulled two chairs close together and shared one computer screen.

"What do you mean you can't use a computer, Beth?"

"Me, what about you? You're the one always telling me how smart you are."

"Beth, you're going to have to go back over there and speak with the battle axe. Just ask her how to do a search."

"You're the man, you go ask her!"

"Fine I'll go…"

"Excuse me, Ma'am, but could you show—"

Irene cut him off again. "Right, follow me," she said sternly. They marched back over to where Beth was seated.

"You see this box here? This is the search box. This is a keyboard. You type what you want in the box, this is the ENTER key. Hit that, the computer will then tell you where to look. I've already described how the library is laid out, now is there anything else?"

"No, that's fine. We'll manage from here, thanks."

"Wow, Robert where on earth do you think they found her?"

"God alone knows, anyway let's get on with this."

SHOE MANUFACTURES…

⋆

"Come on in, Father."

"Did you find the house easily?" asked Martha. "It can be tricky to find once it gets dark. I always try to remember to leave the light on at the front."

"Yes, it wasn't a problem. I'm not from around here, as you are well aware, but I have visited a few of your neighbours, so I'm getting to know the area quite well."

"You can just hang up you jacket by the door and come on through to the kitchen."

"I take it young Simon is away?"

"Yes he left a little while ago. He says to tell you 'hi' and he's sorry he missed you. I can't leave this cooker for too long. Everything is happening at once. The fridge is there just help yourself, Father."

"Thanks, Martha. I wanted to follow up on what you said the other day outside the church. Who is this Linda you mentioned?"

"She graduated with Simon. When Annamae and I went to the graduation party he was dancing with her and they were getting quite close. In fact, since then I know he's been seeing her quite a bit but he's not saying much. He still keeps telling me they are just friends."

"I'm really happy for him, Martha. He seems to be getting on so well with his life now and he's put that episode behind him."

"Oh, you have no idea, Father. As a Mom, to see your son go through what I've witnessed… but, honestly, I don't even want to talk about it. I'm only looking forward for him. He has done great in his exams, he can do anything from here."

"He still has no idea what he wants to do, no?"

"None at all, but Linda, I know for certain, is going on to university and I feel Simon may just decide to do the same. He told me they took similar subjects in high school."

"Do you mind if I use your bathroom?"

"Sure. It's just at the end of the hall, past the bedrooms, last door on the right. Don't be too long, though; this beef is just about ready."

Fr. Mark left the kitchen and noticed there was a silver plaque of the last supper above the doorway. He turned and walked down the hallway slowly, looking at all the pictures on the walls. He passed a bedroom with the door opened. He reached inside and put the light on. The room was tidy, the bed was made and there was a pair of jeans and a shirt neatly folded on a chair. There was a desk in the corner with books and folders. He looked at them quickly; they were all school related. He observed a stack of books next to the bed. He picked them up. There were books on the history of Judaism, Islam and the Hindu religion. He picked up the Quran. There were pages with passages underlined and notes made. He looked around the room. On the wall was a poster of a singer wearing very little, with the name Madonna above it. He turned off the light and continued down the hallway.

A couple yards further on the left was another door. He opened it and looked in. He could see this had to be Martha's room, he felt terrible about what he was doing. He looked back down the hallway and could hear the sounds of cooking in the kitchen. He turned on the light but could not bring himself to enter the room. He felt like he was violating her privacy. Everything he saw just said it was a normal woman's bedroom. He quickly turned off the light and shut the door quietly.

He continued down the hallway, went into the bathroom, and closed the door. He looked around briefly, closed his eyes and said a prayer for guidance. He took out the book Bishop Connor had given to him and opened it at the chapter he had marked with the gold thread. He said the words in Latin, passage after passage. He closed his eyes and waited. There was nothing. He said a final prayer and returned to the kitchen.

"Just in time, Father. Please move that bowl there, so I can put this on the table. But be careful; it's hot."

"Perfect, you can say Grace, Father."

"This tastes fantastic, Martha. You're an amazing cook."

"Thanks, Father. Now I've done my part, it's your turn to tell me all about The Book of Revelations."

"Well, I know what it is about. However, I'm unable to understand it fully myself."

"Why didn't you tell me this last Sunday?"

"I'd have risked missing out on this amazing meal."

"You're definitely worth watching, Father. You're not quite as innocent as you make out!"

"I told you, Martha; when your cooking is as bad as mine, you take every opportunity for a free meal that you can get. Seriously though, I will tell you what I know about The Book of Revelations and, based on that you can read it again and make your own interpretation. How does that sound?"

Martha nodded.

"During or just after the time of Christ, there was a man

called John. There is much debate as to whether he was John the apostle, or a different John. However, John lived on an island between Greece and Turkey called Patmos. It is on this Island that he had visions of the end of the world. He recorded them in what you are reading, called The Book of Revelations.

"John's visions describe the end of the world when Jesus returns and defeats the armies of Satan. It describes Satan's fate and the fate of those who choose his ways. It also speaks of Jesus's love for his followers and the protection he offers from Satan, for those who choose to listen. It is a warning to prompt the self-examination of our lives and to think carefully about what is truly important in this life. Therefore, the word 'Apocalypse' is used as the veil that was lifted on all the events that will come to pass or, to put it another way, the events that were revealed."

"So, Father, how does the word 'Apocalypse', written on the cloth, fit in with all of this?"

"As I told you, Martha, I do not understand the connection between the cloth and The Book of Revelations. I wonder, at times, if there is a connection. I just don't know."

"Father, if we put aside this second part, 'The Apocalypse is written in the back', and look at the first part, 'I have chosen you', it is very worrying for me. I've been trying to ignore it, but Simon was given that Bible, wrapped in the cloth, for his first birthday. This first part frightens me. Has Simon been chosen? And, if so, by whom? And to do what?"

"I know it has been many years, Martha, but the man who gave you this Bible, Dr Brockman, would you recognise him today?"

"Without question, I would. It was over ten years

between seeing him on Simon's first birthday and later seeing him in the hospital, when he had his appendix removed. I know it was the same man."

"Martha, the Bishop, his staff and I, have looked carefully at that Bible. There has been nothing in The Book of Revelations that has been added or removed. I can't emphasise this enough. Please do not worry."

"Father, why is there no publisher?"

"What do you mean, Martha?"

"The Bible is the most sold book in the world. Publishing companies must have made a lot of money selling them. I have looked at other Bibles. They all have publishing companies with their names and details clearly written on the back. That Bible has no such details."

"I had not noticed that, Martha. That is a very good observation indeed."

Martha's eyes filled with tears. "Father, I question that Bible; I question what is written on that cloth; I question Dr Brockman, who no one seems to know about; I question the murder of Julia; and I even question my own son at times. I am truly frightened for him. My life can end today; I know I have lived a good life. I have no fear of death, but this is my only son."

Fr. Mark handed Martha a napkin to wipe her eyes. "Martha, let us look forward, as you said earlier. I think, as you let the events surrounding Julia go, you need to let these questions you have go. Please, for your own good, you need to stop thinking about him."

"You're probably right, Father, but it is so much easier said than done when it's your child."

"I don't have any children, but I can understand."

"Why don't you have a family, Father? Why did you

choose to do this? You seem so much more normal than a priest should be."

Fr. Mark looked intently at Martha across the table. "Martha, I was called to do this. I know there are some of my fellow clergy that sometimes question their decision. I can understand that also, but I have no doubt this is my calling.

"When I was younger, something happened to me where I found myself neither awake nor asleep. It was something between the two states. Like a vision, I was fully aware of what I was seeing. I was outside myself and I saw myself in the future. It was a frightening time for humanity. However, everyone went on with their lives, unaware of what was to come. I tried to warn them. I was screaming, telling them this is the end, but they were too busy to listen. I saw that I was a member of the clergy and I had a great purpose in the events that were happening."

"Father, that scares me almost as much as what I'm going through."

"Martha, you are correct in what you said regarding yourself. You live and have lived a good life. You have nothing to fear. Your life can be taken at anytime but it is only the death of your body – it means nothing.

"Regarding your concerns for Simon, you should have no fear for him. I am genuinely happy that he has made new friends and is interested in girls and having fun. However, at church I have had conversations of such depth with him, they are beyond what I have with senior members of the clergy. He has a spiritual understanding that he really should not possess at his age.

"I have observed Simon in a state of prayer where his body does not move. He does not fidget. He is perfectly still. Your son is very special and you must not fear for him.

Be happy, Martha; you are free to live the rest of your life, however long that is, without any fear. There is no greater gift in this life.

"Martha, have you any idea how many today would give all their wealth for what you possess? It is unfortunate for them that what you have cannot be purchased. Still, they do not understand and continue to try."

"I'm not sure what to say regarding Simon, Father I just want a normal son. I know he studies religion. However, your description of that side of him is something I was not fully aware of."

"I've really enjoyed this chat, Martha, not to mention the dinner. It was amazing. Thank you so much. You have gone to great lengths."

"No problem at all, Father."

Fr. Mark got up from the table. "Allow me to help tidy up before I head home."

CHAPTER 8

"It was never going to be easy, Beth, but I think we have made some good progress over the last week. Get you notes and let's just review where we stand at the moment."

"Okay, Robert. I've broken it down like this, so I'll just read out the item, the status and the plan ahead.

"Footprints. Almost without question the brand of shoe is Converse All Star High Tops, size nine and a half. Sold at two locations within the Sidon area. We have Thursday this week lined up for visiting both outlets."

"John A Holman (suspect's father). Deceased, served in 25th Infantry Division. Died, 8th July 1968. Cause of death is classed as combat related. I called the Veteran Service Records but they will not release any information to anyone who is not an immediate member of his family."

"Leave that one with me, Beth. I have some old friends who served in Vietnam. Perhaps they know people and can get some information on him."

"Murder Weapon. So far, we have not been able to establish where it came from. Looking at the photos of it, there is no manufacturer's name on it, only the unusual symbols on both sides of its handle."

"Sheriff Joe (retired). I called his office and he has agreed to meet us for lunch on Wednesday."

"I'm not even sure if it's worth meeting with him, Beth. Like I said at the time, he looked more interested in playing golf than solving this. But I guess if you have made the appointment then let's go ahead and see him on Wednesday."

"Dr Brockman (medical examiner) I called the coroner's office. They don't have a Dr Brockman working for them. They checked back but came up with nothing. Of course I could not tell them I was looking at his signature on a report. I just gave them the month. I thought he worked there but they said I was mistaken."

"Let's look into that further. I'd like to speak with him and get his thoughts on Simon Holman."

"Hair left at crime scene. The medical examiner's determination, that the hair left at the crime scene did not match the suspect, was accepted. Therefore, his hair and the hair left at the crime scene were never sent off for testing."

"How do they test them?"

"From what I've read, there is a process called Microscopic Hair Analysis, that can match two hairs."

"Unbelievable, Beth. Who cares what the examiner wrote in his report? What the hell were they thinking? They should have just got them tested."

★

At the Bishop's Rectory, Fr. Mark reached into his bag and took out the small black book. "Your Grace, I would like to return this to you."

"Thank you, Fr. Mark. I take it you used it."

"I have. However, I must report there is no infestation, or demonic presence within the home. I have also looked around and there is nothing that would suggest any element of evil. In fact, quite the opposite, I found there to be a feeling of peace within it."

"Very well. I appreciate your efforts and I will continue to look into the matter. However, I believe you have done all you can at this stage but I would still like you to continue to keep close to the family. Please report back to me anything that disturbs you."

"I will, of course, Your Grace."

"I can give the cloth back to you now, Father. Please thank Mrs Holman and do apologise to her for keeping it so long."

"Were you able to determine anything further regarding it?"

"We continue to look for Dr Brockman but, as I told you, he does not appear on any records. As to the writing on the cloth, unfortunately we have been unable to interpret its message, if indeed there is one."

"I have given a report on the matter to Cardinal Phillips, who will pass it on to the Vatican. As you are aware, we have many learned scholars whose life's work is to study ancient texts and messages. If there is a logical message on the cloth, they will discover it."

"And the knife, the Athame, any progress?"

"We still have it. Currently, it is undergoing tests but I have had no feedback on it so far.

"That will be all for now, Father. I wish you a safe return to Sidon."

"Thank you, Your Grace."

★

"Great, you're home. I was getting worried," said Martha.
"You should not worry about me, Mom."

"I'm your mother, it's my job. Anyway, this came today for you in the post."

"I guess, Mom, you read the name on the envelope?"

"'UNIVERSITY OF SIDON'. How could I miss it? So, you have applied then?"

"Well, not yet. This will be the application form in here but I've made up my mind."

"Is it anything to do with Linda going there?"

"No, Mom. You don't give me enough credit; I have put a lot of thought into this decision. I mean what are my options? I can get a part time job for a year doing something but what is the point in that? I may as well go on for another four years and by then I'm sure to have figured out what I want."

"Well, I'm certainly happy. It will keep you close to home, so no complaints from me."

"Have you told Fr. Mark?"

"Actually, it was him that advised me to do this."

"Oh, so you took Aunt Annamae's advice after all then?"

"In a way, but I've become quite close to Father and I trust him a lot. I was always planning to speak with him about it."

"He is a wonderful human being. We are lucky to have him as our parish priest. He thinks the world of you. Any advice he gives you, then listen closely. He has your best interests at heart, son."

★

"Here it is, Beth. This is the café coming up on the right. I'll just park round the corner."

"Sheriff Joe, it's good to see you."

"Robert, Beth. How have you been?"

"Well, we are both doing as good as you'd expect, all things considered."

"I'm glad to hear it."

"You know, Sheriff, I'm retired now and with nothing to do. You have likely heard that Beth and I are reviewing the case."

"I have heard that from some of the guys at the station. Look, I want to apologise to you both. I hated the fact that I retired from the force with that case left unsolved."

"Well, perhaps you can assist us now. We have a few questions regarding some of the evidence."

"Regarding the murder weapon used, were you ever able to establish where it came from?" Beth asked.

"We did a search of the Holman house, but there was nothing there to match it to. We were hoping it was part of a set."

"We have been trying to research it but there is no manufacturer's name on it and we can't understand the symbols engraved on the side of the handle."

"You seem to have a very detailed knowledge of the murder weapon. How did you get access to it? In fact, I don't want to know as I'm implicating myself here, so let's just forget I ever asked that question. Do you understand?"

"We do, Sheriff. We completely understand."

"To be honest with you both, of course we looked at the murder weapon at the time. We ran it by a few guys but no one knew what the engravings represented, so we could not move forward with that line of investigation."

"Fair enough, Sheriff. I'd like to ask you about the hair. There may not have been a lot in Julia's hand but did you look at Simon Holman's scalp yourself?"

"I took the boy into the study in your home the day he showed up after the murder. He was petrified. He knew a lot more than he was letting on. I've not been thirty-five years in the force and without being able to know when someone is hiding something."

"So, did you look at his scalp yourself?"

"I did. You had a good light on your desk. I made him sit forward in his chair and I passed my hand through his hair but it was difficult to know. If it was a good clump she had pulled out his head, I'd have seen that, but it wasn't enough to be sure."

"Just your opinion, Sheriff, but how close do you think the hair in Julia's hand was to the boy's?"

"It's his, not a doubt in my mind. I don't care what the examiner said, and I told him that at the time, because I stayed in there while he checked the boy out."

"If the hair was the same colour and length why do you think he dismissed it so easily?"

"I told him then, I agree there is no clear bald patch but I don't know what he was thinking on the colour and the length. If Bob was there, he would have had a completely different opinion, I'm sure of that. I've worked with him for over twenty-two years."

"Who is Bob?"

"He is the examiner the coroner's office always sends when things like this happen, but he could not make it that day so they sent this other guy."

"You mean Dr Brockman?"

"Yes. That was his name actually. How would you know that? Damn, there I go again. Forget I asked."

"Did you ever see Bob afterwards, Sheriff?"

"I just worked with Bob. A good guy, but I don't know

him on a personal level. I heard one of the guys at the station saying something about he fell down the stairs, coming out of his apartment, so he couldn't make it that day."

"Do you know his full name, Sheriff?"

"Dr Bob Cooper, are you thinking of having a word with him?"

"It's a long shot, but yeah. We probably will try and have a chat."

"What did you make of the prints on the knife, Sheriff?"

"I so wanted them to be the boy's, you have no idea, but whoever it was they did not care about leaving prints. The ones on the knife matched the window. They were everywhere. I'll tell you, my gut says it was the boy, but how do we prove it?"

"That is what we are now trying to do, Sheriff. I have a considerable sum of money and the rest of my life. Beth here feels the same way, if we have to die trying to get him, we will."

"Look, if you need me for anything, you know where I am, okay. I may be retired but I still know a lot of people willing to help nail Holman."

"We appreciate it, Sheriff."

★

"Good afternoon. My name is Robert, this is my wife Beth."

"I'm Donna, the Manager. How can I help you?"

"We just came from the shoe shop down the street. They told us you sold Converse shoes. We are looking for All Star High Tops in a size nine and a half."

"You are a year or so too late. However, we do have the latest version and I'm pretty sure we have them in a nine and a half."

"Sorry Donna, I should have made myself clearer. I'm actually looking for someone who would have come in here just over two years ago and purchased them. Is there any way you can look back in your records to see if you sold a size nine and a half of that type of shoe and if so, how many did you sell?"

"What exactly is this about, if you don't mind me asking?"

"Donna, our daughter was murdered in Sidon—"

"I'll stop you there, you don't need to say anymore. I did not know her but of course I heard about it. I'm terribly sorry for your loss. I've read in the papers they never got the guy. I take it he was wearing All Stars?"

"That's correct Donna."

"Can you leave this with me? I'll look into it."

"Donna, did you work here back then?"

"Yes, I've been here over five years and I'm almost guaranteed to have been on shift. They almost never give me a day off from this place!"

"Here is my number, Donna. I look forward to hearing from you."

"I will, sir, and I wish you and your wife the best of luck with this."

"Thanks, Donna."

"Where to now, Robert?"

"Why don't we head across town to the coroner's office? I'm not sure what hours they work there but, if the traffic is not too bad, we should get there before five."

★

"Good afternoon, is Dr Bob Cooper in today?"

"Your name, sir?"

"Osbourne, Robert. This is my wife, Beth."

"I can check. He may have already left for the day. Just have a seat over there; I'll see if he's still in."

"Bob said he is in a hurry to get home today. If it's important he can give you five minutes now, or you can make an appointment for next week."

"It won't take more than five minutes. We'd like to see him now please."

"Okay, sir. Through the double doors, second on the right."

"Thank you Ma'am."

"Mr and Mrs Osbourne, come on in. I'm really sorry but I have an appointment to run off to, so I can't give you much time today, but what can I do for you?"

"Our daughter, Julia, was murdered a few years ago. We had lunch with Sheriff Joe earlier on today and he said you were supposed to be the medical examiner on that day but you were unable to make it. We heard subsequently that you fell down the stairs. Do you remember what I'm referring to?"

"I'm sorry about your daughter and yes, believe me, I know what you are referring to, but I did not fall down the stairs. I was pushed."

"Are you certain?"

"I'm absolutely certain. I was shoved in the back, but I didn't see who did it. I cracked my head on the wall at the bottom and fractured my leg. That is not tripping and falling down the stairs. That is being shoved really hard by someone."

"The coroner that was sent to Julia's home that day, did you know him?"

"I was off work for quite some time. I know they had a

few different guys who covered for me but I can easily look into it and find out who they sent."

"I have his name here. It was Dr Brockman."

"No, I can't say I know him. He must be a new start. Most of us in this field either know, or have heard each other's names."

"Dr Cooper, can you look into this for us please. Just make some enquiries and see who actually sent Dr Brockman and, if you can, locate where he is working now."

"No problem. I'll see what I can do, but I've got to get going folks. I'm sorry. If you leave your name and number with the receptionist, I'll get back to you with what I find out."

"We really appreciate your time, Dr Cooper."

★

Robert and Beth got in their car to head home for the day. "So, Robert what do you make of that?"

"Very odd. There is certainly no question in his mind that he was pushed down the stairs. Sheriff Joe spoke quite highly about him. He sounds like a straight-up guy, so it's hard to know why someone would do something like that to him."

"I know what you're saying, Robert. I wonder what the outcome would have been if he was there instead of Brockman…"

"I appreciate the prints did not match. I think everyone agrees on that. However, Brockman's report certainly played a big part in the decision not to move forward with charges. One thing seems certain; if Dr Cooper was there, they would have had the hair samples compared to Holman. That really gets me. Why the hell would they just accept the coroner's report? They had nothing to lose in sending it off to be tested."

"Anyway, Robert, it's after 5pm, so let's just switch off for the day. We have got a lot done. In fact, I have an idea. How about we stop by that new restaurant on the way home and have dinner?"

"I don't think either of us are remotely dressed for dinner, Beth."

"If you don't care, I certainly don't."

"Sounds good. Let's go!"

CHAPTER 9

"You sign and date here, Mom, and same on here and the back page here."

"Quite a lot of forms to fill out, huh? You realise you're the first person on your dad's side or, in fact, my side to go to university."

"What was he like, Mom? You've never told me much about him, other than he died in the war."

"An amazing man, I loved him so much but he died, as far as he was concerned, doing his duty for his country."

"The way you put that, it does not sound like you quite agreed with his view?"

"I didn't, son. It's the only thing your father and I disagreed on, but it's what he wanted and I couldn't stop him. His family had a long history of military service going back many generations. I used to tell him the lot of them had been brainwashed. The politicians just feed the poor and uneducated stories of patriotism and duty, while they sit back getting rich off the war. They never send their own and, if they ever do, it's only for publicity to further their careers. They make damn sure their loved ones are never in any danger, but it stops with you, son. As long as I'm alive, you will never join the military to fight their wars."

"Mom, I know I'm not sure what I want to do but, for sure, joining the military won't happen."

★

Robert and Beth Osbourne invited Sheriff Amos over for a drink and updated him on their efforts so far.

"That's actually really well done guys, I'm impressed!" said Sheriff Amos. "Next time the department is looking for recruits, I'll be sure to give them your number."

"Definitely not!" said Beth.

"You have certainly opened up some avenues to investigate further. What do you see as your next step?"

"Well," said Robert. "That is kind of where you come in. I'm sorry, but I want to ask you to get a hair sample from the crime scene and one from the suspect's head. I want to compare them. There is a lab over in Texas that do Microscopic Hair Analysis for private citizens. They charge a lot, but I want it done."

"Robert, getting you in there to take photos was one thing but you are asking me to illegally remove stored evidence from an unsolved case."

"I know. I've thought about it but there is no other way, it should have been done at the time. I don't need all of it, just a few samples of each is all they require for the test. No one would even know they went missing."

"Okay, I'll try later this week, but no promises. It may be into next week before my guy is on night duty down there."

"Thanks again, Amos."

"What you said about Bob earlier is quite interesting. He's been around a long time and is very well thought of, both in the medical community and the force. If he told you he would get back to you, then he will. Let me know when he does. I'd be interested to hear who assigned Brockman that day and what he has to say for himself now."

"Can we just ask you one other favour, Amos?"

"Go on then, it can't be much worse than what you've already asked me to do."

"We have the police photo of Simon but I'd like you to give me a dozen or so other police photos of similar looking guys. They have to look the same, like the one we have, taken front on. I don't want it to look any different, other than the face itself."

"I don't even need to ask what you want this for, I have already figured it out. This request is easy but you'll need to give me them back once you're finished."

"We'll be sure to do that, Amos."

"So, what do you guys have planned for the rest of the afternoon?"

"We are heading back to the library."

"Are we?" asked Beth.

"We need to do more research on the knife. The engraving on it must represent something."

"You don't sound too keen on the library, Beth."

"I don't mind the library, Amos. It's the old woman in there behind the desk that I have to pass by. The other day I heard her from where I sat. She was going on and on about the best clothes hangers. I mean, who speaks about clothes hangers? The poor assistant's ears were falling off. I wanted to go over and rescue her but just couldn't bring myself to do it."

"Wow! Mental note to self – avoid the library!"

★

75

"You see those bags on the back seat?"

"Oh, Mom. Give it a rest. Yes, prices are going up blah, blah. You say the same thing every time!"

"It's not you that has to run the house on a tight budget, it's me. I'm the one who has to get us through to the end of each month."

"And don't roll your eyes either!"

"Mom, why are you turning here?"

"The mechanic has called ahead to the scrapyard for me to pick up the cable mechanism thingy for the bonnet. He promised to fit it for free if I collect it."

"You mean you can't even open the bonnet?"

"Well, I can, but you need the pliers that's on the floor by your feet to pull the wire under here and I've never managed to do it. Normally, I wouldn't care if I could open the bonnet or not, but the radiator has a leak and I need to keep filling it every few days, so I really need the bonnet fixed."

"Wow, this car is such an embarrassment, Mom."

"Have you met Linda's parents yet?"

"Yes. Why do you ask?"

"Well, next time you see her dad, tell him there is a loan application sitting on his desk that he needs to approve. Anyway, this must be the place here."

"You think, Mom? What gave it away? It's not the thousands of junk cars surrounding us, is it?"

"Look you're not too old for me to give you one across the ears you know. Anyway, let's go see if we can find the guy. His name is Sean."

"Come on, Simon. We need to go and find Sean. What are you standing by the car and looking at?"

"I'm just making a mental note where we've parked it.

Surrounded by all of these, it won't be easy to find it again. We could end up leaving in the wrong one!"

"Funny! Now come on."

★

Robert and Beth walked up to the counter of the shoe shop. "Hi, Donna. Thanks so much for looking into this so promptly."

"Not a problem. I'm not sure how much I can help you, but I looked back in our records, from the time we took in the All Star High Tops, to the time of Julia's murder. We only sold four pairs of nine and a halves, it's not the most popular size we sell."

"These are the receipts for the four of them."

"Were you on duty for all the transactions?"

"Yes. My initials are on all of them."

"Look, I appreciate it's a long time ago but do you think, if I showed you some photos you could recognise the guy?"

"I can try, sir."

"Do you mind if I just lay these out on the glass counter here?"

"Sure, go ahead."

Donna looked at all the faces. It did not take her long. "This is the guy! This one here."

"Why did you pick him, Donna?"

"I remember him. He flirted with me at the time. I thought it was cute, as he was so much younger than me."

"How sure are you?"

"I wouldn't swear by it, but I'm pretty sure that was him."

"Thanks so much for your help, Donna. You have certainly done all you can."

"This does not prove anything, Robert. You realise that, right?"

"Beth, what are the chances of her picking Holman out of fourteen mug shots?"

"She could be mistaken. She could have seen his photo in the newspaper."

"Beth, if a guy flirts with you, wouldn't you remember him?"

"Fair point, but still, Robert."

"Look, it's one more thing that confirms our belief. We'll get him, Beth. It won't be easy, but we'll nail him eventually."

★

Sheriff Amos pulled up outside Robert and Beth's home.

"Look, something is going on guys. I went to get the hair samples in the Evidence Room, I pulled the drawer open and the knife was gone."

"Who the hell would have taken it?"

"I don't know, Robert. I asked my man down there. He said his relief told him he handed it over to some religious guy. The order came from really high up. It's not something you question. You just do it."

"What the hell would a religious guy want with that knife, and nearly three years after the murder?"

The sheriff pulled a clear plastic bag from his pocket. "These are a few strands from the crime scene, but there were no samples taken from the boy."

"Are you sure? I thought we had photos of his hair."

"Yes, you have photos, but there are no samples stored. When I checked into it, the reason none were saved into evidence was because the examiner's report ruled him out.

Look, I'm going to have to lie low on this for a while. I'm not going back down there. There is no way my guy will allow it anyway, sorry guys."

"You have done everything for us, Amos. I don't know how we will ever repay you for that."

"Another thing; if you need me, give me a call and we'll meet up somewhere else. I don't want to be seen coming here too much."

"Understood. Thanks again, Amos."

"Okay. All the best guys, I got to go."

"Bye, Amos."

"So Sherlock, what's the master move now?"

"I think, Beth, we need to look at that knife differently. All along we have been comparing knife company emblems at the library and getting nowhere. I think we need to look at some religious designs and see if we can get a match from one of them."

"Fair point, but what about this hair sample? What are we going to do? It's useless without Holman's."

"Do you really need to ask?"

"Hey, there is no way we are going over there!"

"Do you have another option? Think about it Beth; the two are at Mass every Sunday. They live out in the middle of nowhere. I doubt they lock up properly, if at all. We'll just drive over there. We have at least an hour that we know for certain that they are gone.

"We will go in, find his room, or the bathroom. There is sure to be a comb, or brush lying around. We will bag some hair samples and head out. At the most we will be in there ten minutes max."

"Do you remember what Amos said? We can do anything but break the law. You want us to break and enter into someone's home. Can you imagine what would happen to us if we were to get caught?"

"We won't, Beth. Is there an alternative?"

CHAPTER 10

"This is a perfect spot, Beth. They have to pass by here on their way to church. Their house is just a couple hundred yards up the road, we can park here and it's off the road. There is no way anyone passing can see the car.

"We'll come here tomorrow night for 6:15pm. Church starts at 7pm. You wait in the car and I'll see them drive by from behind those bushes. Once I see them go by, I'll run to the house. I'll take this screwdriver and gloves, just in case I need to lift a window to get in. I'll put the hair in this bag and I've got a flashlight so I won't have to put on any lights. I'll be back within fifteen minutes."

"Robert, I can't believe I let you talk me into this."

"Let's get some lunch and then go visit your friend at the library."

★

"What are you reading Simon?" asked Fr. Mark.

"It's the Quran."

"That's a first. I don't think I've seen anyone reading a Quran in church before."

Simon motioned for Fr. Mark to sit next to him. "Rightly or wrongly, Father, I'm beginning to believe that it may not actually matter. I have the Torah in my bag and I'm studying other religions as well."

"You may well be right, Simon. There are good people in all religions. Perhaps a better way is to see religion as a vehicle that takes us to God. We may choose different vehicles but they all end at the same destination. I am interested, Simon, to hear how you see life."

Simon paused for a moment. "Father, I find myself going through the Universe on this planet, I am trapped within this body. I have only five senses to try and understand where I am and why I am here. I have escaped myself only briefly in travelling visions, but I am soon returned and imprisoned. There is a force that will not allow me to stay outside of myself. I must fulfil a destiny within this body, before I am allowed to leave. Only then will I be reunited with God."

"Why do you use the word 'reunited'?"

"I have an awareness, Father, that we all came from him. None of us are much different to God except in degree. He made us like himself and a part of us is in fact Him. When we see each other we are seeing God. He is all around. What can we offer up to a God that has created this Universe? Churches with gold Altars, beautiful Mosque Temples and Synagogues? He does not want buildings with gold. The only service we can offer Him is to help each other make it though this life. Only then are we directly helping Him.

"I see us killing in the name of religion. The horror of war, there is no Holy War. This is a contradiction in terms. When we kill, we are killing God. I have devoted much prayer and thought to this. I am not wrong."

"You are very much correct, Simon. Unfortunately, our leaders and the leaders of other faiths have misled their followers. Many are corrupt and power is a drug that they cannot do without. Like politicians, they create a crisis to take the focus off of their corruption, and the bigger the crisis, the less the focus is on them. War is the biggest crisis of all, so they love war."

"What is the answer, Father?"

"The end is clearly written in Daniel and The Book of Revelations. Jesus, when asked, discussed it in detail. Other religions have also given clear warnings. No one can stop what is to come.

"Simon, treasure blinds many so they fail to see the prophecy happening around them. We are powerless to change the destiny of the world. However, we can change our destiny and that of those around us. We can give no greater gift than to bring someone to Him."

"Father, I have searched for truth. I have prayed that I see without judgement or prejudice and it is the greatest challenge of my life."

"Perhaps, Simon, you are being too hard on yourself. We are human with faults and weaknesses; our job is to overcome them. You are still very young and you have the rest of your life to perfect yourself."

"Thanks Father, I think at the rate I'm going I'll need longer than that!"

Fr. Mark smiled. "Trust me we all feel the same about ourselves."

★

"Perfect timing Beth: 6:15pm. In about 10 minutes, I'll head over to the bushes and look out for them passing."

"Great, I'll just sit here worrying then…"

"It will be fine, trust me. Hey, you know that buddy I

told you about who served in Vietnam? He called me back this morning. From what he found out, John A Holman died of injuries in combat, but that's not all. He said the cause of death was recorded as a bayonet to the chest but one of the guys who was with him that day swears it was not a bayonet."

"He said they were patrolling through thick jungle at the time and a guy came out of nowhere and put a knife into his heart. They shot and killed the guy but the knife was actually left in him. When he told me that, a shiver went up my spine."

"I'm not sure what to make of that, Robert. It has to be just coincidental."

"Yeah, that's what I think as well."

"Anyway, final check: gloves, screwdriver, flashlight and sample bag for hair. I'll see you back here soon, they should be passing by shortly."

"Hang on, Robert. What you done to your shoes?"

"I held them over a candle and melted the soles. The ground is dry I don't want to leave any clear footprints. I'll incinerate them with these gloves when we get home."

"Wow. I wonder sometimes who I married."

"Isn't it great, Beth, when a plan comes together?"

"You got it already?"

"Yep, let's go."

★

"What happened? Tell me, did you have to break in?"

"I just went around the back, the door was open. I went into his bedroom and he had a comb on a shelf so I took some of the hair and put it in the bag and left. See: no drama."

"You have everything with you that you took?"

"Sample bag with hair, flashlight, unused screwdriver, and gloves, check."

"Wow. I'm impressed, Robert. Well done!"

"I've sent off for the two sets of sample kits. They should arrive soon so, hopefully by the end of next week, the lab will start the testing. They said, about two to three weeks after that, they will let us know the results."

"Why do they send two sets of sample kits?"

"They said it's policy. They send two so that if the first set of samples is damaged in testing, they will call me. Then I can send the back-up sample kit to them."

"You know, Robert. Whatever happens, I'm really glad we made the decision to do this. It was so hard in the beginning but, somehow, it is getting that much easier now. I feel it's bringing us closer together as well."

"I feel the same way, Beth."

★

Martha and Simon turned off the main road and headed down the country track towards their home.

"So, Mom, did you fill out the application form?"

"Yes, I dropped it off at the bank this morning. It's crazy the cost of going to university these days. The Manager told me, as it's a student loan, it won't be a problem. I should have gone to him for my car loan instead of Martin Bernstein."

"Mom, he was only doing his job. It was nothing personal."

"Don't you go defending him, I've never had bad credit for anything."

"Yes, Mom, but then you've never had any money either."

"Anyway, Simon, enough of that, before you go into the house stand back and let me show you a thing of beauty."

"That's it, Mom? You opened the bonnet."

"Yep, the part worked. The mechanic said it was not from the same model but he managed to fit it. You're impressed aren't you?"

"I couldn't be more proud, Mom!" Simon shook his head. "Speaking of the model, what type of car is this?"

"It's a Vauxhall Victor, son. Your dad was so proud the day he bought it. Unfortunately, the name fell off the back a few years ago."

"Did it fall off or did Vauxhall send someone round to remove it?"

"Oh, ha, ha. Very funny!"

"I didn't open the bonnet just to impress you. We are going to fix the radiator leak."

"Mom, I know nothing about cars and you know even less."

"Well, what do you make of this?"

"It's an egg you're holding."

"Exactly! The mechanic told me that if I can't afford to fix the leak then just crack an egg and put it in the radiator. It will settle into the hole and stop the leak."

"You are joking, right?"

"Nope. That's what the man said."

"Oh God!"

"Don't you take the Lord's name in vain, Simon J Holman!"

"It was not in vain, Mom. He's the only one that can rescue this car, and it maybe even be beyond Him!"

"Just let's get on with it, but watch out when you take the radiator cap off. It was over-heating on the way here."

For Robert and Beth, this was the day they had waited for. The lab results were in the post and they would almost certainly be delivered today. Robert looked out the living room window.

"This is it, Beth. I can see him across the road. He's just delivered some mail over by the Fullarton's and he's headed over here now."

The letter did not even hit the floor. It was caught as it came through the front door of the Osbourne home. "Come on let's go into the living room and open it."

The lab results showed a 94.6% likely match between samples provided.

"We have him! This has got to be it, Beth. I told you our hard work would pay off. Let me give Amos a call. We'll try to meet up with him for lunch."

"So, what you think, Amos? A 94.6% match! I knew it was him. There was just no one else it could be."

"I don't even want to ask how you guys got a sample from Holman. Well done!"

"Yes," said Beth. "Please don't ask."

"We have to go about this the legal way. I'm going to have to assign someone to look into it. We have to build a case with sufficient weight and get a judge to grant us permission to bring the boy in. The examiner must take a sample. We will then send it off to the lab from there."

"Are you serious, Amos? How long is that going to take?'

"I'll put someone on it that I know well and I'll let him know the background. Don't worry, he will get enough to sway a judge."

"So how long are we talking about?"

"I'm guessing, four to six weeks before we can approach a judge. But once he agrees, we usually get the paperwork, with the warrant back from him in a matter of days. Look, I know you want this to happen by tomorrow, but it can't. You have waited nearly three years. We have to do this the correct way. We can't be seen not to by his defence lawyer. He will pick up on any failure on our part not to adhere to procedure. He will get the case thrown out on a technicality. It's got to be watertight."

"You're right, Amos. We can't screw things up at this stage. Beth and I will continue to build the case against him and I'll let you know if we find anything else. We'll leave you to do your part."

*

"Hi Annamae, come on through to the kitchen," said Martha. "So, you feeling better?"

"Yes, a lot better; I finally got over that cold. It had me feeling really rotten at one point, so I just stayed in."

"What you been up to, Martha?"

"Not too much, the usual. I've actually been thinking recently that, with Simon having finished school and heading off to university soon, he won't need me like before, so I might look for a job."

"You work? Doing what?"

"Well, there is a lot I can do but, when I left school, you remember, I did that Secretarial Course and I learned to type pretty fast. I've been seeing, in the big offices, the girls typing on the computers. So, I could catch up on my typing skills and, at the same time, I can learn about computers."

"Are you serious, Martha?"

Martha took a sip of coffee.

"Yes, Annamae, I've been thinking about it a lot. I want

to get out and meet new people and I can sure use the extra money. With the expense of university, I was kind of hoping you would have encouraged me."

"I'm happy for you, Martha. It's just that I've seen you at home for so long now, I can't picture you working."

"Well, we'll see. First I need to practice my typing and learn about computers. Then I can apply for a job, so it won't be anytime soon, that's for sure."

"Good news, Martha, on Simon going to university. At least we will have him close by for another four years. When does he start?"

"In a few weeks, so I gave him a list of things I want done around the house before he starts. I told him I don't care what his plans are, I want the list completed."

"What's he been up to in his free time?"

"He's been hanging out with Linda and her friends a lot."

"Don't tell me – the same Linda from the graduation party."

"Yes, same girl. He says they are still just friends but he speaks really highly of her."

"I don't like her for him at all. She is far too grown up in the way she carries herself, all smothered in makeup."

"Come on, Annamae. I think that's a bit unfair. You have never spoken to her. You can't just make that judgement from just seeing her once."

"Oh, I know her type. I've seen them thousands of times."

"Anyway, don't go making trouble and, if you come over and she is here, just be nice and don't embarrass your only nephew."

"Come on in Mr and Mrs Osbourne."

"Thank you, Dr Cooper."

"Please sit down and just call me Bob, everyone does. Firstly, I'm sorry it took me a while to get back to you. I actually started looking into what you asked at the time, but I was struggling to make sense of what I was being told, so it took a while. Actually, I still have not understood what happened that day."

"That's okay, Bob. What did you find out?" asked Robert.

"Well, no one from dispatch assigned any doctor to your home that morning. I am certain of that. I've asked around and I've checked the logbook, there is no record of it. In fact, they did not even know about Julia's murder that morning. The first record of it in their books is the actual report Dr Brockman logged and filled out that afternoon. Unfortunately, this was not picked up at the time. Everyone just assumed someone else called him and no one checked the log."

"But I thought Sheriff Joe called here and asked for an examiner to be sent over…"

"I'm sure he made the call, but it did not come through to this Office as it would have been recorded. They log all calls and they sure don't forget to log a call by the sheriff regarding a murder."

"So, how did Brockman end up at the crime scene?"

"I have spent a long time trying to answer that question, as well as who he is, but no one seems to know. I contacted every Medical Professional Body that I am aware of and there is no Dr Brockman. One thing I will say, though, is that I looked at the Medical Report and the other paperwork he filled out and this guy for certain has some form of medical background. He used medical terminology and used it correctly, in a way that a layperson would not have been able to without at least some decent level of training.

"I then spoke to Sheriff Joe. He said there was no reason not to think the guy was a professional. Everything about him, in his words, 'screamed doctor' even though he did not agree with his findings."

"Dr Brockman used our Medical Forms. Actually, he did not have a choice because of where the murder was committed, so I knew he must have come in here both to collect and submit them. I asked around and a couple of people remember seeing him that day. Anne in the back office clearly remembered him. She said, when he signed in, he signed as Dr Brockman. However, he had photo ID hanging around his neck and she noticed it said Dr Brookman. She asked him about it and he said something to the effect that 'it's a typo' and he has never got around to getting it replaced. The photo on it, she swears was definitely him, so she had no reason to doubt what he said.

"I began to think, from what Sheriff Joe told me, the way he filled out the paperwork and the ID he was wearing, he hadn't just studied medicine but been around medical facilities and crime scenes. This guy knew what he was doing, from all accounts. In the checks I had made to locate him, I had used the name Dr Brockman. However, after what Anne told me, I looked for him as Dr Brookman and straight away he showed up in the system."

"That is amazing, Bob. Did you get his details? Needless to say, we need to speak with him straight away."

"Yes, I learnt quite a lot about him. In fact he died

eighteen years ago in a canoe accident on the river. His canoe was recovered but his body was never found."

"This can't be real, Bob. So, what's going on?"

"I wish I could tell you guys, I really wish I knew. Look I've put a lot of time into this and taken it as far as I can. I'll leave you to look into it from here but stop by and let me know what you find out."

"We will, Bob, and thank you so much again, we really appreciate your help."

"No problem. I wish you both all the best moving forward with this."

"Thanks again, Bob."

CHAPTER 11

Robert and Beth were in the spare bedroom that they had converted into an office. They were surrounded by all the paperwork and evidence they had uncovered.

"Have a look here, Robert. This looks almost identical to the knife we are looking for. Look at the symbols. They are the same on both sides of the handle. You were correct; the knife was not a regular knife. According to this, it is an Athame, which it says was used by pagans in sacrificial ceremonies."

"I agree, Beth. It looks very much the same, not just the symbol engraved on the handle but the shape of the blade as well. What does that mean for Julia? Why would such a knife have been used on her? Look, let's go over everything we have."

"Okay, Robert, let me get the folder from the cabinet."

Footprints:
"We have established that the type of shoe is Converse All Star High Tops, they were likely purchased on High Street. The store Manager, Donna, identified Simon Holman out of fourteen photos."

Hair:

"The lab report confirmed a likelihood of 96.4% likely the same individual, using Microscopic Hair Analysis, Amos has started work on getting enough evidence to go to a Judge, to bring suspect in for the medical examiner to take a hair sample."

Fingerprints:

"Expert ruled they did not belong to Holman – yet to be matched to an individual."

Suspect's father, John A Holman:

"Eyewitness claimed he was killed in Vietnam, combat related injury. He was stabbed in the heart and the knife left in him."

Murder Weapon:

"Almost certainly identified as an Athame. Further investigation needed."

Dr Brockman:

"All enquiries have failed to track him down. Nevertheless, he was in fact at the crime scene because Dr Cooper fell, or was likely pushed, down a flight of stairs that morning. Turns out, Dr Brockman's ID has his name spelt Brookman, who died in 1968 in a canoe accident – body never recovered."

"Look, Beth, we need to get Amos in on this. He can find out a lot more about Dr Brookman than we ever could. I feel terrible asking him to help us yet again."

"I know what you mean, but we don't have a choice. You know, Robert; I'm trying to look at this objectively. The strongest evidence, the prints on the knife and window, don't match Holman. However, the hair analysis almost certainly does. On one hand, Julia knew no one capable of doing something like this, but on the other hand Amos says murders are almost always committed by someone the victim knows. Not to mention, we still have Dr Brookman to find, along with the mystery behind the knife that was used."

"Beth, don't you go having doubts. We both know exactly who did this. There is no one else it could be. Now, just dismiss any doubts in your mind. We are going after Holman and we will get justice for Julia. Anyway, Beth, that was Amos on the phone earlier on. He wants to meet us at the bar tomorrow to discuss the meeting they had with the judge."

"Did he indicate how it went?"

"No. He did not say much. He was very matter of fact and told me he will discuss it in detail tomorrow."

★

Martha and Simon were on their way home following a trip into town.

"You're joking right? Tell me, Simon J Holman that you're not serious?"

"No, Mom. I'm very serious."

"Are you really asking me to teach you to drive, after all you have said about this car over the years?"

"Yes. I went down to the centre and got my learner's permit, who else is going to teach me? I can't afford lessons."

"Okay, so let's say I teach you to drive and you get your license, exactly what car are you planning to drive?"

"Well, until I can afford my own, I was thinking this thing."

"Really! This thing?"

"This car, Mom."

"That's a bit better, but I'll tell you now: I'm thinking of getting a job, so if I need the car, I don't want to hear a moan out of you. If I don't need it, then you're welcome to use it – deal?"

"Okay, Mom. Fair enough. Where are you thinking of working?"

"I'm not sure. I'd like to learn about computers and brush up on my typing, then see from there. I'm going to the library next week. They have some computers I can use for free. I've also seen a few adds in the papers, advertising for temporary secretaries, so I'll give it a go."

"Best of luck with that, Mom. You would be a great secretary, and I appreciate the sacrifice you're making."

"Teaching you to drive is no sacrifice. I'm happy to do it."

"No, Mom. Going out to work. You're doing it to help with my university expenses. I know you are, but you don't have to. I plan to get a job each summer and it will help to pay for it. In that way, I won't have that much left to pay off when I graduate."

"No, son. That is not the only reason I'm getting a job. I'd like to meet new people, have some responsibility. Yes, a bit of extra money coming in will also be good. Anyway, Simon, let's run inside quickly; this rain is going to get worse."

★

Martha put her handbag and keys on the table. "Do you have everything ready for your first day tomorrow? Let me know now if you need anything ironed."

"I'm good, Mom."

"So, what time do you need me to drop you at the bus stop in the morning?"

"Bus is at 7:45am, so we can leave here by 7:30am. Thankfully it goes right past the university. You can pick me up at the same bus stop about 4:10pm, but if I don't see you there, I'll just walk home – no problem."

"Now, you know I'll be there."

"I know, Mom. Anyway, I'm just going to get a shower."

"Don't be long, I just need to heat up the dinner."

★

Martha and Simon were clearing the table after dinner.

"You know, Mom, I'm just going to go straight to bed now."

"You all packed?"

"Yes, all packed and ready."

"I'll finish tidying up, and then I'd like us to say prayers together tonight."

"Okay, I'll see you in a bit."

Martha went into Simon's room soon after. He was already in bed reading a book.

"Did you see the new socks I got for you? I put them in the drawer here."

"Yes. Thanks, Mom."

"What's the book you're reading?"

"The hint is here on the cover, where it says 'The History of Religion.'"

Martha looked at Simon narrowed her eyes and showed him her fist. "I really could hit you now, Simon."

"You couldn't hit me, Mom. You always say you're going to and never do."

"One day I might surprise you."

"Yeah. You always say that too."

"Anyway, son, let's say prayers together. We have a lot to be thankful for. A new chapter of your life starts tomorrow."

"Just one thing, Mom, when you pick me up tomorrow can you park a bit away from the bus stop?"

"Are you ashamed to have your mother collect you after school?"

"It isn't so much you collecting me. It's more what you're collecting me in…"

"Do you want to learn to drive or not?"

★

Sheriff Amos walked into the bar and saw Robert and Beth waiting for him.

"Hi, Robert. How's things? And how are you, Beth? You're still managing to put up with old grumpy here?"

"Just about, Amos. It's not easy but I'm hanging in there. We ordered a beer for you. I hope that's okay; its after 5:00pm so you must be off duty by now."

"That's perfect, Beth, thanks. Sorry I'm late. I had to take a call just as I was leaving the station."

"No problem. So, tell us: how did you make out with the judge?"

"I'm afraid it's not good news. We built more than a strong enough case. However, the FBI has just announced that Microscopic Hair Analysis can no longer be accepted as a science that can match hair to one individual. Therefore the judge has refused to grant permission to move forward and bring Holman in. I'm really sorry."

"I can't believe this," said Beth. "The lab said it was a 94.6% likely match and they are saying that's not good enough?"

"The timing could not have been worse. This procedure has been accepted science since the fifties and they have just, in the last couple of weeks, come out with this ruling."

"So, where do we go from here? Robert and I have put so much time into this."

"I appreciate that. You can certainly continue to look into the other leads you have developed. Regarding the hair sample, that is a non-starter. No judge is going to listen to us after what the FBI has said. I'm so sorry."

Robert then told the sheriff everything Dr Bob Cooper had found out about Dr Brockman.

"Wow! Robert, that is an unbelievable story. I will certainly get my people to look into Dr Brookman. That won't be hard to do, but well done. At least, finally, we have his actual name now, but I'm struggling to piece this together. So it's one of two things either: Dr Brockman is Dr Brookman – he never died but had just changed his name for some unknown reason; or, Dr Brookman died and someone, with some level of medical knowledge, is impersonating him. Do I have this correct?"

"I think so Amos. Now, let me order another couple of beers and a glass of red wine. I'll tell you what we've found out about the murder weapon."

"Robert, the more you look into this, the weirder it seems to get. I mean, I've never even heard of a knife called an Athame."

"I don't think most people would have, Amos."

"Okay. I'll look into that as well, but I'm not even sure where to start. I don't know any pagans or wiccans in Sidon. Let me see what I can find out. Needless to say, it would be a huge step if we could establish where the knife came from."

"Amos, what do you think?" asked Beth.

"Honestly, I don't know. I have always suspected Holman, but now, with everything you are finding out, I'm starting to have my doubts. It's like there is more to this than we thought. You must have noticed that almost every piece of evidence you have looked at has turned up something really unexpected? I mean, not much is really normal about the case."

Robert quickly jumped in. "You two are letting your minds play tricks on you. There is no one other than Holman. Why can't you see that? If this thing was investigated properly at the time, Holman would be locked up and that would have been the end of it."

"Robert, relax; Beth and I are on your side, but take a step back. Look at the evidence. It is certainly not a slam-dunk case against Holman."

CHAPTER 12

Martha sat at the breakfast table counting the minutes. She could not wait to leave and collect Simon. *What is wrong with me?* she thought. *He is nearly eighteen years of age and I'm worried about his first day at university. I've got nothing done in the house and I've spent the entire day thinking how he is getting on.*

Finally, for Martha it was time to go. *I don't mind being a bit early, I can sit in the car and read my book*, she thought. Martha left home and drove slowly, but still she was far too early. She sat in her car with one eye on her book and the other eye looking out for the bus. *Here it comes*, she thought. The bus door opened and out came Simon, followed by Linda. He kissed her and walked towards the car. *Well,* she thought, *so much for 'just friends'. I'll be speaking to him about this.*

"Hi, Mom. You waiting long?"

"No, I just got here. I almost forgot I had to pick you up today… what do you think? Of course I've been waiting for a long time! I spent the whole day thinking about you. So tell me; how was your first day?"

"Oh, really good. I thought it would just be orientation and getting our syllabus but, once we found our classes and sat down, the lecturers were straight into it. They asked questions to make sure we were paying attention and even gave us assignments to do on our first day. Can you believe that?"

Martha smiled. "I'm thrilled to hear that. You know the university has an excellent reputation; leave there in four years time with good grades and you will be set up for life."

There was then a couple of minutes' silence as they drove along the country roads. Simon took a folder from his bag and reviewed some notes he had taken.

"So just friends huh?"

"Oh, Mom. I just knew you had to say something. You could not just let it lie could you?"

"Well, I must ask; I'm your mother."

"I told you I liked her, she reminds me of you. She is really nice and has a good group of friends who I've gotten to know quite well over the last few months."

"Is she sitting next to you in class?"

"Well, yes – for the classes we are in together."

"I'm not sure I like the idea of that; I hope she will not be a distraction."

"No, Mom. She actually had better grades than I did in high school. She is pretty studious."

"I'm happy to hear that, so when am I going to meet Linda?"

"Oh, I don't know. I'll see what I can arrange but don't hassle me about this. I'll keep it in mind and let you know."

"Okay, I won't hassle you, but wow talk about defensive."

"Anyway, when are you going to teach me to drive?"

"Oh, I don't know, Simon. I'll see what I can arrange, but don't hassle me about this. I'll keep it in mind."

Simon turned and looked at Martha. She kept her eyes on the road and then laughed out loud. "Okay, we'll start this weekend."

"Thanks. So, how did you get on with your typing at the library today?"

"I didn't go. But I'll definitely go tomorrow."

★

Sheriff Amos spent most of the day on the phone. He was finally able to determine that, over eighteen years ago, Dr Brookman lived and worked over 300 miles away in Louisiana. He died on the 7th April 1968, and the cause of death was suspected drowning. Body was never recovered and his last listed address was: 12, Mountain View Apartments on Cornhill road. He could have assigned one of his officers to go there but he wanted to do this himself, even if it meant over six hours of driving.

The following day, Sheriff Amos left Sidon long before dawn but it was not until after lunchtime when he pulled up outside the apartment he was looking for. There was no missing the huge "MOUNTAIN VIEW APARTMENTS" sign. On the door it said "Vacancies".

"Hi, my name is Sheriff Amos. I'm from the town of Sidon."

"I'm Larry Summers. How can I help you, Sheriff?"

"How long have you owned these apartments, Larry?"

"I'll tell you what: would you like to come in? It's a bit hot to be talking outside, and you probably could use a drink as well."

"Thank you. That would be great."

"Iced tea okay?"

"Iced tea sounds fantastic, thanks."

Larry poured a couple glasses of iced tea and sat down. "To answer your question, Sheriff, my wife and I have lived here for over forty years but it did not look like this originally. We have done a lot of work to the place; most of the apartments you see we added ourselves."

"I'd like to ask you about one of the tenants you had here about eighteen years ago."

"Oh, with my memory the way it is, I may need to get the wife to help me here. That is quite some time back. What's the name of the person you want to know about?"

"His name is Dr Brookman." From the look on Larry's face, Sheriff Amos knew he recognised the name.

"I don't think I need to call the wife, I remember him well."

"What can you tell me, Larry?"

"I remember just about everything. He was a young doctor, really well mannered and an extremely likeble guy. However, a few months after he moved in, he asked me if anyone had stayed in the apartment before him, so I said, 'of course'. He wanted to know if they had complained about anything strange going on in there. I asked him, 'strange like what?' He said he was having trouble sleeping at night. There was a voice and he swore he had seen a figure in there.

"I told him tenants complain about things from time to time but never anything like that. I could tell he was quite spooked by whatever happened to him. Over time it must have gotten worse. The wife and I used to hear him shouting in the middle of the night."

"What was he saying? Larry, do you remember?"

"He kept shouting 'leave me alone', there were screams as well. I spoke to him again and he told me there was a demon attacking him."

"I met him one day. Well, actually I walked up to him from behind when he was going into his apartment. He must have sensed I was there as he turned quickly and looked at me with the most terrified expression on his face, and it made me feel real uneasy. He was trying to control himself, but he was clearly shaking, the poor guy. He composed himself and I told him if he wanted I could move him to a different apartment. However, he didn't answer me, he just nodded. I was really happy he took me up on the offer as some of the other tenants had started complaining to me about him screaming during the night.

"Anyway, we helped him pack up his stuff and he moved all the way to the other side: over there, closest to the road. It's about as far away from where he was as he could have been, and it was away from most of the other tenants as well.

"Unfortunately, it did not help. In fact, things got worse. Whenever I saw him, he was really shaken up. My wife was very worried about him. He had gone from this fresh-faced young doctor to looking really terrible. Eventually, he came to me and said he wanted to break the lease agreement and he would be leaving at the end of the month. I said to him, forget about breaking the agreement, you won't owe me anything, just square me up at the end of this month.

"I think it was a Saturday or Sunday, but it was the weekend for sure when the police knocked on the door to tell me about the accident."

"You're referring, of course, to the canoe accident."

"Yes, it was terrible. I couldn't believe it. The police looked around his apartment but they did not stay long."

"Do you know if going out on the river was something he did a lot?"

"He never mentioned it to me, but he should not have gone. We had terrible rain for days and the rivers were really swollen and running fast. They warn folk not to go but I guess, for some people, that is the best time, although obviously not for him."

"I understand his body was never recovered, Larry."

"That's right, Sheriff. They found the canoe smashed but never found him."

"What happened to his belongings in the apartment?"

"Well, when there was no sign of the body, I read in the papers that he had been declared dead. I contacted the police and told them I had all his stuff in the apartment. However, they told me they had no information on relatives to forward it to, so the wife and I packed it into boxes, cleaned the apartment and continued renting it."

"Did anyone ever complain about the apartment after he left?"

"No complaints, well nothing like what he was seeing and hearing that's for sure."

"Did anyone ever show up to collect his belongings?"

"No, it doesn't seem like he had any family at all."

"What eventually happened to them?"

"We kept them along with things other tenants leave in a store room in the basement. We've had people come back a year or more after they've checked out, asking about something they left, other times it just sits in the storeroom year after year."

"Would you mind if I went through his possessions"

"No, I don't think that would be a problem, Sheriff."

"In fact, Larry I'm not driving all the way back to Sidon, do you have a spare apartment I can rent for the night?"

"Yes, I'm sure we do."

"Great, if you have one near the store room, I'd like to have it. I'll look through his stuff and I'll check out in the morning."

"Hang on, Sheriff. Let me have a look in the book here and see what would be the best room for you."

"I have one upstairs from the storeroom, that's about the closest I have available."

"Perfect, Larry. Thanks so much. If you could take me to your store room and show me which are his boxes, that would be great".

Sheriff Amos went for lunch and then spent the rest of the day and into the night going through Dr Brookman's belongings item by item.

★

"Well, Sheriff, did you get some sleep last night?"

"I got a bit, thanks."

"Did you find anything interesting in the boxes?"

"Yes and no, actually. I have a photograph here; can you confirm this is Dr Brookman?"

"Yes, that's him. Quite a handsome, clean-cut guy. It must have been taken a while before he died; he didn't look much like that in the last few weeks."

"Do you know if he ever spoke about Sidon, or visiting Sidon?"

"I don't believe so, Sheriff. Why do you ask?"

"I have a 1968 journal of his here. He kept a good record of his life. He has an address listed in Sidon. Would you mind, Larry, if I took both the journal and this photo of him?"

"I'm sure, after this long, no one is going to miss them. Not a problem, Sheriff."

"The other thing I noticed is there wasn't a single magazine, or even an item, that would connect him with being interested in canoes, rivers or the outdoors. I found that quite strange for someone who would go off in a canoe at one of the most challenging times."

"Yes, that is a bit strange, Sheriff. But, like I said, he was an absolute gentleman when he arrived here. I've no doubt something really strange happened in the apartment that affected him badly. I take it you're leaving us today?"

"Yes, I'm going to head back to Sidon shortly. What do I owe you for the night?"

"Oh don't be silly, it was a pleasure having you, Sheriff. Just leave something in your room. I have a young girl who does the cleaning, single mother. She would really appreciate it."

"Consider it done, Larry, and many thanks again for all your assistance with this."

Sheriff Amos jumped into his car and placed the photo of Dr Brookman behind his steering wheel, almost completely covering the speedometer. This is a face he wanted implanted in his memory. He then flicked through the journal one last time before he drove off. He had not actually been honest with Larry when he said he got a bit of sleep; in fact, he was up all night.

The journal detailed the life of a young man who had gone from a dedicated medical professional to becoming something akin to a paranoid schizophrenic. It was not written by someone with a wild imagination, it was an actual account of demonic possession and this young doctor's experiences were recorded in detail. It was truly frightening.

The journal started on January 1st, 1968. It contained the neatest handwriting, which recorded courses, lecture dates, daily routines and medical books for reference. Suddenly, on March 5th, 1968, the handwriting changed completely, as if it belonged to someone else; there was no similarity.

It was untidy and unreadable in places. The words were written with such pressure the pen went through the pages and then the next day the handwriting returned to normal.

By the third week in March, there were numerous entries written with untidy handwriting. There were torn pages, followed by pictures drawn of faces contorted in agony. One particular demonic figure had his hand held high above his head and in it was a knife that was dripping with blood. The pages with the neat handwriting were getting fewer and fewer.

At the beginning of April, there was a picture drawn of a young woman holding a baby with an address in Sidon. Then, for the remainder of April, to his last entry, there was no neat handwriting. The pictures drawn became more horrifying. Sheriff Amos thought, if this is what the young man was seeing it's no surprise he was screaming out. The last entry was dated April 6th, 1968, the day before he died.

Sheriff Amos was absolutely shattered when he got to the outskirts of Sidon. He had driven with the windows down most of the way to try and stay awake. As much as he wanted to go straight home and sleep, he could not. He had to visit the address in Sidon. With the sun just setting, he turned off the tarmac and made his way through the fields along the bumpy dirt road.

"Good evening Ma'am, my name is Sheriff Amos. I'm sorry about coming by at this time, but I wanted to have a word with you, if that's alright."

"Sure, Sheriff, my name is Annamae. How can I help you?"

"I've a photo here. I want to know if you recognise this gentleman."

The sheriff showed Annamae the photo of Dr Brookman and looked closely to see her reaction.

"I'm sorry, Sheriff. I'm pretty sure I don't know him."

Sheriff Amos was not convinced; her words came out strong but her face said otherwise.

"Are you sure, Ma'am? Why don't you take another look?"

Annamae did not look at the photo a second time. "I'm excellent with faces, Sheriff. If I tell you I don't know him, then I don't know him. Now, why would you come to my house just before dark asking if I know this man?"

"He was reported missing so we we're just asking in the area, that's all, Ma'am. In fact, may I ask how long have you lived on this property?"

"I moved here in 1964. I like the isolation and, for the most part, people don't disturb me."

"I feel the same way, Ma'am, I'm not a city person myself. If I could, I'd move the office out of town but, anyway, thank you for your help."

"Good night, Sheriff."

"Sorry, Ma'am, I'm a bit tired and I'm trying to remember, but have we met before?"

"No, I've not met you. I've seen you in the local paper, but we have not met before."

"And one other thing: do you have any children?"

"No, Sheriff. I live alone, no husband and no children."

"Okay, thank you Ma'am and have a good evening."

Sheriff Amos got into his car and drove off. He knew without question the woman was lying to him but his training always taught him never to show it. Allow the person to think you believe them, while you try and figure what reason they have for lying. There is something that connects this woman to the picture, drawn in the journal, of the woman holding a baby at this address, he told himself. Anyway, it's time to go home; it's been a long two days.

★

Robert and Beth sat outside, enjoying a cup of coffee, whilst watching the sun setting below the fields.

"Robert, I don't wish to sound negative. We have been so busy these last few months, however, I feel we are running out of leads to follow-up on. We really need to turn up something from the murder weapon. If that fails then we are down to just hoping to find Dr Brookman, whoever he is."

"I'm aware of what you are saying, Beth, I've been thinking the very same thing myself, but we can't give up until we exhaust every possibility."

"Is it time to take a break from this? Perhaps go off for a week somewhere and get away?"

"I don't know, Beth. Let's see what Amos comes up with from his follow up on Dr Brookman and we'll take it from there. You know, I'm really sorry the way I reacted the other day. I've been so convinced all along that it was Holman and, honestly, I'm beginning to have doubts. As Amos said, whenever we look into something it gets really strange. Not to mention the murder weapon, I mean, what the heck is that doing in a place like Sidon?"

"I know how you feel, Robert. It's so difficult to be objective when it's about Julia. I guess that's only natural. Anyway, as we said at the start, we'll do our best and it's all we can do."

CHAPTER 13

Sheriff Amos woke suddenly and looked at the alarm clock, it showed 10:38am. *Good thing I'm the sheriff,* he thought. He had a shower, ate breakfast, jumped into his car and looked at the photo through the steering wheel. *I'm going to get you, Brookman,* he thought. On the way to the police station, it suddenly hit him and he knew exactly why he found Annamae familiar.

At the next junction, he turned around and headed back into the country. He drove down the path towards the old house. He walked over to the parked car, put his hand on the bonnet, and it felt warm. He walked up and knocked on the front door.

"Good morning, Ma'am. I'm sorry to trouble you unannounced like this. My name is Sheriff Amos, I have a few questions I'd like to ask you if you have a minute."

"I just got back from the library, Sheriff, and the house is a bit of a mess, but you're welcome to come in."

"Thank you, Ma'am."

"Call me, Martha. Would you like a coffee, Sheriff?"

"That would be great, Martha."

"So how can I help, Sheriff? I really hope it's nothing to do with Simon. I've answered enough questions about him over the years."

"No, Martha, it's nothing to do with your son. I have a photo of someone and I wanted to see if you could identify them for me."

"Sure, let me have a look."

Sheriff Amos watched Martha's expression suddenly change.

"I take it you know this man?"

"Yes, Sheriff. His name is Dr Brockman."

"Can you please tell me what you know?"

Martha then told Sheriff Amos the times she had seen him but avoided telling him about his gift of the Bible and cloth, or anything to do with the fact that the clergy were also looking into him.

"Can I ask how you came across that photo?"

"It's a long story, Martha."

"I've got a lot more coffee here."

Sheriff Amos smiled. "I'm not sure, actually, if you want to hear the full story as there are some disturbing elements to it."

"Sheriff, you must know what I have been through with my son. There is little that can be as disturbing as what I have witnessed. Please, I've shared with you my experience of Dr Brockman, and the difficulty I have had trying to find him. I really would like to know the background to this photo."

Sheriff Amos assessed Martha. There was something very likable about her. He decided to tell her what he knew, hoping that perhaps it would encourage her to share any information that she had, but he avoided any mention that he was helping Robert and Beth investigate Julia's death. He spoke about the demonic pictures in the journal but thought it best not to mention the picture of a woman holding a baby whom he was certain had to be Simon.

"So it's Dr Brookman? That is unbelievable. That explains why I could not find him. That account in his journal is truly frightening. I'm not sure what to make of all of this. However, I know for sure that is the man I saw on the occasions I mentioned, so he must be alive, but why do you think he would fake his own death?"

"Yes, I'm trying to understand that myself, Martha."

"And why is my address in his journal?"

"Actually, it's not your correct address. It's a house not far from here. I'm guessing it's your sister that lives there?"

"Yes, Annamae, but why then would her address be in his journal? I definitely need to ask her that."

"Actually, I went there last night and spoke with her. I only realised this morning that the reason I thought I recognised her was that you two look similar and, of course, because I was dealing with Julia's murder, I had seen your picture in the files. As soon as I made the connection that you two were related, I came by here to see you."

"So, what was her explanation when you showed her the photo?"

"Unfortunately, she said she did not recognise him."

"Annamae said that?"

"I'm afraid so, Martha."

"She knows exactly who he is, she knows him better than I do. On Simon's first birthday, he sat in the chair you're sitting in and Annamae sat opposite him. So why is she telling you she does not know him?"

"I don't know. I don't understand a lot of what is happening."

"I'm just thinking, Sheriff; how do I approach this with Annamae? I'm guessing she does not know you came here?"

"She does not know that for certain, but she may suspect

I'd figure it out and I'd come here eventually. As to what you say to her, I'm not sure whether you should confront her or not, that's entirely up to you."

"Sheriff, you know, just when I thought I'd put this whole thing behind me and moved on, you have opened it up again."

"I'm really sorry about that Martha."

"No, I did not mean it like that. It's not your fault. I am happy that you have answered some questions I've always had, but you have certainly created a lot of new ones."

"Speaking of moving on, do you mind if I ask you how Simon is doing?"

"No, I don't mind you asking, Sheriff. Actually, he had a very difficult year after Julia's death but he slowly got back on his feet in time to finish high school. He graduated with honours. He has just started university now and is doing really well."

"I'm really pleased to hear that. I can't imagine what both of you must have gone through."

"Sheriff, I lost my husband, who I loved dearly, but that pain could not compare to what I watched my son go through. I thank God every night that it is behind us now."

"Martha, thank you for the coffee and the chat. I don't want to influence your decision either way but, if you do end up speaking with Annamae regarding Brookman, do you mind letting me know what she says?"

"I'm not even sure how to answer that question. Annamae and Simon are all I have in this world and I don't want to promise you anything – you do understand, don't you?"

"It was an unfair request. I'm sorry. I should not have put you in this position."

"That is okay, Sheriff. If I were in your place I would likely have asked me the same."

"You are a very honest person, Martha. In my line of work I don't come across that quality very often."

"Thanks for the complement, Sheriff. You have a safe journey."

"Bye, and keep in touch."

Martha closed the front door and stood in the hallway. All the memories came flooding back of Annamae denying that it was Dr Brockman coming out of the operating theatre. Now she was denying she knew him. Suddenly, she thought, how did he show up on the night of Simon's birth, who called him? Why have I not even thought about that before? And Simon's words I can never forget. 'You do realise, Mom, he is not a doctor.' Why did he say that?

Martha spent the next few hours trying to understand what she should do. The hours went by quickly, she needed more time to think this through but she had to leave and pick-up Simon at the bus stop.

"Hey, Mom."

"Hi, son. How was your day?"

"Great! I've got a big assignment to work on when I get home, but it's an interesting topic so I don't mind too much. It will probably take me about a week to complete."

"Well, the main thing is to do it right."

"Do you mind if, perhaps, Linda came over and worked on it with me tomorrow after university"

"No, not at all. Finally, I'll get to meet her. Will she stay for dinner?"

"I'll ask her, but make extra just in case."

Martha drove the remainder of the journey home without saying much. The memories of Annamae from years ago just replayed over and over in her mind.

"You're pretty quiet today, Mom. Everything okay?"

"Yes, I'm good. I went to the library this morning. My typing is not too bad after all these years and I'm learning about the computer as well."

"That's good to hear. When do you think you will be ready to start applying for jobs?"

"I'm not sure. I want to get a bit more proficient, not so much with the typing, more with the computer."

Later that night, Martha had thought enough about it. She was still unsure if she should confront Annamae, but she decided Simon was old enough now and he would not be too affected with questions about the doctor. Simon had already gone to bed but she knew he would be up reading so she knocked on his door.

"Can I come in?"

"Sure, Mom. What's up?"

"Ah, I just wanted to ask you about something."

Simon sat up in bed and Martha sat next to him. "Do you remember, a long time ago, you were about ten and you went into hospital to have your appendix removed?"

"Yes, I remember it well, Mom."

"When I came to see you the next day in the hospital, you told me that you knew I had seen a particular doctor and you said 'you realise, Mom, he's not a doctor.' Do you remember what I am talking about?"

"The reason I said he is not a doctor, was because the individual that owned that body was no longer there. That body you and others saw as a doctor was possessed by a demon."

Martha tried to stay calm as she felt a chill run through her body. "How do you know this?"

"Mom, you remember the day after Julia died? I went to her house after school and the sheriff had a medical examiner look at me. It was him that checked my head and hands for cuts. He argued with Sheriff Joe at the time and insisted that I could not have killed Julia. He defended me."

"Are you sure it was him?"

"He is a demon. He is aware that I know he is a demon whilst others do not. I was so scared at the time. This is what gave me nightmares for so many months. However, at church I found books and learned about demons and possession."

"What did you learn?"

"They are evil but powerless in the spirit world. They roam amongst us, desperate to find a body. They target the spiritually weak, the drug and alcohol addicted and the non-believers.

"When they find a body, they will try to take as much control of it as possible but the individual will resist and there will be an internal battle. The fight can go on for the entire life of the body. On most occasions, it sends the individual insane."

"Is this what happened with the doctor?"

"I do not know what happened to him, but I know he has been driven out from that body and the demon has total control."

"Do you know what the demon wants, Simon?"

"I don't know his purpose, but it is not to harm me."

Martha held Simon's hand, she was frightened to ask. "That day after Julia's death, was it the last time you saw him?"

"Yes. Mom, that was the last time, but I sense he is never far away. He has a definite purpose."

"How can you be so matter of fact about this, Simon? I am scared just listening to what you are saying."

"Mom, I have spent so much of my life being afraid. I

have lived with a level of fear you would not understand. I decided a few years ago to try and conquer it. I have not succeeded completely, but I no longer live like I used to."

"I love you so much, son. Now let's say prayers, it's late."

Martha went to bed later that night and thought much about what Simon had said. She decided she could not put if off any longer and it was time to confront Annamae. After dropping Simon at the bus stop, she invited her over for a coffee the next morning.

★

"Hi, Annamae, I must ask you something. Sheriff Amos came here. He had a photo of Dr Brockman and he told me he showed it to you but you said you did not recognise him. Is that correct?"

"That is correct, and you should have told him the same thing."

"Why do you say that?"

"He is nothing but trouble for us, Martha. He is just pretending to be looking into Brockman, but he is really looking into Julia's death."

"Why do you say that?"

"Oh, Martha, you are so naïve. Julia's parents have been spending months trying to get Simon arrested. That sheriff is their good friend. He and Julia's parents are going around asking a lot of questions. I take it he conveniently forgot to mention any of this and just focused on Brockman's photo, right?"

"Who told you that, Annamae?"

"Martha, I go out a lot more than you do and I speak with people. All you do is attend church and go to the grocery store. I've seen him in town with Julia's parents, they are always together. Be very careful what you say to him, he is trying to trap you. They have not given up on going after Simon."

"He told me Dr Brockman's real name is Brookman. That explains why I could never find him and in Dr Brookman's journal he had your address. Why would he have your address Annamae?"

"Wow! You actually believe him, Martha?"

"Well, yes."

"You really need to wise up. This sheriff has spent his life tricking innocent people and forcing confessions and he is good at it. Think about it; the sheriff before failed to get Simon arrested. This guy would look like a real star and he doesn't care if Simon is innocent or not. What he wants, when he retires, is to run for governor. Solving Julia's murder would give him lots of publicity."

"Annamae, let's forget everything about the sheriff. I know for a fact I saw Dr Brookman come out the door when we were in the hospital. You denied it then but I know what I saw."

"I think you are really letting your mind run away with you. I don't think it was him and you thought it was – big deal."

"Tell me, how did Dr Brookman end up being there the night Simon was born?"

"You will remember there was just me and a few concerned neighbours from around the area in that room. None of us could have performed a home birth, so I called the hospital and explained your situation. They told me not to attempt to bring you in, they would send a doctor straight away and that was who they sent. Look, take my advice and stay far away from that sheriff, or you will end up regretting it."

Annamae left shortly after and Martha sat at the breakfast table, thinking the conversation through. This was the first time in her life that she had trouble believing her sister. She decided to turn to the only person she knew she could trust, but first she needed to make a phone call.

"Good Morning! American Medical Association, how can I help...?"

"Hi, Father, it's Martha."

"Hello, Martha. How are you?"

"I'm fine, Father I just wanted to have a chat. Are you busy tomorrow, or can we meet for lunch?"

"Hang on, let me check my diary. I'm taking Mrs Johnson to the doctor but I only need to drop her off and her daughter will collect her, so I could meet you about 12:30pm."

"That would be great, Father. Same café?"

"Yes, if you don't mind."

"Not at all, I'll see you there tomorrow."

★

"Hi, a table for one, Ma'am?"

"No, actually I am meeting someone here. Can I get that table over there in the corner, please?"

"Sure, would you like to order drinks to start with?"

"I'm not sure – perhaps. I'll wait a few minutes. Actually, there he is just coming in the door. I'll take a coffee please."

"Hi, Father. The waitress is just taking a drinks order. What would you like?"

"I'll have a glass of orange juice to start with please."

"So, Martha, how have you been? And how is Simon getting on at university?"

"Oh, he's doing great. Lots of assignments to complete and lots of study."

"I'm happy to hear that. I met him in town the other day and he introduced me to Linda. She is quite an attractive girl."

"Yes, he told me they were dating now. In fact, I met her for the first time recently when she came over and stayed for dinner. She made a good first impression, I liked her a lot."

"That is great to hear, Martha. I'm so pleased for him."

The waitress approached the table. "One cup of coffee and a glass of orange juice. Would you like to start with the soup?"

"Yes, that would be great. Thanks," said Martha.

"Well, Martha, what's on your mind?"

Martha shared with Fr. Mark everything she had been told by Sheriff Amos, as well as her conversations with Simon and Annamae.

"So, Fr. this is why I wanted to speak with you; you're the only one I trust."

"Thank you, Martha. So, let me get this straight: if the American Medical Association has confirmed everything Sheriff Amos is saying about Dr Brookman, why would Annamae try to convince you otherwise?"

"I don't know, Father. There must be a connection between her and Dr Brookman, but I've no idea what it is."

"Martha, are you planning to ask Sheriff Amos if he is actively looking into solving Julia's murder?"

"Yes, I think so."

"Simon is due to stop by the church this week to help me move some furniture. Do you mind if I discuss what you have told me with him?"

"Not at all, Father. I think he would like to speak to you about this. He is very matter of fact, as though he has some inner strength and is dealing with it better than I am."

"Martha, you have had to raise Simon without your husband, as well as helping him overcome everything he has been through. You are coping remarkably well. Don't think negatively and don't put yourself down; have faith."

"I try, Father. Believe me, I try."

★

Robert and Beth sat in their living room and listened intently to everything Sheriff Amos said about his trip to Louisiana, what he found in Dr Brookman's journal and his discussions with Annamae and Martha.

"This is a lot for us to take in," said Beth. "It tells us much we did not know, but I'm not sure if it gives us any new leads that Robert and I can look into. If you can't find Dr Brookman with the department's resources, then we don't have much chance."

"I understand fully what you are saying, Beth. It's just another instance of the recurring theme of this case: we look into something and end up with more questions than answers."

"I agree with Beth," said Robert. "As much as we appreciate the work you are putting into this, Amos, we are definitely running out of leads to follow up on."

"I know, Robert. I feel the same way myself. The most promising lead, if you can call it that, is to establish why Annamae would deny knowing Dr Brookman. There must be a reason for that and why her exact address was in his journal."

"What did you make of Martha?" asked Robert.

"I found her to be very welcoming, unguarded with her words and believable. She is basically the polar opposite of her sister, Annamae, who without question and for reasons unknown, was lying to me."

Amos left, promising to look further into Annamae and Dr Brookman.

★

Fr. Mark and Simon sat in the church canteen resting and enjoying a drink. Fr. Mark was very troubled by what Martha had told him. He felt he had an obligation to inform the Bishop, especially of the fact that Dr Brockman's real name was Dr Brookman. However, he wanted first to speak with Simon.

"Well, Simon, that was a great morning's work, how is your hand?"

Simon raised the blood-stained tissue to inspect his knuckles.

"It's just about stopped bleeding now. I knew I scraped them against the wall coming down the stairs with the bookcase, but I didn't think much of it at the time."

"It was a little bit my fault. Simon, you were walking backwards and I should have slowed down a little more."

"Yes, Father. I noticed I was not only the one walking backwards most of the time. I usually ended up lifting the heavier side of each piece of furniture as well."

"Tricks of the trade, Simon. It's not the first time I've moved furniture, you know."

Simon laughed out.

"On a more serious matter, Simon, I was speaking

with your mother the other day and she told me about the conversation she had with you, about Dr Brookman. I found it very interesting. Why do you see him as a demon?"

"I don't know, Father I just do. He is possessed. I can feel the presence of evil when he is around."

"Do you have any idea what he wants, Simon?"

"As I told Mom, he argued with the sheriff and protected me. Why would he do that, Father?"

"Simon, I don't know. You must tell me if you see him again. What level of control do you think he has over the doctor's body?"

"It is absolute. The doctor has been completely cast out and he has completely taken over his body."

CHAPTER 14

Over the next four years of university, Simon continued to experience life as any young man would. His relationship with Linda grew and the two were nearly inseparable. They both worked hard and dedicated themselves to university. This was not to say they never got into trouble.

During the summer break in 1987, following a late night party, Simon, Linda and a few friends went down to the lake to watch the sunrise. They sat on the jetty looking out across the water. There was a small rowboat alongside the jetty with a number of boats further out, tied to moorings.

Everyone had a bit too much to drink and a few of their friends were smoking weed. Suddenly, someone started singing, "Roll... roll... roll the joint, pass it down the line, take a toke and hold the smoke and blow your fucking mind."

Everyone was laughing so much, no one noticed the two policemen on the shore. They were all rounded up, taken down to the station and released later that day with a severe warning.

For the most part, these four years for Simon consisted of study, spending time with Linda, summer jobs and continuing to help Fr. Mark; it was the happiest time of his life. Martha taught him to drive and he passed his test on the first attempt. Suddenly, the car he had spent his life criticising was worth its weight in gold. He even started cleaning it.

Simon felt he had found a balance between all the competing aspects of his life. He continued to study religion and pray, and his relationship with God became stronger. As he matured, he started to see Martha differently. He began to realise how much she had sacrificed for him and how difficult it must have been for her, raising him on her own.

In the past, he would go with Fr. Mark to help some of the elderly and now he found himself driving them to the doctor. He would pick up groceries for them and run errands; this was what he thought life was about.

Martha's trips to the library paid off. Her typing skills came back within a few weeks and, after six months of computer classes, she plucked up the courage to apply for a secretarial position. She was offered a part time job at an accountancy firm working three days per week. It did not pay much, but she could not have been happier. She enjoyed the responsibility, and getting out of the house did her a world of good.

Annamae continued to visit with Martha but things were different. Since the conversation about Dr Brookman, she viewed Annamae with some suspicion. She was convinced she was hiding something. Though she tried not to let it show, she felt Annamae could sense things were not quite right between them. Despite the issue with Annamae, these four years were the happiest time of Martha's life. Just seeing Simon growing into a man with values and character was worth more than anything else in the world to her; not to mention the fact that she really liked Linda a lot.

★

Robert, Beth and Sheriff Amos continued to look into Julia's murder but it was increasingly frustrating. None of the evidence ever led to anything, and the only two outstanding lines of enquiry that remained unresolved were that the knife used in the murder could not be traced, nor could the elusive Dr Brookman.

Fr. Mark often thought about Simon. He went over and over the conversations he had with the Bishop, Martha and Simon. Too much had happened for him to dismiss it as bad luck or coincidence. Simon had to be central to everything. The words "I have chosen you" on the cloth and the Bible, were given to Martha as a gift from a doctor possessed by a demon. Initially, when Martha first showed him the cloth, he had for the most part dismissed it but, as the years passed, he became certain that there was a definite message in it that he just could not interpret. This same doctor was at Simon's birth and was protective of him, yet Simon and Martha were, without question, very spiritual individuals; nothing seemed to make any sense.

Fr. Mark became increasingly convinced that the visions he had all those years ago, which called him to the priesthood, were in some way connected to Simon. There was an inevitability that they had a shared destiny. He wanted to discuss the Bible and especially the words on the cloth with Simon, but he knew Martha had never told Simon about this and he could not betray her trust. Perhaps Martha was correct in not telling him, no one would want to be told they were chosen.

Bishop Connor always presented a problem to Fr. Mark. Every few months he had to meet him, and the message on the cloth and Simon often came up. Fr. Mark had made the decision not to tell the Bishop what Dr Brockman's real name was, nor did he reveal to him the fact that Simon saw him as possessed. He knew, if he did, it would bring a lot of unnecessary difficulties for both Simon and Martha, as Bishop Connor would be sure to question them.

During one of their meetings, Bishop Connor told Fr. Mark that the cloth had been examined fully and the message was determined to be meaningless. He returned the cloth to Fr. Mark, who passed it onto Martha. The Athame had also been examined. However, a definite determination could not be made as to its authenticity. It was quietly returned into police evidence. Bishop Connor told Fr. Mark that he would like to meet with Simon. However, he did not want it to be formal, more of a chance meeting.

Fr. Mark arranged for Simon to be helping him one day at the church and the Bishop just 'happened' to be in the area and stopped by. Fr. Mark introduced Simon to Bishop Connor and they decided to have pizza delivered.

Over lunch, the conversation was light-hearted. The Bishop asked Simon if he was enjoying university and asked about the subjects he was studying. Gradually, he turned the conversation to more spiritual matters. They discussed life, religion and the interpretation of verses in the Bible.

The Bishop was stunned at Simon's knowledge. He could not believe someone so young could have this level of understanding; Simon's beliefs were certainly rooted in traditional Catholic doctrine. However, he had a way of encompassing the beliefs of the church with the beliefs of many other faiths and could draw parallels between them and, all the while, he spoke with such authority on difficult matters. The day after Bishop Connor met Simon, he was on the phone to Fr. Mark expressing how impressed he was with Simon.

"That is certainly a young man we need to watch closely; there is something very special about him."

"I agree totally, Your Grace. I am very fond of him. His mother has done an amazing job instilling these values in him."

"Surely, Father, it is not only his mother. You must take some credit for this. I can see the bond you share with him you are doing a fine job for the church. Keep up the good work."

CHAPTER 15

Simon and Martha were having dinner at the kitchen table.

"You have to go, Mom. It, will look terrible if you don't. You know Linda really likes you, and she has told her parents that, so they are looking forward meeting you and this is the perfect opportunity."

"Let me think about it, Simon."

"Come on, Linda is planning it to be the most informal graduation party ever. It won't be all students either – plenty of parents are invited. Linda has put a lot of thought into it. There will be finger food, a buffet, a barbeque, and an indoor and outdoor bar. If you want to sit and eat at a table inside, you can – or you can just eat outside. It will be very relaxed. They have a large garden where they have set up a small stage for a hired band. You will really enjoy it."

"I don't have anything to wear to a graduation party."

"You are just making excuses, Mom."

"It would have been so much easier meeting them if her father had not turned me down for that car loan. It's going to make meeting him a bit awkward."

"Mom, I've told you for years now, he is a great guy. You will like him a lot and you have so much in common with her mother, you see her all the time at church. Occasionally her dad goes, but her mom is always there. She usually sits at the back and leaves before us, so you have not met her, but for sure you will recognise her straight away when you see her at the party."

"Alright, you have worn me down. I'll go."

"Great, I guarantee you will tell me the next day that you really enjoyed it."

"We'll see…"

"And you never know, Mom, if you make a good impression you might even get your car loan approved."

Martha's eyes narrowed. "Now let me tell you something, Simon J Holman. If you think I am going there to try and…"

"Relax, Mom. I'm just joking. . ."

"Well, for that comment, you my son can do the dishes, and I'm not joking!"

★

Robert sat back in his favourite chair, put his feet up and looked out from his porch towards the hills. Beth put a cup of tea on the table next to him and handed him the newspaper.

"I'll join you in a few minutes, Robert. I just need to check the roast in the oven."

Robert started flicking through the paper and a headline caught his eye: "TOMMIE LEE ANDREW'S CASE, A REVOLUTION IN SOLVING CRIME."

Beth sat down next to Robert and picked up her pen and crossword book from the side table.

"Tommie Lee Andrews, does that name mean anything to you, Beth?"

"Should it?"

"It definitely will when I tell you what I've just read."

"Who is he?"

132

"He is a guy who raped a woman in Florida. He had an O Positive blood type which is the same as 65% of the population. He became the first person convicted in the US using something called DNA. It stands for Deoxyribonucleic acid. It says here it's found in many things, including a person's blood, semen, hair and saliva. It contains the genetic blueprint that gives each person their individual identity. DNA testing has a greater than 99% accuracy."

Beth put down her pen and crossword book. "I've never heard of this before. Did it happen recently?"

"He was convicted a couple of years ago. His lawyers recently appealed the use of DNA at trials, but the District Court of Appeal ruled against him and accepted DNA as credible scientific evidence."

Beth was lost for words.

"Do you know what it means, Beth? We need to call Amos straight away and get him onto this."

★

"You look amazing, Mrs Holman. That dress fits you perfectly," said the young sales clerk at the boutique.

Martha was indeed surprised at how good she looked. It had been years since she dressed up for any occasion. "I'll take it and the shoes. I just need to go now and find a gift for Linda."

"Any ideas what you are getting her?"

"The only thing I can think of is jewellery, she has everything else!"

The sales clerk folded the dress carefully and put it into a bag. "Well, you can never go wrong with jewellery, Mrs Holman. I'm sure she will love whatever you get her."

"I hope so, I've really gotten to like her a lot."

"When is the graduation?"

"It's this weekend coming. Actually, the closer it gets, the more I'm looking forward to going."

"You will have a great time, Mrs Holman. Say hello to Simon for me. Between you and me, I had a secret crush on him in high school. I wished I had the courage to let him know back then. He must have been going out with Linda for over four years now, so my chance has surely gone."

"You'll find someone. Ah, sorry, I didn't get your name…"

"It's Jane. Just tell him Jane from high school said 'hi'. He'll remember me."

"I will, Jane, and thanks for your help today."

"Bye, Mrs Holman. Enjoy the party."

★

Simon packed the lunch box, drove over to Linda's house, and the two headed for the nearby hills.

"So, Linda, how are the preparations coming for this weekend?"

"There is nothing left to do. I just told my folks a few weeks ago what I wanted. We made a list and they have done it all. There are a few small things regarding the music. The band gave me a set list, which I'm happy with. However, I also need to speak with the DJ regarding what he has lined up."

"Does your dad need me to come over to help move furniture, or set up tables? Actually, we can get a few friends to help out."

"No. It's all taken care of. The guys building the

temporary stage for the band will do all the heavy lifting. Mom has arranged all the food. As I said, there is nothing that needs to be done."

"Okay, please tell your dad, if he needs any last minute help, to call me."

"I will. By the way, how did your mom make out with the dress hunting? Did she find anything yet?"

"Yes. She told me yesterday; she is all set and looking forward to it."

"Did she really say that?"

"Well, she said she is all set and looking forward to it, more than she thought she would be – I just cut off the last bit of the sentence."

Linda laughed out. "I've no idea what she is thinking. She will have a great time. I told her that the other day."

"You know, Linda, she is not used to going out and meeting lots of people. However, since she started working, she is a bit more sociable. Her main issue is the loan thing."

"What loan thing are you referring to?"

"I never told you, but years ago, long before I met you, Mom applied for a loan to buy a new car and your dad knocked it back."

Linda smiled and shook her head. "Wow, Simon, you could not make this up. And now we are together. Yep, I can see why your mom would be hesitant to go, but she shouldn't worry. You know my dad. He will just make a joke of it."

"I know. I told her that."

"What did she say?"

"She told me she was thinking, on the day of the graduation when she gets to your home, she will drive past all the fancy bankers' cars and park her car right in the middle of the front lawn. And, just for good measure, she will make sure it's overheating with steam coming out the bonnet."

"Oh, your mom kills me, with the stuff she comes out with."

"Trust me, I only tell you a fraction of it."

"So, tell me, Simon: what is this place your taking me to? We've not been up in these hills before."

"It's just around a few more bends. Then we get out and walk for about thirty minutes and we'll be there. I don't want to spoil the surprise."

Linda and Simon walked through the trees and suddenly came out into an open area. There was a small waterfall, which cascaded down onto the rocks, with a pool of water that was crystal clear.

"Wow, Simon, I've lived in Sidon all my life and I did not know this place existed. It's beautiful. How did you know about it?"

Simon unfolded the blanket, placed it on the ground next to the lunch box and poured a couple of glasses of wine.

"When I was ten years old, I had my appendix removed. It was a bit of a difficult time for me. Shortly after I got home and recovered from the operation, I took a bus and got off a few miles down the road. I started to walk towards these hills and discovered it, I've not been back since."

"Why not? This is such an amazing place, so peaceful."

"Back then, I promised myself that the next time I come back here, it would be to ask the girl of my dreams to marry me."

Simon got down on one knee and held Linda's hand. "Linda Bernstein, there are many beautiful women in this world, but you are the finest of them all. Will you be my wife?"

This was the last thing Linda was expecting. She did not have to think about it for very long. "Yes, of course I will. Simon, I love you so much."

★

At the Archbishop's house, Bishop Connor hesitantly broke the red and gold seal on the letter. He knew what it would say. Tears came to his eyes. This surely marked the beginning of the end for him.

At the age of seventy-two, his resignation on the grounds of ill health had been accepted. Yet he felt he was letting the church down. Life was so short and there was so much left to do. However, he knew he could not go on much longer. He was asked to recommend someone who could succeed him. Only one name came to mind.

★

"So, Mom, are you all set for the graduation tomorrow?" asked Simon.

"As ready as I'll ever be. You will be pleased to hear I won't be driving there, so you won't be embarrassed by the car."

Simon smiled. "That's a relief, Mom. Why the change of plan? I thought the mechanic sorted out the problem a few weeks ago."

"He did, but I could not get it started last Wednesday. I ended up late for work."

"What did Mr Caine say when you showed up late?"

"Oh, he is no problem. He's still pushing me to hire on full time but I told him I'm happy with just three days a week. He says I am the longest serving part time employee in the firm's history."

"He obviously thinks you're doing a good job. Anyway, who is taking you tomorrow?"

"I'll go with Aunt Annamae to the ceremony and then, I guess, someone will give me a lift to Linda's house afterwards. I can't ask Annamae to drop me there. I already feel a bit guilty that she has not been invited. As you say, Linda's folks really don't know her at all."

"Did you explain that to her?"

"Yes, she came over yesterday so I mentioned it, but I can see she's clearly upset."

"Yes, but Mom, she is coming to the graduation, so that is far more important than the party afterwards."

"Somehow, son, I don't think that she sees it that way."

"Mom, I've been wanting to ask you something regarding Aunt Annamae. Do you find she's a bit cold towards Linda? I mean she is polite and everything, but I get the impression she does not like her much."

"Oh you know your Aunt. No girl is every going to be good enough for you in her eyes."

"I hope that's what it is, Mom."

Martha knew exactly what Simon was speaking about. It had always bothered her and, in a way, she was happy Annamae had not been invited. She knew she would find fault with everyone and everything.

"Linda mentioned her mom invited Fr. Mark. So, if you're stuck for conversation, you always have him."

"What! Why didn't you tell me that ages ago? Well at least I'll know someone there. What a relief. It won't be so bad now. Also, I can get a lift with him straight from the graduation over to Linda's house."

"You know where she lives, right?"

"I think everyone in Sidon knows where her family lives. Just look for the mansion in the town centre," Martha replied. "Oh, before I forget, I'm telling you now I want at least one dance with you; and I don't want to hear anything about you being embarrassed to be dancing with your mother... got it?"

"Sure, no problem, Mom. By the way, speaking of being embarrassed, please do not bring that camera of yours tomorrow. The university will have dedicated photographers there and we can just choose and order up what we want after."

"So you're embarrassed by my car and now my camera as well? Do you know, when I was pregnant, your father worked two jobs on his time off from the military to buy it. This is the only reason we have all those precious baby pictures of you to cherish forever."

"Seriously, Mom? That camera is from the sixties. If you really want that dance, you will have to leave it at home."

★

Beth came home, put the shopping on the kitchen table and went out to the porch. It was spring and Robert was sitting in his favourite chair. She kissed him and sat down.

"So Robert, how did it go? Did you finally manage to get hold of Amos?"

"Yes. He'd been tied up at meetings, so he couldn't take our calls. He said they are restructuring the department – again!"

"Do you have good or bad news?"

"A bit of both really. He said they got an internal memo when DNA was used to convict Andrews. However, they knew it would go to appeal. Until that ruling comes down it changes nothing. Now that the District Court has ruled that

DNA can be used, it sets the precedent. Each jurisdiction can now make a list of unsolved cases with the evidence in question, subjected to DNA analysis."

"So what does that mean for us?"

"That's exactly what I asked. He said, apart from police departments submitting evidence for DNA testing, every convict that has heard of DNA analysis, innocent or guilty, is asking their lawyers to file to have their cases retried. The laboratories where the testing is done are overwhelmed at the moment. It's going to get worse before it gets better as more and more people find out about it."

"So about how long are we speaking?"

"He said that it's difficult to say. Department guidelines clearly gives priority to cases where suspects who pose a risk to the public can be locked up, or where it is thought a conviction can be attained with DNA analysis."

"It's logical. So can Amos not argue that Holman poses a risk?"

"He can try, but unfortunately Julia's murder has been classified as a cold case. It's much further down the list of priorities when compared to more recent crimes. Amos still has the hair sample from the crime scene in evidence. Of course, he has to go before a judge to have Holman brought in, to get a hair sample from him. If the judge rules in our favour, we can get Holman's sample sent off together with the hair from the crime scene to be compared. He could not give a timeline, but it won't be quick, he said."

"I thought the lab in Texas that we used for the Microscopic Hair Analysis sent us two kits, one we sent off which was the A Sample and the other was a back up B Sample. We still have that up stairs. Over the years it's made its way to the back of the cupboard."

"You're right, Beth. Let's look into it and see if we can find a lab that does private DNA testing. Even if there aren't any now, with the demand, it won't be long before they are everywhere."

★

It was a stunning morning; the weather could not have been better. Martha was dressed and ready with more than an hour to go before Annamae arrived. She usually wore her hair up but, on this occasion, she thought it looked better down. She looked in the mirror again. It gave her the confidence to overcome the nerves she felt inside.

Martha and Annamae arrived at the graduation ceremony fifteen minutes before it was due to start and sat together in their allocated seats. Martha looked around, desperate for familiar faces, and spotted Fr. Mark and Linda's parents. There were a few other faces she recognised, but none of them she knew well.

There was the usual long introduction, welcoming everyone and speaking about the achievements of Sidon University. Martha thought, please stop and just get on with handing out the awards. She wondered if everyone else was thinking the same.

At last the students started walking onto the stage to collect their awards. Martha could not wait, and then finally the name was announced: "Simon J Holman, Business Graduate, with honours." As she watched her son walk onto the stage, suddenly John came to her mind. She was sure he would be looking down and seeing what his son had achieved. She took a tissue and dried her eyes.

As Martha walked out of the ceremony with Annamae, her eyes were fixed on Fr. Mark. She caught up with him outside and they all got photos taken together with Simon. Martha said goodbye to Annamae but it was a frosty farewell. She got into the car with Fr. Mark and drove the short distance to Linda's home.

"Have you been by the Bernstein's before, Fr?"

"No, but I've a rough idea where they live. My plan is just to follow all the fancy cars up ahead."

Martha smiled. "Yes, good idea, Father. I think anyone who is anyone in Sidon will be there."

"Speaking of being there, I'm guessing your sister wasn't invited."

"No, but I tried to explain to her the other day that Linda's parents really don't know her."

"From the look on her face a few minutes ago, it does not look like she is taking it very well."

"It was that obvious, huh? Hang on, Father. I just realised… what is Linda's mom's name?"

"It's Brenda, but you must know her from church, don't you?"

"Only if I see her. We've not spoken before."

"I'm obviously not doing a very good job of bringing people together am I?"

Martha smiled. "No, Father It's more a that I don't know that many people. Actually, you are just about the only person I'll know, so I'm afraid your stuck with me for the evening."

"That's okay, Martha, I should know quite a few of them so I'll introduce you. It won't be so bad."

Fr. Mark and Martha followed the line of cars through the granite front pillars and along the tree-lined driveway towards the house. They drove around a large white fountain and a man with a cap directed them to park on a pebble stone area.

"Perhaps I should have washed the car this morning," said Fr. Mark.

"Never mind that. Thank goodness I did not bring my car, could you imagine the looks I'd get?"

Fr. Mark laughed.

Martha reached into the back seat and picked up the carefully wrapped gift. She turned down the visor, one last look in the mirror, a deep breath and she was ready to go.

"The music is loud from here," said Martha, "and good, it looks like everyone is just walking straight in. I don't like those formal handshake greetings."

"Stop stressing, Martha. It will be great."

Martha and Fr. Mark walked up the steps and through the front door. There were decorations in the colours of the university, with banners, balloons and confetti everywhere. There was a table on the right where people were leaving their gifts along with a book for guests' comments. To the left was a doorway that led into a large room. Martha could see buffet food along the entire length of one wall, with a graduation cake that must have been at least two feet tall.

"This is hugely impressive, Martha, and we have hardly even entered their home."

"I'm pleased you like it," said the gentleman.

Fr. Mark and Martha turned around.

"Martin, Brenda, how are you?" said Fr. Mark.

"Keeping well, thanks. A bit nervous about tonight," said Martin. "Hoping everyone will have a good time. Martha, you look stunning, I'm so glad you made it, I'm sure you know my wife, Brenda from church."

Martha kissed Brenda. "I was saying to Father on the way here that I feel terrible; we see each other every Sunday, yet we've never spoken."

"That's okay, Martha," said Brenda. "I always sit at the back so I can make a quick escape once the Mass is over."

Fr. Mark raised an eyebrow.

Brenda put her hand on Fr. Mark's arm. "Ah no offense, Father."

Fr. Mark laughed. "Brenda, at least you make it to the end. I had one guy that used to get up and walk out half way through the Mass!"

A waiter approached with glasses of champagne on a tray. "May I offer anyone a drink?"

"That would be great," said Fr. Mark.

Martha nodded and Martin handed the champagne to them.

"Martha, Father, you must excuse us. Brenda has to follow up with the caterers and I have to go outside. I'm told our parking plan is not coping too well with the number of cars. I'll catch up with you later on. Go ahead and enjoy the night."

"Thanks so much," said Martha. "You have both gone to so much effort to make this a special night, we'll chat later."

Martha and Fr. Mark made their way into the house.

"That went pretty well," said Martha.

"I told you not to worry."

"I didn't know priests were allowed to drink."

"There is actually no rule against it. We should not get drunk but otherwise it's not a problem."

Over the next few hours, Fr. Mark introduced Martha to many new people. The band played a mixture of sixties, seventies, and eighties music. She danced with people she hardly knew. She even got Fr. Mark on the dance floor but, most of all, she got to dance with her son. *Life could not get better than this*, she thought.

"Well, Martha, what do you think?" asked Martin.

Martha raised her voice above the music. "Oh, I can't thank you enough. I'm having a great time – I think everyone is. You and Brenda have put so much thought and effort into this, down to the very last detail."

"It was mainly Brenda. She is the creative one. I've not seen her for a couple of hours now, but I'll let her know what you said. I must tell you, Martha, that Brenda and I think the world of Simon. You have done a great job with him."

"Oh, you beat me to it. I was going to say the same about Linda. What a wonderful girl! I'm so happy they met each other, she has certainly brought out the best in Simon."

"How is work going? Your boss told me he's unable to convince you to go full time."

"Oh, do you know, Mr Caine?"

"His firm audits the accounts for the bank. I've gotten to know him fairly well over the years. He's tough but very fair."

"That is a good assessment of him, Martin. He is tough, as you say, but I really enjoy working for him. Three days a week is perfect for me. As my sister says, it's not like I'm going to climb the corporate ladder at this stage of my life."

Martin smiled. "Yes, she described you as happiest when you're home."

"Oh. You know Annamae as well?"

"I sort of just met her a little while ago."

"What… she's here?" Martha looked around briefly but could not see her. "Oh. I'm so sorry about this Martin."

"It's okay, Martha. Annamae being here is not a problem."

"No, Martin, it is a problem. She was not invited. She had no right to show up. This is so embarrassing."

"Perhaps it was our fault. Being your only sister, we should have thought…"

"No, Martin. Stop right there. That has nothing to do with it. You were right not to invite her. Neither you nor Brenda know her at all."

"Look, please don't allow this to ruin your night, Martha."

"I need to find Brenda. I must apologise to her. Please excuse me, Martin."

Martha spotted Fr. Mark and told him what had happened.

"I know it reflects badly on you, Martha, but you need to calm down. You have done nothing wrong. Annamae is the one that should feel ashamed."

Suddenly, the music stopped and there was an announcement from the band. "Linda and Simon would like to say a few words. Can we ask Martin, Brenda, Martha and Fr. Mark to come forward and for everyone to gather in front of the stage."

Martha looked at Fr. Mark. "What is this about? It sounds very formal."

"It's probably just to thank everyone for coming, I guess."

Martha grabbed Fr. Mark's arm. "Come on, let's go."

The two made their way through the crowd and stood next to Martin and Brenda. A few feet in front of them, Simon and Linda stood on the stage. Simon took the microphone and looked up at the crowd.

"Good evening, everyone. Firstly, I'd like to thank you all for coming. I'd also like to say a huge thank you to Mr and Mrs Bernstein for the amount of work they have put into hosting this party."

The crowd shouted their approval.

"Fr. Mark, over the years you have become far more than a parish priest to me. Thank you for your support and guidance. Last, but not least, I'd like to say thank you, Mom, for all you have sacrificed to bring me up, I love you."

The crowd cheered again. No words could describe how Martha felt at this moment.

Simon handed the microphone to Linda. She looked nervous and held his hand.

"Simon and I have some news we would like to share with you all. We have been desperate to tell everyone, but thought we would save the announcement for tonight, when all our family and friends are together."

Martha glanced quickly across at Martin and Brenda. From the look on their faces, they clearly had no idea about this.

"Three days ago, Simon and I drove up to the hills for a picnic, he got down on one knee and asked me…"

Emotion got the better of Linda and she could not complete the sentence. Martha, Brenda and Martin ran onto the stage and hugged the two of them. The crowd cheered and whistled and the band started playing, Martha looked up to tell Fr. Mark to come up on stage and share the moment. Suddenly, she spotted Annamae walking quickly, with her head down, out the back of the room.

CHAPTER 16

Martha put the kettle on. She was feeling quite rough; she had not drunk that much in decades, but what a night. It exceeded any expectation she could possibly have had. While the kettle boiled, she took a couple of headache tablets with a tall glass of water. Fr. Mark made her promise that she would not dwell on what Annamae did, and how could she? There was so much to celebrate, so much to be thankful for, but today was a new day and, when she thought of what her sister had done, she was livid. Still, she reminded herself to keep calm and count her blessings. *I'll deal with her later, but first I need to phone Fr. Mark.*

"Morning, Father. You asked me to give you a call at 10am. Are we still on for lunch today?"

"Are you sure it's ten?" a tired voice asked.

"Yep, definitely ten o'clock. You sound pretty bad, one or two too many?"

"No, well maybe… I guess…"

Martha laughed.

"Don't worry, I'm not feeling great myself. I doubt anyone is this morning. We can skip lunch if you like."

"No, let's meet up. I have things to do this afternoon, so let's do lunch and then I'll get started. Same place for about 11:30am?"

"See you then, Father."

★

Martha sat at her favourite table in the café and looked out for Fr. Mark. He's not usually this late, she thought.

"Hi, Father. A bit of a struggle getting here this morning?" she asked with a smile.

Fr. Mark sat down. "A little bit, but I'm feeling better."

Martha smiled. "You feeling better or are you or trying to convince yourself you're feeling better?"

Fr. Mark laughed. "No. Honestly, I had a shower, a coffee, and a slice of toast, so I'm not too bad. I didn't drink much you know." Martha smiled and gave him a knowing look. "I went ahead and ordered for you, Father. It should be here shortly. In fact, here it comes."

The waitress placed the breakfast on the table.

"I have to say, that was a thoroughly enjoyable night, Martha."

"Oh definitely. I think everyone enjoyed it. I can't wait to see the photos."

Fr. Mark's expression changed.

"Oh I know! You're worried aren't you?" Martha burst out laughing. "You're worried you may not look your usual dignified self perhaps?"

Fr. Mark smiled and looked around the cafe. "Keep your voice down, Martha. You know I can just see some outrageous headline in the newspaper and below is a photo of me on the dance floor, with a glass of champagne."

"Oh, that's too funny. Sorry for laughing, but I wouldn't worry about it. As you said, there is no rule against drinking or dancing, so no problem, huh?"

"I suppose you're right. I'm so happy for them, though. They will make a wonderful couple."

"I'm going to miss not having him at home."

"You will have him for a while yet, Martha. He told me that the wedding wouldn't be for some time. They have to find jobs, save some money, find a place to live and so on."

"I know, Father, but you know how time flies. I'm going to treasure every moment I can with him."

"So what plans do you have this afternoon, Father?"

"I promised Mrs Thomas I would visit her. She's not doing well – she is ninety-two. Her daughter is really worried and, after that, I need to pick up a prescription for Jean. She is laid up in bed," he replied. "What are you up to?"

"Well, I'm going over to see my sister and tell her what I think. But I will not get emotional, I will just be very matter of fact and tell her how I feel."

"That sounds like the right approach, I wish you well."

"On a happier subject, Martha, last night Martin told me he wants to have us all round to an engagement dinner."

"Yes, he mentioned it to me when we were saying goodbye, but Linda was saying, 'No, Dad, you have done enough'. However, he was insisting and he said he will let me know when.

"Actually, thinking about it now, I should invite them over – I wish I'd thought of that last night. Then again, to go from his home to mine, stuck around a small wooden kitchen table for dinner, that won't really work, will it?"

"Not exactly. Perhaps you could invite them over for a drink and put out some finger foods. That would definitely work."

"Good idea, Father. I'll probably do that after."

Martha left the café, jumped into her car and composed herself. She knew exactly what she was going to tell Annamae and she was not going to hold back. Initially, she was going to call her and say she was coming over to speak to her, but then she thought otherwise. *I'm just going straight there right now. It will be better to catch her off guard.*

★

Martha knocked on the door.

"Hey, sis, what a nice surprise. Come on in."

"No, Annamae. I am not coming in. I will tell you what I have to say right here."

"But I'll put the kettle on so we can chat inside."

Martha stood at the door. "Have you any idea what you did last night. Do you know how embarrassed you made me feel?"

"But I spoke with Martin when I arrived and he said that he was okay with it."

"No, Annamae. He was not okay with it. No one was okay with it. You knew you were not invited."

"I think you are over reacting, Martha."

"No, I am not over reacting. This is the final straw. I have put up with you and your ways for long enough."

"What's that supposed to mean?"

"It is everything. From you lying about Brookman, to your attitude towards Linda. How uncomfortable you make everyone feel when she is around. Turning up univited last night, you should be ashamed of yourself, but you are not. You act as if nothing is wrong. Well, I am sick of pretending nothing is wrong. Something is wrong and it's with you!"

"But I like Linda."

"You're lying to me again, Annamae. I saw you walk out the back of the room when she announced their engagement. If you liked her, you would have celebrated like everyone that was there. Anyway, you keep away from me and my son. I want nothing to do with you, is that clear?"

"You don't know what you are saying, Martha. It's bigger than you think."

"And what is that supposed to mean?"

"You think you can stop me, Martha? You think you can change what is to come? You have no idea what you are dealing with. I am a part of this. I am a part of Simon's life and you can change nothing."

"You stay away from my son, you hear me."

"Oh, Martha, this is bigger. It's so much bigger than you could ever know."

"You just stay away."

Martha stared at her sister for a few seconds. Annamae had a distant, almost evil look, that she had never seen before. She turned her back, walked to her car and drove off. As she was leaving she heard Annamae shouting, "You don't know what you are dealing with…"

★

"Hey sleepy head. Nice to see you're finally out of bed," said Martha.

Simon slumped down at the kitchen table. "What time is it, Mom?"

"Only 2:30 in the afternoon!"

"Oh my head!"

Martha smiled and handed Simon two tablets with a glass of juice.

"So you enjoyed last night, Mom?"

"Oh, it was a fantastic night. Everyone did."

"I told you that's what you would say. You were worrying for nothing."

"So you're keeping secrets from me, huh?"

"Mom, I was desperate to tell you we'd gotten engaged but Linda and I promised each other that we would not say anything to anyone."

"Actually, I was not speaking about that."

"Oh no, what did you hear?"

"Only that you and a bunch of friends were caught smoking marijuana and taken down to the police station."

"Oh that."

"Yes, oh that… forgot to tell me did you?"

"How did you find out?"

"I overheard some of your friends recounting the story and laughing last night."

"We weren't charged or anything, Mom. They let us off."

"You were very fortunate. I hope you learnt your lesson."

"Mom, Linda mentioned that she heard someone saying that Aunt Annamae was there last night. That's not true is it?"

"I'm afraid so, Simon."

"What was she thinking?"

"You're older now, so I guess I can tell you. I went over a little while ago and had it out with her. As always, she tried to pretend nothing was wrong and I was blowing it out of proportion. She invited me in for coffee but I just stood at her door and told her exactly how I felt. I've not been happy with her for a number of reasons and what you said about her attitude when Linda's around was correct. I've noticed it and it's really annoyed me and then last night – well, that was it. I told her to keep away from us. I turned my back, got in the car, and left."

"What did she say?"

"Oh she's not happy, as you'd expect; she started screaming at me as I drove off. I'm sorry that it has come to this."

"She brought it on herself, Mom. I'm glad you noticed how she was with Linda. It has been a bit awkward; Linda's asked me a few times in the past if my Aunt did not like her."

"Please apologise to Linda for me. I really should have dealt with this years ago. It's terrible that she felt uncomfortable around her. Anyway, you can let her know that I've addressed the matter."

"I will, Mom. In fact…"

"'In fact' what. Simon?"

"No forget it…"

"No, I want to know, Simon – tell me."

"I was just picturing you letting her have it, turning your back, getting into the car and it fails to start…"

"Your right! Oh thank God it started, could you imagine? I don't even want to think of what I'd have done then."

"Yeah, Mom, it would not have exactly been the ideal time to ask her for a jump start, huh?"

"Oh, on a different subject, Simon, I forgot to tell you Jane from high school, said to say 'hello'."

"Jane, really? Where did you see her?"

"She was working in the shop where I bought the dress, she said you would remember her."

"Yes, of course I remember her. I used to fancy her back then, but I knew I never stood a chance."

Martha shook her head.

Over the next week, Martha heard nothing from Annamae. She suspected this was really it for their relationship. They had argued before and her sister was always quick to come over, apologise and give her a hug. Not this time; Annamae must have really gotten the message and, in a way, Martha was happy she was not around.

Martha could not decide. They had been at the studio now for over an hour and basically she wanted every photo she looked at.

"You're going to have to put some back, Martha," said Fr. Mark.

"I agree, Mom. This will cost you a small fortune."

"I know, but it's so hard to decide; I like them all. I bet you're a bit relieved, Father. I'm not seeing any that are too damaging."

"Yes. Thankfully they focused more on you than me!"

"Oh, Mom. Please just make a decision."

Finally, Martha made her choice.

"That is great, Ma'am," said the photographer. "So, we have twenty-eight in total. Now, what sizes do you want them in?"

"Oh no, Father. We're going to be here for another hour," said Simon.

Fr. Mark looked to the heavens and motioned to Simon to follow him to the door.

"Where do you think you two are sneaking off to? I need help with this," said Martha. "Now, what sizes can you do them in, sir?"

CHAPTER 17

Martin and Brenda Bernstein had everyone over for the engagement dinner. Martha had not spoken much with Brenda at the graduation party but she really connected with her now. The two women had never realised they shared so much in common. They agreed to meet up every Tuesday for a coffee and Brenda started to stay back after Mass, just to chat with Martha on the way out.

Martha had no plans to stop working at the accountancy firm for Mr Caine. It got her out the house and she enjoyed the job. Annamae never made contact, but Martha and Simon saw her on a suspicious number of occasions – so much so that, one evening, Martha met Simon for lunch at the café and caught Annamae looking in at them. Martha stormed out of the café and confronted her in the street, Simon had to step in and calm Martha down. He told Annamae, in no uncertain terms, to stop following them around.

After Simon proposed, Linda wanted to abandon her plans of going on to complete her Master's and instead to find a job. She knew Simon was working towards the down payment on a mortgage and she wanted to help. She calculated that doing her Master's, would mean another eighteen months at least before they could get married, and she could not wait for that day. After much persuasion, her parents and Simon convinced her to continue her studies.

Shortly after their engagement, Simon was offered a job working for Martin Bernstein at the bank. He was twenty-two years of age but still had no idea what he wanted to do. He explained this to Martin, who completely understood the young man's position. He advised him to take the job and, if he did not like the banking industry after a year or two, he was still young enough to change his career.

Simon settled quickly into his new role. He remained open minded about a career in banking but continued to look around and research other prospects. He lived at home with Martha, who refused to accept any money from him. "You and Linda have to save and plan for the future," she would say.

At one time, he contemplated buying a car but he could not justify the expense. Martha worked Monday, Wednesday and Friday and they would drive into town together. On Tuesdays and Thursdays, he would take the car, if Martha didn't need it, or occasionally he would get the bus.

Simon shared an office with Charles Rankin on the second floor of the Horizon Bank in the centre of town. The two had a good working relationship but it didn't go beyond that, Charles was in his late forties and always looked unhappy with life. He kept to himself and would only reluctantly attend office functions.

"Can you take my calls please, Charles?" asked Simon. "If Mr Robinson does call, tell him his account is set up and we have sent him a letter with the details and his new cheque book."

"Where are you going to eat, Simon?"

"I'm thinking, I'll walk up to Subway today. I'm tired

of the café food. I can only eat so many hamburgers and chips."

"Where did you go today?"

"Not far, just round the corner, and had a hotdog."

"Any good?"

"Don't waste your time."

Simon smiled. "Okay, Subway it is. I'll see you in a bit, Charles."

★

"That was a short lunch break!" said Charles.

"I had to eat quickly as I saw it was going to rain. I ended up running most of the way back and still got soaked."

Simon took his jacket off and hung it up, hoping it would dry quickly. "Looks like my jacket took the worst of it. Thankfully my shirt is still dry."

"On your way out of the bank, Simon, you should have grabbed one of those customer umbrellas at the entrance."

"You're right. I need to get in the habit of doing that, especially at this time of year," Simon said. "Any calls, Charles?"

"Just one, a guy. I told him you had gone to lunch and he just hung up – so rude. Anyway, Simon, if anyone is looking for me, I'm just heading downstairs. They are short-staffed and one of the girls asked me to cover her for lunch."

Simon looked at the time: 12:25pm. *Great*, he thought, *I can close my eyes for couple of minutes*. He pulled the lower drawer of his desk open, reclined his office chair, and put his feet up.

★

The bedroom door was ajar. He looked in and saw his victim across the room, she was studying at her desk. He squeezed the handle of the knife and approached her slowly from behind. He stood over her and as he positioned himself, the wooden floorboard below the carpet creaked. She turned around, but it was too late. She did not even have time to rise out of her chair. He covered her mouth and brought the knife down into her heart. She slumped into the chair.

"It is done," he said.

★

"No!" he screamed.

Simon awoke violently. The drawer he had his feet on slammed closed and he fell over in the chair. He got up off the floor and looked around, but he was badly shaken. He focused his eyes, the clock on the wall said: 12:53pm. He looked at his hand, it was shaking but he could feel the knife in it. The memory had returned from all those years ago and it was as true and violent as it was then.

"Are you okay, man?" asked the voice.

Simon looked over to the doorway but he struggled to focus on the face.

"Ah, yes. I'm fine. . . I'm fine, Charles."

"I was coming up the stairs and I heard you scream out. You don't look okay, and why is your chair lying on the floor?"

"Ah, I tripped... I tripped and grabbed the chair, but it's on wheels, so I ended up pulling it over."

"I just came up to get this folder, and I need to go back downstairs again. Are you sure you're okay?"

Charles took the folder off his desk. "I'll be back shortly, Simon."

Simon picked up the phone immediately, but he felt he was holding the handle of the knife. He panicked and dropped it on the desk; his hand was still shaking. He composed himself, picked it back up and dialled Linda's number but there was no answer.

Tuesday, he thought, *Mrs Bernstein is probably with Mom, having a coffee or more likely on her way back home.* He was struggling to think. He held his head, he could feel a bump had formed. He looked down and realised he must have hit it on the corner of the wall behind him. He picked up his chair and wheeled it forward; *I need to call Mom,* he thought.

"Hi, Mom. Is Mrs Bernstein still there?"

"No. She left about twenty minutes ago."

"Is she heading back home?"

"I didn't ask, but I assume so. Are you alright? You sound uptight."

Simon closed his eyes and put all his effort into trying to sound normal. "I'm fine, Mom. I'll try her again at home. She should be there anytime soon."

"How's your day? You busy?"

"Yes, pretty busy, Mom. I got to go, love you."

"Love you, son. Bye."

Simon stood, trying to think what to do, and then suddenly he heard the sound of sirens. *God no, please no.* He sat down and put head in his hands *no... no, please no...* he tried to think but, between the emotion and the blow to his head, he couldn't.

"Simon, Simon... SIMON!" the voice yelled out.

Simon looked up from his desk.

"Something terrible has happened; Mr Bernstein just got a call to go home immediately. I think you should go."

Simon got in his car and drove the short distance over to

the Bernsteins' home. He kept hoping he would wake from this nightmare but he knew it was too real. He sped through the front pillars as he approached the house. It was like a flash back to all those years ago; approaching Julia's home, the many cars, flashing lights and an ambulance. It was all horrifyingly familiar.

★

Sheriff Amos sat in his office the following day, reviewing the initial murder findings with the senior members of his team. The press, who were camped outside the station, needed to be addressed. The murder was front page news and there were wild rumours and speculation. He knew he would have to form an official position and give a statement.

"Sheriff, are you telling me you don't think he did it?" asked Deputy Blaine.

Sheriff Amos shook his head.

"Come on, Sheriff. It's like his signature. The guy is a monster. It bears all the hallmarks of his last girlfriend and you're telling me there is no connection?"

"I'm not saying that. For God's sake, of course there is a connection. Two young girls stabbed through the heart with what looks like identical murder weapons. Yes, there's a connection. I just don't think it's Holman."

Everyone in the room shook their heads.

"Sheriff," said one of the officers, "we have statements from three eye witnesses so far, saying they saw him leave the bank, and we have four statements from other eye witnesses who said they saw Holman running back to the bank approximately twelve minutes before the mother found the body. Now, I'm not sure, between the history of this guy and what we know so far, how much more evidence you need to bring him in."

Sheriff Amos looked at the faces gathered. "Guys, the seven of us in this room have worked together for many years, in some cases for over a decade. I completely understand why you all feel the way you do. I don't want to go into the details but I have put a lot of time into investigating the Osbourne murder. Julia was like a daughter to me. I was convinced, like everyone at the time, it was Holman. It looked a slam-dunk case, yet today I'm almost certain it was not him.

"All I ask is for everyone to keep an open mind and, wherever the evidence takes us, that is the direction we go. Remove any preconceived opinions you have gentlemen.

"Gaby, please inform the press that I will be out to give a statement at 11am. After that, Deputy Blaine and I will drive out to Holman and question him."

Sheriff Amos approached the barrier. He looked around and the large crowd of reporters fell silent. He could see not only local news media but also large corporations from outside the state which had sent their people to cover the story. He cleared his throat and addressed the crowd.

"Ladies and gentlemen, I'd like to read a brief statement," he said. "At approximately 1:05pm yesterday, we received a report of a suspected homicide. Units were dispatched and a twenty-two year old girl's body was found and confirmed deceased by the coroner at 1:40pm. At this time, we are continuing our investigations.

"The deceased's name is Linda Anne Bernstein. Her family is well known to many of you here and I would like to ask you all to respect their privacy at this difficult time. We have posted officers at their home and you will be arrested if you trespass. Additionally, no one is to enter the Horizon

Bank, unless his or her intention is legitimate banking business. There will be no questioning of bank employees on the premises.

"Finally, we have set-up a hot line for anyone who believes they have information related to this case. We have handed out cards with the details and ask you please to share this with the public. Thank you."

As one the assembled crowd roared their questions at the sheriff, he shouted back. "One at a time!"

"Sheriff, is it true the victim was stabbed?"

"Yes."

"Sheriff, should the general public be concerned?"

"At this time, I'll ask everyone to be extra vigilant. Lock your doors, keep in touch with your loved ones and report anything that you think is in the slightest way suspicious."

"Sheriff, is there any connection to the Osbourne murder?"

"That will be one of our lines of enquiry."

"Sheriff, did the police's failure to catch the killer in the Osbourne case result in the death of this young girl?"

"That will be all for now. Ladies and gentlemen, we will update you in the coming days and weeks. I remind you all to respect the privacy of everyone involved."

Sheriff Amos and Deputy Blaine left the police station just after lunch and headed out into the country.

"Have you met Simon Holman before, Sheriff?" asked Deputy Blaine.

"I've met the mother, Martha, but not Simon. However, I've heard so much about him over the years, I feel I have."

"When do you think we will hear from the coroner?"

"He is doing the autopsy as we speak. He told me he should have the initial report by the end of the day and, within a few more days, the toxicology results should come in."

"Look, Sheriff, I did not mean to challenge you in front of everyone in the room this morning. I'm sorry about that. As it stands, I'll keep an open mind, but I just can't see it being anyone else."

"Hell, that's okay Blaine. I would not have made you deputy if I wanted a yes man. Now, you keep giving me your honest opinion on everything – you understand?"

Sheriff Amos and his deputy approached the wooden house.

"Hang on, there are two cars parked outside. I recognise the old banger. She must have a visitor," said Sheriff Amos.

"I know the other one, Sheriff. It's the priest's car. Fr. Mark is his name, a real nice guy. The wife and I like him a lot."

★

Martha was sitting crying in the kitchen with Fr. Mark when she heard a car pull up, she looked out the window. "Oh no, Fr. It's a police car." She started to shake.

"Do you want me to get the door for you?"

Martha shook her head, pulled some fresh tissue from the box, and walked slowly towards the front door.

"Good morning, Martha. I'm sorry, but I would like to ask Simon some questions, if that's okay. Do you mind if we come in?"

"Come in, Sheriff," her voice was barely audible.

The two officers entered the kitchen and greeted Fr. Mark.

"Martha, perhaps I should really go," he said.

Martha put her hand on his shoulder and indicated for him to remain seated. Fr. Mark looked up at the officers and Sheriff Amos motioned for him to stay where he was.

"I'll have to get Simon," said Martha. "He's in his room."

Sheriff Amos looked around the kitchen. Martha has clearly been crying for hours but so had the priest, he thought.

Martha entered the kitchen. "He will be a minute," she said.

"I understand, Martha," said Sheriff Amos.

As they waited for Simon, nothing was said. They all stared down at the floor. Simon entered the kitchen after a couple of minutes. He was dressed in a green towel robe. He half nodded at the officers and sat down.

Sheriff Amos thought it would be better if he sat down too. He was a large, intimidating man and he wanted Simon to feel as at ease as possible. He pulled up the last empty chair.

"Simon, my name is Sheriff Amos, this is Deputy Blaine. I appreciate this is very difficult for you, but can we ask you a few questions?"

Simon nodded. Deputy Blaine stood against the kitchen door and quietly took the small notebook out of his pocket.

"I understand you work at the Horizon Bank. Can you tell us as much as you can remember from the time you got to work yesterday? Please, I know it's hard to remember exact times, but if you could try and be as accurate as possible…"

Simon related his day to the officers. He told them everything he could remember, except regarding the dream he had.

"Thank you for that Simon. You have given us a lot of information. I've just got a few things I'd like to clarify. You said you got back early from lunch. Did you run all the way from Subway?"

"Shortly after I left, it had just started to rain, so I ran the rest of the way to the bank."

"What is Charles's last name?"

"Rankin."

"You said you tripped and hit your head. Was there any blood or just a bump?"

"No blood."

"Can you show me where?"

Simon turned the back of his head and pointed to the spot. The sheriff could feel a small bump. Instantly, Simon's mind flashed back to all those years ago, when Sheriff Joe was inspecting his head.

"That's not too bad now Simon, but I'm sure it was sore at the time."

While Simon was speaking, the sheriff observed him carefully. He knew how Linda was killed. He suspected she may, for a second, have had a chance to fight back but he could see no signs of scratch marks on his hands or face.

"Simon, I have one last request and then we will leave. It's entirely up to you, if you want to or not. I'd like you to lower just the top half of your bathrobe."

"Sheriff!" said Martha.

"It's okay, Mom."

Simon stood and removed his bathrobe. The two officers looked closely at his arms and neck. There were no marks or scratches on him.

"Simon, Martha, I'd like to thank you for your time today. I'm terribly sorry for your loss. I appreciate it must be especially difficult to have to answer my questions. I will be in touch over the coming weeks. In the meantime, can I please ask you to keep your doors locked, especially at night, and leave the outside lights on."

Sheriff Amos was going to put the police siren on to get back to town quickly, but decided otherwise. He wanted time to process what he was told.

"So, what do you think, Blaine?"

"You know how I feel. I've not changed my mind, but he is very believable. Is it because he has been through this before? I don't know."

"What are your thoughts?"

The sheriff passed his hands through his hair.

"Oh man! I hope this does not turn out to be like Julia."

"What do you mean... unsolved?"

"Unsolved is one thing. There are a lot of unsolved crimes, but that case had some really weird things connected with it."

"What do you mean, weird?"

"Just that. Weird, strange, unusual. . . Things we looked into just constantly left us with more questions than answers."

"So, where to now? Are we heading back to the station?"

"No, I sent Dominic late yesterday afternoon to Horizon Bank he got the CCTV backed up. We have Holman's times when he said he went for lunch, so we will be able to verify that at least. Actually, we were supposed to have met Dominic at Horizon ten minutes ago."

"Is that the young kid that just got promoted again? I've heard a lot about him."

"Yeah, a future star in the making, that boy."

"I tell you, Sheriff, if we find Linda's murderer, we find Julia's."

"That statement I agree with... definitely!"

Sheriff Amos and Deputy Blaine arrived at Horizon Bank and were escorted to the security room, where they met Dominic.

"Hi, Sheriff. My name is Adam. I am in charge of the CCTV system. Please have a seat in front of the monitor."

"Okay, Sheriff," said Dominic. "There are a total of eight different cameras positioned in the lobby of the bank. I've backed them all up. However, in my opinion, camera three provides the best view to see the faces of those entering the bank and camera seven for leaving. Also, I have made a note here, sir, of the times Holman arrives and leaves."

Sheriff Amos looked at the piece of paper Dominic handed him.

Arrived for work 7:25am.
Left for lunch 11:42am.
Returned from lunch 12:21pm.
Left bank for the day 1:16pm.

"I've reviewed every camera angle, Sheriff. There are no other times Holman arrives or leaves the bank."

"That's good work, son. Now, Adam, please play for me five minutes either side of each of the times on this paper."

The sheriff watched intently. The CCTV was in black and white but the image was clear. Officer Dominic's times were spot on but there was nothing to be seen five minutes either side of Holman's arrival or departure.

"Well, Blaine, the times are pretty close to Holman's account, are they not?"

"Yes, Sheriff. In fact extremely close, if you take into consideration that he works upstairs. It would take him a minute or two to come down."

"What's the story with Subway?" asked the sheriff.

"The cashier on duty described him perfectly, sir. He said he was the only one sitting and eating in a suit," said Dominic.

Sheriff Amos turned and looked the young officer up and down. "You look in good shape. How old are you, son?"

"Twenty-eight, sir."

"Tomorrow, I want you to dress in a suit with the same shoes as Holman. Leave the bank, walk down to Subway, eat a sandwich, then run as fast as you can back to this bank and time each part of it."

"Yes, sir."

"I'm not finished, son. I then want you to catch your breath, walk back to Subway and then run from Subway to Bernstein's home and run back here."

"Understood, sir."

"Come on guys, let's review this again. This time, give me ten minutes on either side of when he arrives and leaves."

Sheriff Amos started reviewing the tapes again. There was nothing of note then suddenly...

"Stop! Rewind!" he shouted.

The group of men looked at him.

"That guy with the low brim hat and the long coat standing next to the fire extinguisher. He's the same guy we saw when Holman returned from lunch. Remember, he was seated over here next to this plant? Show me that other tape when Holman returns."

"Look, it's not just the same guy but you can see his head is turning. He's watching Holman. Can you zoom in on him? Damn, he is not lifting his head! What business is he doing in the bank for that length of time? Show me that guy from the time he comes in, to the time he leaves. I want every camera angle of him."

"Stop, there! Who is that girl that goes up and talks to him?"

"That's Margret, she works for us downstairs."

"Get her in here, now!"

"Rewind. He lifts his head when she approaches him, right stop and zoom in."

Sheriff Amos blinked his eyes a few times, not believing who he was looking at, but there was no mistaking the face. He had watched it for three hundred miles from Louisiana to Sidon.

"You recognise him, Sheriff?" asked Blaine.

"Yes, his name is Dr Brockman. I mean Brookman… Dr Brookman. But, if his past is anything to go by, we are going to have a hell of a time tracking him down."

"What cameras do you have outside the bank?"

"There are two pointing in opposite directions, up and down the high street," said Adam.

"Get them on, let's see which direction he goes."

"Here, Sheriff. That's him on the pavement, coming into view. He looks to be on his own. He now enters the bank," said Blaine.

"What we got of him leaving?" asked the sheriff.

"Here he is, just leaving the bank, walking. Then look: you can just see him at the top of the screen. He gets into the passenger side of that car over on the far side of the road. Damn, they drive off around the corner."

"Zoom in, Adam. Can anyone make out what type of car it is?"

"This other car is in the way. At best, we can just see the top of it and part of the back windscreen, Sheriff. It could be anything."

"It's a dark-coloured car. Does anyone see anything else?" asked the sheriff.

"Anyone? Any guesses? I'll take anything."

"I'm not sure but, if I had to guess, Sheriff, I'd say it was a Ford Mark IV Cortina," said Adam.

The sheriff looked at Adam. "You joking right? How the heck can you tell that?"

"I used to own one. I've cleaned it often enough. To me, the slope of the roof down to the back windscreen looks the same."

The sheriff looked around the room. "Anyone got any other ideas?"

Blank faces steered back at him.

"Okay, we've nothing else, lets run with it. I want a list of everyone in Sidon and the surrounding area who owns a dark-coloured Ford Mark IV Cortina. Dominic, I want you to send that tape off to Ford Headquarters to see if they can confirm it is a Mark IV Cortina.

"Adam, who else has CCTV on the High Street and Orchard Street, where the car turned up?"

"I can't think of anyone else, let me get back to you on that, Sheriff."

The door opened.

"Excuse me, I'm Margret. I got a message to come here immediately. I work as a teller."

"Hi, Margret, I'm Sheriff Amos. We were just reviewing the lobby tapes from yesterday. In them you approach a customer wearing a long coat and a low hat. Do you remember? Or do you need me to show you?"

"No. Of course, I remember him."

"Tell me, word for word, that conversation."

"It lasted less than a minute, maybe thirty seconds or less. I noticed him when I was working. He was just standing there and later, when I was going for lunch, he was still there. I just went up and asked him if he needed any help. He said no, he was waiting for someone. I told him he could have a seat, but he just stared at me. It was a bit unsettling. He gave me the creeps. So I left, and when I came back from lunch he was gone."

"Thanks, Margret. That's all."

★

"I'm sorry, Father, but no one is allowed through the gate," said the officer.

"Please, I am a friend of the Bernstein family. They are expecting me."

"Hey, Jim, it's okay," said the senior officer. "I'll escort him to the house."

"Make your way up the path, Father. I'll catch up with you in a minute."

Fr. Mark walked up the drive between the trees. He could see the top floor of the house come into view. He remembered the happiness of the graduation party and later the engagement dinner. Now, it has all come to this. *Why, Lord, why?* he asked. As he walked further, he looked up at the magnificent trees. The blue sky broke through the thick foliage only briefly. Suddenly, a feeling of déjà vu came over him. He slowed his pace and looked around, why is this so familiar? He was overwhelmed by a feeling that everything was happening as it was meant to.

Linda was the only daughter of Martin and Brenda Bernstein. They had an older son who had made a successful career for himself in the Navy. Brenda was utterly traumatised. She had come home and found Linda covered in blood. Her body, slumped in the chair, was halfway under the desk. Martin was trying hard to be strong for his wife. She needed him, but losing his only daughter was devastating. The police, upon seeing Brenda's condition, advised him to have a doctor come over. Martin agreed and, after a brief look, the doctor put her on medication.

Fr. Mark entered the house. To the left, he could see blue and white police tape blocking access to the upstairs. He walked in and met Martin in the living room. He expressed his sympathy, but there was little else he could do. Brenda was seated on the couch with her head down, sobbing. Fr. Mark went over to her, crouched down, and held her hand. She opened her eyes and looked at him. She pulled him towards her. She hugged him and cried. No words were spoken. Brenda sat back in her chair, tears were streaming down her face. Fr. Mark stood up and started to walk towards the door. Martin put his hand out and stopped him.

"How is Simon?" he asked quietly.

Fr. Mark was caught off guard by both the question and the tone of Martin's voice. It carried more of a caring quality than one of anger. He knew there was no way a man like Martin Bernstein, with all his contacts, would not have looked into Simon's background.

"I just came from there. He is not good."

"And Martha?"

"She asked me to pass on her condolences. She tried to call but was unable to get through."

"Yes, I know. There were a number of prank calls, so the police have blocked the line. Father, I know Simon's past and I have got to know him well over the last five years. I do not believe he did this."

CHAPTER 18

As the years went by, Robert and Beth's investigation into Julia's murder began to wane. They had slowly started to believe that Simon could possibly be innocent. However, when the news of Linda's murder broke, they followed the case closely. Suddenly, this latest murder shattered any thoughts they had regarding Simon's innocence. There was no way two young girls, from the same town, who were killed in the same way, were not related. The common denominator was only one person: Simon Holman.

The day after Linda's murder, Sheriff Amos made a brief call to Robert and Beth. He gave them only a little more information than the statement he had made to the press and promised to come back to them as things developed.

★

Fr. Mark related the conversation he had with Martin Bernstein to Martha and Simon. This was a massive relief to both of them. Shortly after, Martin called Martha and expressed the same feelings to her. He also told her to pass on to Simon, that he wanted him to take at least a month off of work, or as much time as he needed.

As tragic as Linda's death was, Sheriff Amos knew it presented an opportunity to finally get justice for Julia. As deputy Blaine said, "catch Linda's killer and we will catch Julia's." He knew killers always made mistakes, especially in subsequent murders. They begin to believe they can't be caught, overconfidence sets in and they become careless.

Four days had passed since Linda's murder, Sheriff Amos arrived at the station and he knew he had another long day ahead of him. Finally, the coroner's report was on his desk. He opened the brown envelope and reviewed the report. One word screamed off the page.

"She was pregnant?" asked deputy Blaine.

"That's what it said – approximately eight weeks."

"Did she know? Did anyone know?"

"That's what we need to find out."

"Was there anything else in his report?"

"Cause of death was as we all knew. Whether he will call me to discuss it off the record, I doubt it. Actually, you know, I really miss Bob…"

"You mean the previous coroner?"

"Yeah. I don't know about this new guy. He is three days late with his report. He gave me some BS the other day. I had to tell him to get his ass over to Bernstein's house. Well, we'll see how long it takes him to have the toxicology results on my desk. They won't release her body for burial until everything is completed. I really feel for the family.

"We have a long day ahead of us, Sheriff, and it's only 7:50am. You need to take it easy big fella."

"You're right, Blaine. Let me get a coffee, you want one?"

"I'm okay. The guys should be here soon for the eight o'clock morning meeting."

Sheriff Amos took his place at the head of the conference table. There were seven other officers in the room.

"Dominic, let's start with you."

"Sir, I rented a suit yesterday and these are my times to Subway, the Bernstein's house and back to Horizon Bank." Dominic handed the sheriff the paper and passed copies around the room.

"What is this time at the bottom with a question mark next to it, son?"

Dominic distributed a drawing of the house and surrounding area to the officers. "As you know, sir, there are two possibilities: he either approached the house up the main driveway, or he went around the side and in though the small gate on Bermuda Avenue. Unfortunately, the drive is tarred and the side entrance is pebble stone. Without footprints, we are not sure which approach he took. It's further complicated by the fact that both the back door and front doors were unlocked. Therefore, the time at the bottom is estimated, based on the quickest approach. This is through the side entrance and in the back door."

"Okay, so adding everything up and using the fastest approach, there was just enough time for Holman to leave Subway, commit the crime and make it back to Horizon Bank. Is that what you're saying?"

"Correct, sir, just about."

"What have we got for fingerprints?"

"Holman's prints are throughout the room and house in general, as you would expect. I just had it confirmed, on my way in here, that the back and front doors are clean of prints as well as the knife. This is their report here, Sheriff."

The sheriff shook his head.

"What about the couple in the parked car on Bermuda Avenue. How credible are they?"

"Sir, they are adamant, especially the wife. They both saw a man leaving through the side gate. He walked right by their car. I showed them a photo of Holman. They are certain it was him but the clothes they described him wearing were incorrect."

"Ali, any word on the jacket?"

"Yes. We took it from his office and sent it to the crime lab. They confirmed late yesterday that there was no trace of blood on it."

"Look, there is no way he buried that knife in her without getting covered in blood."

"Did anyone here see him when he got to Bernstein's house that day?"

"I did, Sheriff," said Nick. "I stopped him from entering the house. He was wearing a long-sleeved white dress shirt. He was clean."

"Tom, what do you have on the Mark IV Cortina?"

"I got the owner details yesterday afternoon. I told them to give me two lists. One is registered dark-colour Mark IV's and the other consists of all the light colours, in case the car was repainted. We have started knocking on doors, sir, but so far no leads."

"What about Ford?"

"They have reviewed the image, Sheriff. They are saying there's not enough to know one way or the other."

"Look, it's all we got on the car. Keep your men on it. The CCTV guy, what's his name...? Adam. He sounded fairly certain. In fact, leave me a copy of that registered owners list please, Tom."

"Rankin, Charles; the guy who shares the office with Holman. What's his story?"

"He is confirming Holman's account," said Nick.

"Did we find out what calls were made from the office phone?"

"Two calls were made after Holman got back from lunch. One was to Bernstein's address and the other was to his mom's house. Before that, they appear just work related."

"What we got on the murder weapon?"

"Almost identical to the Osbourne murder. We are trying to trace it but it has no manufacturer's name on it," said Nick.

Sheriff Amos thought to himself, *good luck with that*! It also reminded him that the last time he had looked in Julia Osbourne's evidence draw, the knife had been removed.

"Has anyone actually compared this knife with the Osbourne murder weapon?"

"I have, sir," said Nick. "I've got photos of them side by side next to a ruler. The dimensions are identical."

How the heck did that knife end back up in the evidence drawer? he wondered…

"Good, Nick. I'll need a copy of those pictures."

"Okay guys, I got the coroner's report this morning and Linda was eight weeks pregnant. Whether she knew or not, I'm not sure."

"Oscar, you're more familiar than most in here with the medical side of things. Find out if they have a family doctor and see if she visited him. If not, then start with the clinics closest to her home and see what you come up with. Additionally, guys, I do not want to tell the parents, or anyone at this stage, that Linda was pregnant. So keep it within these walls."

"Did we hear back on the CCTV? Is there any building near Horizon with it?"

"No luck, sir. What little CCTV that exists is all indoors," said Dominic.

"Gaby, anything on the hotline?"

"Nothing significant, Sheriff. A few nuisance calls but no solid leads so far. Needless to say, the press are insisting on another statement."

"Hold them off for another day or two please, Gaby. Okay guys, that just about wraps up this morning's meeting. Anyone got anything else?"

The room was silent.

"All right, let's get to work."

★

Catholic doctrine states that, for a priest to become a Bishop, he must meet the following requirements: As well as being at least thirty-five years old and a priest for at least five years, he should be "outstanding and in strong faith, good morals, piety, zeal for souls, wisdom, prudence and human virtues", and should possess the other qualities needed for fulfilling the office.

In May 1989, the Apostolic Nuncio notified Fr. Mark that he had been short listed, along with two other priests, for the position of Bishop. In a few months time, he was to be interviewed by a representative of the clergy.

Fr. Mark had mixed emotions about this. He was proud that his work had been recognised by the church. He could not help but think that this was about the worst possible timing; he was needed by not only Martha and Simon but the Bernsteins too. In addition, so many others in the community had come to depend on him. He prayed that God would find a way.

★

Martha was reliving her nightmares from all those years ago. Thankfully, though, Simon did not wake during the night screaming. For her, that used to be the worst part of it. Otherwise, there was little difference. Simon spent the day in his room and only came out to eat. There was nothing Martha could say. She felt that all the promise of his life had been taken away. Rumour and suspicion lingered everywhere. As the days went by without an arrest, the newspaper editors printed the most outrageous theories. Everyone had an opinion. Even at the supermarket Martha overheard people discussing the murder.

Sheriff Amos had not called or visited her since the day following the murder. She could not relax, every time she walked into a room and passed a window, she glanced out to see if there was a police car approaching. She was desperate to find out what direction the case was taking, but she knew no one in law enforcement. She lived on her nerves waiting for a knock on the door.

Martha had spoken to Mr Caine and explained that she needed to take time off and he understood completely. At times, she wondered if Annamae would use this tragedy as an excuse to come over and try and make good with her. However, there was no visit or call from her and she was happy about that.

Unfortunately, it meant that Fr. Mark was her only outlet and she felt guilty that she was taking him away from so much of the other good work he did. She tried to get through a day without calling or meeting him, but if she did not call him he would always pick up the phone to check on her.

Martha went into Simon's room to see if he wanted

lunch. He was staring at the ceiling and his eyes were moving back and forth. She stood for a short while watching him, but he was oblivious to her presence. She called out to him. He turned and looked at her.

"Are you alright, son? Seemed like you were far away."

"I'm fine, Mom."

"Would you like anything to eat?"

"Is Fr. Mark coming over today?"

"I'm not sure, I've not arranged anything with him but I'm sure, if he knows you want to see him, he will make the time."

Simon nodded.

"Sure, son, I will give him a call. Are you hungry? I've got soup ready."

"No... no, thanks, Mom."

★

Sheriff Amos put the siren on and led the four car police convoy out of town and into the country. He felt like it was the first decent break he had gotten in the case. Finally, there was a clear connection and a piece of the jigsaw had fallen into place. He approached the old wooden house and saw her car outside. He stopped and signalled to the other officers to stay in their patrol cars. He knocked on the door and waited a couple of minutes, the door opened slowly.

"Sheriff Amos," she said.

"Good morning, Ma'am. If you don't mind we would like to ask you a few more questions."

She stared at him. "You are making a bit of a habit of this, aren't you, Sheriff?"

"Just doing my job, Ma'am."

"Yes, I see… you're not very good at it, are you?"

Deputy Blaine looked at the sheriff but his expression was that of a poker face.

"Annamae, I'm going to ask you some questions. You can answer me here or down at the station – it's your decision. Now, where were you on the day Linda Bernstein was killed?"

"I was here at home all day and, before you ask, I have no witness to that. I live alone."

"Your car was seen outside Horizon Bank around lunch time. You want to explain that to me?"

"You must be mistaken, Sheriff."

"We know it was your car, when last did you see Dr Brookman?"

"I've told you before, I don't know him."

"Yeah, I was almost certain you were lying then, but now I know you are." Sheriff Amos looked her up and down. "You know, in my line of work, I question a lot of people. Most of the time I just use gut instinct to figure out if they are lying. But every so often I get a level of proof that is beyond doubt. I then return to question them again. As I observe them, I get a sort of sick enjoyment out of it. You know, right now, Annamae, I'm enjoying this."

Annamae's eyes searched the sheriff's face for a hint of what he knew.

"Now, I'm going to ask you again. Did you leave this house, in that car, on the day of Linda's murder? Secondly, when was the last time you saw Brookman?"

"You're bluffing, Sheriff. Do you think I'm stupid?"

"Last chance, Annamae."

"I told you I was at home all day, and I don't know any Dr Brookman."

The sheriff shook his head. "No Annamae, I was not

bluffing. ~~We have him~~ on CCTV leaving Horizon Bank and getting into your car. A bit of a stupid mistake on your part, wasn't it?"

For the first time, Annamae's expression changed. "I broke no law, Sheriff. You have nothing on me."

"You do realise, Annamae, I know what Dr Brookman is. After this mistake, you present a direct link to him. If I'm right about him, he will come after you; it's only a matter of time."

"You get off of my property now!" she screamed at him.

Sheriff Amos nodded to deputy Blaine. "I have a search warrant here, Ma'am. I will escort you to my car. You can wait in it while your home is searched. If you choose not to comply, we will take you down to the station until our search is complete. Additionally, Ma'am, we have signed authorisation papers here to impound your vehicle. We will notify you when it will be returned."

★

Simon, Martha and Fr. Mark were sitting at the kitchen table. Simon had just finished telling them what he saw when he fell asleep in the chair at work.

"Who exactly did you see, who was holding the knife?" asked Fr. Mark.

"I saw myself, Father. The same as with Julia. It's as if I left the office, did it, and returned. However, my return was so violent I fell out the chair. I could not explain this, so I lied to Sheriff Amos when I said I tripped."

"From you description, I'm certain you somehow witnessed this event but there is no way you did it. So, make sure you have no doubt in your mind about that."

184

"Was I astral travelling, Father? Is that what happened to me?"

"What is that?" asked Martha.

"Astral travelling, Martha, is something that is both ridiculed, as well as accepted as fact by some. It is where a person's soul leaves their body and they travel on what is referred to as an astral plane. They are fully aware and can see events happening far away. They then return back into their body. This return can be normal, as well as violent, just as Simon described happened to him."

"Do you believe in it, Father?"

"I don't know, Martha. I have not practiced it. However, as I said, Simon must fully understand that, despite seeing what happened, there was nothing he could have done to save Linda or, for that matter, Julia."

It did not take long for word to get out in the community that four police cars had been seen at Annamae's home. It did not help either that one of the officers that was involved in the search had also mentioned it to his wife. The following morning, it was front page news, along with further sensational coverage.

Sheriff Amos updated his team on the status of the investigation. He had only made the connection to Annamae because he recognised her name was on the list Tom had given to him of registered Ford Cortina Mark IV owners. He asked Gaby to contact Adam at Horizon and pass on the department's thanks for suggesting the model of car. Unfortunately, no direct link to the murder was discovered during the search of Annamae's home. However two items of significance were found; the first was a 1968 newspaper clipping with the headline: "POLICE DECLARE MISSING DOCTOR DEAD". The second item was a piece of paper with an address in Louisiana that Sheriff Amos recognised immediately. It was the first hard evidence of contact between Annamae and Dr Brookman.

Sheriff Amos gave his team of officers only enough information on Dr Brookman for them to understand he was a central figure in both homicides. He did not include anything regarding his demonic possession, which he recorded in his diary.

"Okay, Sheriff," said Nick. "Let's say, for arguments sake, Holman is innocent. It can't be Brookman, as he was in Horizon throughout the murder. It leaves us with Annamae. She dropped Brookman off at Horizon as a lookout and went over to Bernstein's. Did she do Julia as well? Or are we still looking at Holman?"

"As I told you guys, we need to follow the evidence and, at the moment, we just don't have it on either of them. Hell, for all we know, it's someone else."

"What about Linda's mother, Sheriff?"

"Yes, I've been thinking about her, but I just can't see it. Again, we have nothing on her. In fact, guys, we can't rule anyone in or out. We did confirm the father never left the bank, yes?"

"That is correct, sir. There is nothing on CCTV," said Dominic.

"Is there a back entrance he could have left through?"

"I'll look into that, sir."

"How long are they going to take with Annamae's car, Nick?"

"Forensics informed me not before next Friday, at the earliest. I tried to push them on it but they said it's not just fingerprints they lift, it's an entire science involved with it these days. It takes time to process, they say."

★

"What?" said Martha.

"You heard me correctly. They searched her home and took the car," said Fr. Mark. "I don't want to sound like a gossip. I'm just telling you what I'm reading in the papers."

"Are they saying why they went there?"

"From what the article says, no one knows for sure. There is just a lot of speculation that her car was seen close to the Horizon Bank that day. There is a police news conference scheduled to start at the top of the hour. Channel eighteen will have it live."

Martha and Simon counted down the minutes, along with almost all of Sidon. Sheriff Amos approached the microphone. "Good morning, ladies and gentlemen. I'd like to provide you with a brief update with regards to the Bernstein homicide investigation. The coroner's initial report has confirmed the cause of death was a single stab wound to the heart. The knife used was of the same type as the one in the Osbourne murder and, in both cases, the knife was left in the victim. At this time, the investigation is on-going; we have not ruled anyone in or out. We are continuing to gather evidence and I will again ask anyone with information on this, or the Osbourne murder, to please contact us. I would like to thank all the members of the force for the hours they have put into this. Finally, I would like to remind you to continue to show respect for the privacy of the families involved."

"Sheriff, what can you tell us about the home you searched yesterday?"

"A person has been questioned, their home was searched, and their car is being processed as we speak. No arrest has been made, we class the individual as a person of interest."

"Sheriff, is this person the aunt of the deceased's fiancé?"

"That is correct. However, I emphasise that she is only one of many people we are looking into. She deserves privacy and no one is allowed onto her property without her permission."

"Sheriff, can you confirm that her car was seen outside Horizon Bank on the day of the murder?"

"That is correct."

"Are the prints on the knife the same as in the Osbourne murder?"

"Unfortunately, we were unable to recover any prints from the murder weapon. I will take one more question."

"In your opinion, Sheriff, did the same individual murder both these young girls?"

"Yes, at this moment, that is my opinion. Thank you all and I remind everyone to be extra vigilant at this time and to look out for each other."

"Okay," said Martha. "So he's confirmed Annamae's car was outside Horizon Bank but they are not saying much else."

"Was she following me, Mom?"

"She may have been, but I can't see them looking into her for that. They must have something else on her. I'd love to know what it is."

"She's been acting really strange for quite a while now. I'm not saying she did it but, let's be honest, she never liked Linda."

CHAPTER 19

Three weeks had passed since the death of Linda Bernstein. Her body had been finally released by the coroner and her funeral arranged. Fr. Mark presided over the service and Linda's brother read the eulogy. In a touching gesture, Martin asked Simon and Martha to sit with him and Brenda. The church was overflowing with people who had come to pay their respects. Linda was buried in a family plot in Sidon's main cemetery, on the eastern side of the city.

The funeral gave Martin and Brenda some form of closure and, to some extent, Martha and Simon felt the same. They talked it over and they both determined that they had stayed home for long enough. It was pointless living life like that, they needed some distraction and they both decided to go back to work.

★

It was shortly after eight o'clock in the morning when Sheriff Amos and his officers took their seats around the conference table.

"Good morning, everyone. Deputy Blaine, I think I'll start with you today."

"As you know, Sheriff, from the initial forensics report on

the car, they found no prints or hair. They took a few swab samples from the floor mats and front seat. The results came in yesterday. They should be dropping the report off this afternoon but, in speaking to them, they said they basically got nothing from the car.

"That is what I feared, Blaine. Brookman is an educated man. That pair of gloves we saw him put on before he left the bank, I'm sure he kept them on throughout. Anyway, fill out the paperwork and arrange for the car to be returned."

"Oscar, any luck with the hospitals or clinics?"

"Someone called me from the main hospital, Linda visited it three days before she was killed."

"The main hospital? I thought they said about a week ago, that they had no record of her?"

"That is what they said, sir. Initially they entered her date of birth to do the search and nothing showed up on the computer. However, yesterday someone called me to say that they had made an honest mistake."

"Call me old fashioned, but I think sometimes the system worked better with files and cabinets. Anyway what time are you going there today?"

"The doctor that saw Linda is on the morning shift, so she gave me a ten thirty appointment. Her name is Dr Allison Dearth."

"Damn, that's a bit of an unfortunate surname for a doctor. Anyway, Oscar, if you don't mind I'll come with you. I'd like to have a chat with Dr Dearth."

"Young Dominic, what you got today?"

"Sir, there is another way out of the bank, using the emergency fire escape which opens onto Baker Street. The door is designed to only open from the inside. Unfortunately, they do not have CCTV covering it and the alarm on it is only active after office hours. I did an experiment with bank security yesterday and I was able to exit the bank. By simply jamming a coin in the lock and closing the door slowly, it prevented the door from locking and I was able to re-enter."

"Damn, I was hoping to be able to eliminate the father but, based on what you said, we can't – but what motive would he have to kill his own daughter? Dominic, I want you to start making some… how shall I put it?… gentle enquiries. I think we should start building a profile of him as well."

"Gaby, anything on the hotline?"

"I'm afraid it has been pretty quiet, Sheriff. Nothing to speak of."

"Yes, it's only going to get quieter as people lose interest. Get the press to remind people we are still seeking information."

"Will do, Sheriff."

"Okay, anyone got anything else?"

"I do have one thing I'd like to share with the team," said Nick. "I've been looking into the Bernstein family. Martin Bernstein enjoys a good career at Horizon Bank and, because of who his parents are, he has been fast tracked from Loan Officer a few years ago to Branch Manager today. His parents who live in New York are, by all accounts, fabulously wealthy, again from banking. They actually have the title deeds to Martin's home. He does not own it, they do.

"Linda's brother in the Navy is a bit of an oddball and has been, in a way, cast out of the family. I have it from a reliable source that Linda was the grandparents' favourite and was in line to inherit, not just the family home but most of the grandparents' estate. Is that the motive? I don't know, but I thought it was quite interesting."

"Good research, Nick, well done. I think, like everyone,

I just assumed he owned that house. He is definitely worth looking into but I just can't see it."

★

It was a Thursday morning in November of 1989 and Martha had dropped Simon off at the bus stop. Her plan was to do a bit of cleaning around the house and then go to the supermarket after lunch. She was sitting in her living room with a coffee, trying to make sense of it all. There was so much that she could not explain. A couple of Mountain Bluebirds landing by the window caught her eye. Martha looked over to the fireplace. On the mantle were pictures of John and herself, taken on their wedding day. Another featured baby Simon and there was a picture of her and her sister, taken when they were children down at the lake. Suddenly, it dawned on her. There can be no other explanation; it was the only way everything could make sense. *I must tell Simon*, she thought.

"Horizon Bank. Good morning, this is Charles, how can I help?"

"Charles, it's Martha. Is Simon there?"

"Sorry, Mrs Holman, he went downstairs a little while ago. He is in a meeting. Shall I ask him to call you when he comes back?"

"No, it's okay, Charles. On second thought, perhaps it's better if I wait till he comes home."

★

Oscar knocked on the door of the young lady's office at the main hospital. "Excuse me, Ma'am, I am officer Oscar Rae and this is Sheriff Amos."

"Hello, gentlemen. Come on in and have a seat. Now, how can I be of assistance?"

"We understand Linda Bernstein came to see you a few weeks ago. We would like to ask you some questions, if you don't mind."

"It's tragic what happened to her, Sheriff. I'll assist you in any way I can."

"Thank you, Ma'am. I've learnt from the coroner's report that she was pregnant. I assume that is what she came to see you about?"

"That's right, she was very nervous. We gathered at the time that she had not told anyone."

"What exactly did you check when she arrived?"

"Just one minute please, guys. I'll need to get her file." Dr Dearth left her office and returned shortly after. "Okay, so this is it here. She was approximately eight weeks pregnant. Everything appeared normal. We took her weight, height, blood pressure, blood sample and urine tests, ultrasound which… let me see… were all were normal."

"Did she say why she chose to come here and not her regular doctor?"

"I thought about that and I was going to ask but, wait, hang on…"

"What is it, Dr?"

"I'm just noticing something. Someone has changed her birth date on the form. She was born 11th March 1968. It's been changed to 17th March 1968. I would remember doing this."

Sheriff Amos looked at the form. It was clear to see the date had been altered.

"That would explain why the hospital told us, initially, that she was not here. You used the word 'we' earlier when you said, 'we gathered at the time that she had not told anyone'. Who else was here?"

"There was a new nurse on duty, very helpful. Asked Linda lots of questions, and very keen."

"Do you remember her name?"

"No, Sheriff. It wasn't a girl. It was a male nurse. Looked a bit old to be just out of nursing school but came across as extremely knowledgeable."

Sheriff Amos looked at Oscar, "Are we thinking the same thing? Wait here, Ma'am. I'll be back in two minutes." Sheriff Amos ran out to his patrol car and returned with the picture of Dr. Brockman. "Have a look at this photo, Ma'am. Could this be the nurse?"

"Yes, that's him."

★

"Hi, Father. End of month transactions again, is it?"

"I'm afraid so, Simon. I made sure and queued up over there to get Marian. I dealt with her last month, she is so efficient. I was in and out of here in five minutes."

"You almost did not make it; we are just about closing. In fact, look, they have just flipped the sign on the door. Remember, we close a little earlier on a Thursday, I'm just on my way home."

"Have you got the car? Or has your mother got it today?"

"Mom has it. It's her supermarket day, so I'm going to take the 3:15pm bus."

"Well, actually, I'm heading out your way to visit with Mr Taylor, so I can run you home."

"That would great, Father. Thanks."

★

Sheriff Amos was back at the station when the emergency call came in. He knew the address instantly. He grabbed his gun and charged out of the office. With the siren on, he raced through the streets and out to the country. When he pulled up at the house, there was already a patrol car there. Officer Ben approached him as he got out of his car.

"Sheriff, it's Mrs Holman. She was shot."

"What else do you know?"

"The priest, Fr. Mark, arrived here with Simon, her son, and found her. They are still inside the house."

"It looks like she came home and surprised a robber, sir. As she went in the front door, she was gunned down. There are footprints to and from the living room window."

"Call dispatch. I want the dogs here now!"

The young officer radioed for the dogs. Meanwhile, Sheriff Amos looked around. Next to his car and the young officer's patrol car, were Martha's and Fr. Mark's cars. The ground was relatively dry and he could see clearly tyre marks from each of them.

"I think he came though the field, sir, and entered into the house through the living room window. There is definitely no sign of any other vehicles."

"Park your car at the top of the drive, Ben. Everyone approaching the house will go along that fence on the far side. Have you got tape in your car?"

"Yes, sir."

"Barrier off that side of the house with the living room window – no one goes there. How long before the dogs are here?"

"They will be about forty minutes, sir."

Sheriff Amos entered the house. A few feet inside the door, the lifeless body of Martha Holman lay on the floor, along with her car keys and her opened handbag. In the living room, he found Simon and Fr. Mark, both in tears. Clearly, neither of them were in a condition to speak to him. He walked over to the window: there was glass on the floor and a large rock lay across the room. Looking through the window, he saw footprints, both to and from the window. Clearly, this was how the attacker both entered and exited the property.

Five days later, Sheriff Amos and his team assembled for their morning meeting.

"Nick, please take the team though everything we have to date."

"Okay, Sheriff. I'll bring it up on the projector so everyone can follow."

Entry

"The person definitely approached the house walking from the road down the field, which is parallel with the driveway. He then entered through the living room window and left through the same window. He went into the field and came out at the road. They used hounds and German shepherds but unfortunately both teams of dogs lost the scent at the road, so it's pretty certain the suspect got into a car. There is an area, just off the road, where a car could be parked, that is pretty hidden from people passing. There are no tyre tracks in it but it does not mean the person did not drive out of there and clean them before leaving."

Footprints

"Nine and a half, same size as the Osbourne homicide. Different tread pattern, but sports-type track shoe. It's definitely Adidas, we are checking on the exact type."

Fingerprints

"No prints recovered. Almost certainly wore gloves."

Items taken

"Mrs Holman's purse and possibly some items out of a jewellery box. We will need her son to go back to the house to determine exactly what has been removed. There were a lot of drawers opened upstairs."

"Hang on, Nick. Is Simon still staying at the church?"
"Yes, Sheriff. I'm pretty sure he is."
"Okay. go ahead please."

Re-enactment

"We believe, Sheriff, that the person was in the house when Mrs Homan arrived home. From what we can establish, Mrs Holman parked her car. Her footprints clearly show her exiting her vehicle, going around the back (we assume to get something out of the trunk). She then walked through the front door, where she was shot twice in the chest. Her purse is removed from her handbag, along with possibly other unknown items from the house."

Motive

"Robbery is what it looks like. However, we are all aware that Mrs Holman was not by any means a wealthy woman, other possible motives are unclear."

Suspects

Her son, Simon J Holman, would be the most likely suspect, but he has a rock solid alibi. He was in meetings for most of the day. The bank closed early on the Thursday.

He did not even go for lunch and Fr. Mark took him home where together they found the body. There is only one other family member, her sister. Her alibi is that she was home all day as her car was at the mechanic shop. Her story checks out.

Martha made one phone call to Simon at 10:38am and his colleague, Charles, took the call. He said Martha just told him it was something she wanted to tell Simon, but not to bother as it would be better to tell him when he gets home. Simon tried to return the call at 2:10pm but there was no answer. He assumed she was at the supermarket, so time of death is somewhere between 10:38am, when Charles spoke to her, and 3:35pm, when the priest called the police."

"Thanks for that, Nick. I got the coroner's report late last night. Mrs Holman was killed by two gunshots to the chest, one was directly to her heart, the other was to her stomach. The bullet to the heart lodged in her spine, there is an exit wound from the stomach shot, out the left side of her back, and that bullet is missing. Now I find it incredibly difficult to believe that our team of guys, along with forensics, missed that bullet. We need to find that bullet gentlemen. The bullet recovered from her spine, was from a Smith and Wesson model 30 revolver. Unfortunately, an extremely common weapon. Forensics will be another week at least. However, I'm told 'off the record' they have again found nothing on the car.

"We will go back today and we will again try and find that missing bullet. There is a possibility she was shot before she closed the door, so we will set up a grid pattern outside and I want every square inch of that ground searched. Needless to say, a bullet does not disappear. Blaine, I'd like you to put together a team; you are in charge of this. Dominic, you come with me. We will go and visit with Simon and the priest and perhaps we can get something out of them. I tried the day after the murder, but the kid was a mess. I'm told his father died in the war and his mother is all he had. Go ahead and get started with the search and I'll meet you guys at his house later on.

"Gaby, what you got today?"

"Same as usual, Sheriff. The press are demanding more information. I'm sure you have seen the headlines. The department and you, in particular, are coming in for a lot of criticism and there is a petition going around for a vote of no confidence in you."

"I don't know what to tell you, Gaby. Try and hold them off. The Governor was on the phone yesterday and, from how he spoke to me, I think he will fire my ass before the vote of no confidence happens."

Sheriff Amos and Dominic left the station to make the short journey across town to the church.

"Sheriff. That guy is surrounded by death, don't you think? One girlfriend, a fiancé, his father and now his mother. What are the odds of that?"

The sheriff was too lost in thought to reply to the young officer.

★

Sheriff Amos knocked on the church door.

"Morning, Sheriff," said Fr. Mark in a subdued voice.

"Hello, Father. This is officer Dominic. I'd like to apologise for coming over the other day. I know it was not a good time, but do you think Simon and yourself will be able to answer a few question for me now?"

"Come on in, Sheriff. Have a seat through there in my

office. Simon is in the church, I'll go and speak with him." A few minutes later he returned, "Okay, Sheriff. He won't be long. I have coffee there if either of you like."

"No thanks, Father." Sheriff Amos looked around the office and noticed a mattress against the wall. "Is this where he's sleeping, Father?"

The priest nodded. "Come on in Simon and have a seat," said Fr. Mark.

"Hi, Simon," said Sheriff Amos. "This is officer Dominic. Firstly, thank you for seeing us and, as I said to Fr. Mark, I'm sorry for coming over a few days ago. I appreciate it is a very difficult time."

Simon did not raise his head but just looked at the floor. "That is fine, Sheriff."

"I'd like to say, Simon, I know you have had a lot to deal with in your short life and you have my sincere sympathy for what happened to your mother. Needless to say, you are under no suspicion. All we want to do is ask you a few questions, in the hope that we can find out who did this to her."

Unfortunately, Simon was unable to provide the sheriff with any information that would be useful. Sheriff Amos asked him if he would consider coming back to the house to identify anything that was stolen but Simon refused. The sheriff thought it best not to pursue it any further and to leave it for now. At the end, Simon asked the sheriff how long it would be before he could bury his mother. Sheriff Amos promised that, as soon as the coroner's work was complete, he would let him know.

Sheriff Amos and officer Dominic left the church and headed over to Martha's home.

"Well, Blaine, what have you got?"

"Nothing so far, Sheriff. We have looked inside the house and the search of the front yard is almost complete."

"I don't know, Blaine. Something is not right here. If you look at this photo of the position of the body, this is how she was. The priest told me they did not move her; it was clear she was dead. Now, the front door opens in towards the hallway. Her body was about four feet inside the house, so I'm thinking the gunman sees her drive up, stands in the kitchen and as soon as she closes the door she is trapped in the hallway. He opens fire, so the bullet can't be outside. It must be in here but it's not. It does not make sense. There is no way any gunman would open fire until that door is closed. The coroner's report clearly states two entry wounds: one wound was to the chest and one to the stomach with an exit wound out the left side of the back. She had to be facing the gunman. Standing or slightly crouched, the bullet would likely exit her back and hit the door somewhere here."

"I know what you are saying, Sheriff, but look around. It's not here. I can't see it on the floor or someone kicking it and not noticing."

"Blaine, my gut tells me this was not a robbery. What the hell is there of any kind of value in this place? This was a pretty simple woman living off a VA pension with a part time job. I'm telling you, it is connected to what's been happening. It may not be the single stab wound to the heart but the size nine and a half prints are consistent. If Holman did not have a rock solid alibi, I'd have him locked up now. So who the hell did this?"

★

On 10th December, 1989, a service was held for Martha Holman at St Mary's Church in Sidon. It was without question the hardest service Fr. Mark ever had to perform; on a number of occasions he had to pause and compose himself. Unlike Linda's funeral, this was a far smaller gathering. Along with Simon, there was Martin and Brenda Bernstein, Mr Caine, a girl from the supermarket... Also, there were a few of the women from the surrounding community, some of whom were in the room when Simon was born and who had not seen her since, came to pay their respects. However, noticeably absent from the service was Martha's sister.

The record showed that Martha L Holman, aged forty-two, was laid to rest at 3:10pm on 10th December 1989. She was buried alongside her husband John on the outskirts of Sidon, approximately twelve miles from where she spent most of her life.

CHAPTER 20

More than nine weeks had passed since the death of Martha. Simon told Fr. Mark he would like to return home. Early the next day, they got into Fr. Mark's car and headed out of town. For the entire journey not a word was spoken. They were both lost in their individual memories of Martha. They had tried to prepare themselves but, as soon as they opened the door, they both pictured Martha on the ground. The emotion was too raw and they broke into tears.

Fr. Mark pulled Simon's arm and motioned to leave but he ignored him and walked slowly down the hallway, imagining what had taken place that day. In the living room a piece of wood had been hastily nailed onto the window frame. Simon looked into his bedroom, his wardrobe was open and his books were on the floor. Further along the corridor, in Martha's bedroom, there were clear signs that the person had rummaged through her cupboards and draws.

"Will you be okay, Simon?"

"I'll be fine. Thanks for everything, you can head off, Father."

"You be sure to call me if there is anything you need, okay?"

Simon nodded.

Sheriff Amos sat at the head of the conference table and looked at his team. He could not detect even a hint of optimism. The faces were drawn from weeks of hard work without reward. He was feeling the same but knew, as their leader, he had to remain motivated.

"Okay, Blaine, what have we got?"

"Look, Sheriff," the exasperated deputy said, "we have to accept the facts. We are running out of options here and, unless something comes up, it's not looking good."

"I know what you are saying, but we don't have much choice. Perhaps it's time to go public, we can head over there, film a re-enactment and see if it generates public interest in the case. Perhaps someone will call in. Guys, come on. Give me something. Oscar, what have you got?"

"Sheriff, I know we have nothing on the sister, but I just can't see past her. Okay, her car was definitely at the mechanic. We know that and we know she did not walk there and back, as the dogs would have tracked her. She either borrowed a car, or got a lift, perhaps with Brookman. We know it can't be the son, so who else can there be? I mean she basically had a boss who, from all accounts, thought the world of her and a priest as a friend. That's it. We are speaking about a woman who had no enemies and I don't care how the house looks, that was not a robbery. Did she find something out and call Simon to tell him that morning? We know the sister drove Brookman to Horizon. Perhaps she did Linda and Martha."

"Fair enough, Oscar, I'll tell you what. We have nothing on the sister but what the hell? Let's go over there today and try and rough her up a bit. I need to blow off some steam anyway."

Sheriff Amos, Deputy Blaine and Oscar jumped in the patrol car and drove out to have a word with Annamae.

The door opened slightly, her face was like thunder. Before the sheriff could utter a word, Annamae left him in little doubt that she was not interested in talking to him. As she put it, "get to bloody hell off my land, if you don't have a warrant," and then she slammed the door.

"Well, that didn't exactly go to plan, Sheriff!"

"Bitch! I know somehow she is involved. She's only made one mistake so far: thinking if she turned up Orchard Street the camera would not pick her up. I tell you, she is no fool and, after that mistake, she is probably even more careful than ever."

"Let's pass by Holman's house again. We must be missing something."

★

"Hey, look, Sheriff: the kitchen window is open. The boy must have returned home."

Sheriff Amos knocked at the door.

"Hello. Sheriff."

"Hi, Simon. How are you? When did you come home?"

"I just came back a few hours ago."

"Did Fr Mark drop you off?"

"Yes, sir."

"Have you had a chance to look around?"

"Come on in, Sheriff. I've made the list of the missing items you asked me about. It's on the kitchen table."

1 x gold chain
2 x rings
1 x pendent with flower
Unknown number gold earrings
1 x pair of shoes

Sheriff Amos glanced down the list and spotted the shoes instantly. "What did these shoes look like? Tell me, son, how sure are you they are missing?"

"They were track shoes, sir. I don't have a lot of shoes, so I know they are missing."

"What brand were they?"

"They were Adidas."

"That's it, Sheriff," said Deputy Blaine. "I bet they match the footprints."

"Where did you get them, Simon?"

"Linda bought them for me. I don't know where she purchased them."

The sheriff looked at Oscar and Deputy Blaine. "Come on, guys. Let's figure this out. How did it go down?"

Deputy Blaine took a piece of paper and started writing possibilities. The sheriff sat there looking up at the ceiling. For a few minutes, there was silence in the kitchen.

"It's got to be!" he shouted out. "Look, Blaine, she was not killed here. She was killed over at the sister's house, that is where the missing bullet is."

"But, Sheriff, how did she get the body here? Certainly not in through the window, there would be a trail of blood and I doubt she would be strong enough to carry it all the way from the road and down through the fields."

"Sheriff, if we are all thinking the same, and she put on Simon's shoes to leave so it looked like a man, how did she get tracks to and from the window that led into the field?"

"Damn, yeah. How did she do it? Think, guys. This woman is pretty smart but we are on the right track. I know we are."

The three officers sat at the kitchen table, each writing a sequence with how the murder was committed, in line with the evidence.

"Okay, guys. How is this?" said the sheriff. "For her to be killed at the sister's home, Martha must have gone there in her car. She goes into the house, something happens and Annamae shoots her. She puts her in the car and drives over here and dumps the body by the door."

"Yes," said Oscar, "but Martha's footprints are clearly seen getting out of the car. Actually, that's it... in fact, yes that is it. Annamae was wearing Martha's shoes, making it look like Martha. She got out and that is why she went to the trunk of the car as that is where the body was and she carried it inside."

"Exactly!" said the sheriff. "That all fits the evidence. Now she puts the shoes back on Martha, which means she has no shoes, also she has to make it look like a robbery. So, the purse is taken along with some jewellery and, while going through the house, she comes across Simon's shoes, takes them and thinks 'perfect: nine and a half'. Convenient match for Julia's murder."

"So, what about the footprints to and from the window?" asked Oscar.

"I have that," said Deputy Blaine. "She needs to show she did not arrive in the car; she has to show tracks coming through the window. She opens it from the living room side, climbs out and closes it. She walks to the field. Those are her tracks leaving the house. She then finds a stone and throws it at the window. She has to show tracks approaching the window, so she walks up to the window and then backs up in the same tracks, leaving one set of tracks to the window and one from it. This fits because, if you remember, one set of footprints had a fairly distinct pattern. The other, not as clear so that must be her back tracking."

"We have the bitch now," said the sheriff. "There is no other explanation that fits all the evidence. She was just really fortunate that her car was at the mechanic. It gave her a great alibi."

"One last thing, Sheriff," said Oscar. "There has to be a driver that collected her when she walked up to the top of the road. Was it Brookman?"

"Definitely, you're correct, Oscar. She had a driver, but we have enough to bring her in and then, believe me, I will make sure we get all the information we need out of her, including who her accomplice was."

Simon looked at the officers. They were so lost in thought that they were oblivious to the fact that he had been seated at the table throughout.

"I'm sorry you had to hear all of this. We got a bit excited putting it together. It involves the death of your mother by your only aunt."

"Actually, Sheriff, I sat here hoping you would find a way to get her."

"I'm pretty sure we have, son."

"So, are you going there now?"

"As much as I would love to, I would prefer to wait till morning. We will get the arrest warrant issued this evening and, at dawn tomorrow, we will go there. I like arresting people at that time as they are least prepared. In the meantime, you are not allowed to say a word of this. In fact, with your aunt just down the road, I would prefer it if you didn't spend the night here on your own. I've a spare room by me which you're welcome to use, or we can drop you back to the church."

"I don't want to bother Father again. I'll go with you."

"Blaine, I want the house watched overnight. Put a couple of guys on it 'til we get there in the morning. If she leaves, have her followed and I want to know right away."

That evening, an arrest warrant was granted and, the following morning, Sheriff Amos dispatched two plainclothes officers to be dropped off at the top of the road. They were directed to make their way through the fields and cover the back door of the house. Once in position, Sheriff Amos approached the house. There were two other patrol cars behind him with a forensics van following them. Simon was in the second patrol car and had been told not to exit the vehicle until he was given instructions.

Sheriff Amos stopped his car, got out, and looked in the front window. He could see the TV was on. As he walked towards the front door with Deputy Blaine, a single gunshot rang out and the two officers both hit the ground. In the second patrol car, Simon was violently shoved to the floor by an officer. Sheriff Amos and Deputy Blaine stayed below the level of the windows and listened for movement inside the house. They heard nothing but the sound of the TV. Sheriff Amos looked into the field. One of his officers shook his head indicating that Annamae had not exited out the back. He waited a few more minutes. There was definitely no sound of movement in the house. He lifted his head and looked through the living room window; it looked clear. He crawled forward past the front door and looked into the kitchen. On the floor, he could see a body.

CHAPTER 21

The coroner's report classed Annamae's death as suicide, due to a single bullet that was fired from a Smith and Wesson Model 30 revolver. The bullet penetrated the roof of her mouth at a 65 degree angle and lodged in the cerebellum area of her brain. The day her body was released by the coroner, it was sent to the crematorium. Her ashes were never collected.

Sheriff Amos and his team, who had come in for so much criticism, were now viewed in a much more favourable light, despite the police's insistence that Linda and Julia's murders remain unsolved. The media judged Annamae guilty on all three counts. Slowly, the topic of conversations in the streets and cafes went from murder, back to local everyday news and gossip.

Robert and Beth could never make up their minds, completely, as to who was responsible for their daughter's death. As much as they wanted to believe it was Annamae, they just could not see any motive for her to have killed Julia or, for that matter, Linda. They were quietly pleased that, from a law enforcement point of view, their murder investigations remained active.

Simon was now completely alone for the first time in his life. Other than Fr. Mark, he had no one. The sudden death of Martha and the fact there was no goodbye, was difficult for him. He wondered what she thought about in her final moments, as she collapsed to the floor. He had only recently returned to Horizon Bank, following the death of Linda but then, when Martha died, he felt he could not give his best. He asked Martin Bernstein for time off and again Martin told him to take as much time as he liked. There would be a job waiting for him when he was ready to return.

Financially, Simon was comfortable. The legal formalities were settled without difficulty and the house was transferred to his name. Unexpectedly, Annamae Jackson had it in her will for Simon to inherit her home. Martha also had a small life insurance policy, which Simon got. He had his savings, including the mortgage down payment he had planned to put on a home for Linda and himself. He knew, at some stage, he would have to return to work but, for the moment, living expenses were not an issue.

Christmas Day of 1989 came and went. Simon could not face the thought of spending Christmas without Martha. He did not want to even switch on the TV to be reminded of it. The home he thought of as so small, suddenly became larger. As the weeks passed, he tried to make the adjustment to living on his own. He spent his time reading and praying. Suddenly he was living in a silent, lonely world and, after a while, he began to long for human interaction.

He remembered going to visit the elderly with Fr. Mark. He started to understand a little about the mental and physical deterioration brought on by the loneliness that they had spoken of. For many, their partner had long since passed away. Their children seldom made contact. Lifelong friends were either in hospital or had died, and the isolation of country life led to a desperate loneliness, which eroded their will to live.

Some were in a lot of pain physically, but the pain of loneliness was greater and they would walk long distances to get the bus into town, just to sit in a café with a cup of tea. Sadly, the cup would go cold in front of them as they looked around hoping for a smile, or a brief conversation with someone, anyone.

On many occasions, they told Fr. Mark that they had nothing left to live for. The sadness and despair had gotten to them and they just wanted to die. Some had contemplated suicide but could not bring themselves to do it. Others simply slept out in the cold, hoping they would not wake up.

Now, suddenly with no family of his own, Simon wondered how they were getting on. He felt terrible. He had only experienced a fraction of what their lives were like and it had taken a toll on him. He swore he would never pass another elderly person again and not smile or say hello. He tried to make a list of the ones he could remember, but he could only come up with four names. *I'm going to have to call Fr. Mark,* he thought.

It was, indeed, a sad time for Simon. He would dream about marrying Linda and the life they would share only to wake up and remember the reality. No Linda and no Mom. Being alone meant such a lack of mental stimulation, he could feel his brain wasting away. He was replaying the same thoughts over and over in his head. What was it that made Mom go to Annamae's house that fateful day? She had made it clear, she wanted nothing to do with her. She must have either discovered, or suddenly understood something that was so disturbing that, when she confronted Annamae with it, she lost her life. Simon tried repeatedly to recreate Martha's movements that day. She had not done much cleaning, so he knew she would likely have sat back in her chair by the fireplace. He became increasingly certain it must be something she figured out, instead of something she physically found and confronted Annamae with. She did say to Charles that there was something she wanted to tell me. If only I was not in a meeting that day, I would have taken her call and perhaps she would not have left the house.

★

Sheriff Amos was reviewing the case files. It was certain Annamae Jackson had killed Martha Holman, that was without question. What about Julia and Linda? Did Annamae kill them as well? And, if so, what was the motive? He had taken the coroner's report, which showed that Linda was pregnant when she was killed, over to the Bernsteins'. It was further heartbreak for them, but they had to know.

The clock ticked round to 8am at Sidon police station and Sheriff Amos convened the morning meeting.

"Good morning everyone. Oscar, I'll start with you. Can you bring the team up to date with where we stand?"

"We have traced all calls made to and from Annamae Jackson's phone. We have come up with nothing that would link her to Dr Brookman. It is unclear how she communicated with him. It could be at arranged dates and times, or it could be she used a neighbour's phone or pay phone.

"Oscar, I'd like a copy of all the calls to and from her phone, going back to when Julia was killed. So, all the way to 1983. In fact, tell them I want everything they have from the time she moved into that house and got a phone."

"Gaby, I want to go to the public with this. I want Dr Brookman's picture in every media outlet. Make it known that he is wanted in connection with the murder of the two girls. We have had no success tracking him down so let's try and hinder his ability to move around. In fact, he is likely to go where he feels safe, so get it over to the media in Louisiana as well. I want everyone looking out for this guy... sorry, Oscar please go ahead."

"We have fully completed the search of Ms Jackson's house and the surrounding fields. We are unable to find any of the jewellery, or the Adidas, size nine and a half shoes."

"Yes, Oscar. I'd be surprised if we did find those. I'm sure she properly disposed of them. From her point of view, she was pretty unlucky that one of the bullets exited Mrs Holman and she did not notice."

"Sir, the Smith and Wesson gun has been traced to Louisiana, where it was reported stolen by a Mr Benson, on the 14th July, 1985. Ballistics has confirmed that both the bullet removed from the bottom of the door at Ms Jackson's home, along with the bullet recovered from Mrs Holman's spine, were fired from that weapon."

"Louisiana is where Brookman spent a lot of time. Dominic, head out there tomorrow and speak with Mr Benson. Find out if he recognises that photo of Brookman. Actually, take Annamae Jackson's photo as well. What else, Oscar?"

"That's about it, sir—"

"Thanks, Oscar. I went out and spoke with Simon Holman yesterday. He told me his mother and Annamae had a big falling out after his graduation party and they had not spoken since. As far as his mom was concerned, that was the end of the relationship. However, after that, they caught Annamae following them around on a number of occasions and confronted her. The kid said there is no way his mother

214

drove over there to make up with Annamae. He is convinced she found out something, or figured something out and, whatever it was, she paid with her life."

★

Simon parked just outside the church and got out of his car. It was early March, the air was cold and fresh, but he had not dressed for the weather. He knocked on the side door of the church and waited momentarily, but it was too cold. He opened the door and saw Fr. Mark coming down the small hallway.

"A bit too cold out there, is it, Simon?"

"How did you guess?" Simon responded with a smile.

"Well, I'll say one thing. There is no way your mother would have let you outside dressed like that!"

"Come on in. We'll go through to the office and have a coffee to warm you up a bit. I take it, the heater in the car is still not working?"

Simon shook his head. "Not unless you count the engine when it overheats."

Fr. Mark laughed. "Nothing changes, huh?"

"Here, have a seat by the radiator, Simon."

"So how are things with you, Father? I know I've not seen you for a couple of months, or so. I'm going to start coming back to Mass on Sunday. I just needed some time on my own."

"Oh, that's completely understandable, Simon. I would not worry about it… ah, so how are things with me, you ask? Well, I do have some news."

"Good or bad?"

"It depends on how you look at it, I guess. I've been offered the position of Bishop."

Simon paused; it was not what he was expecting at all. "Well, I have to say congratulations. You deserve it. Of course, we will all miss you, but it will give you the opportunity to have more influence and expand your work further afield than Sidon."

"I have not accepted yet. I asked for a period to consider it, but the current Bishop is not well, so they have not given me much time to make up my mind. Of course, I would be in touch often, as I'll be based just over an hour away, so I won't be too far."

"I'm sure you will make the correct decision, Father."

"Thanks, Simon. I've not told this to anyone, so please don't mention it."

"Of course, Father. I understand."

"So, that is my news. What have you been up to?"

Simon explained to Fr. Mark everything he had been through since Martha had died. He stressed his surprise at the impact. Living alone had taken a toll on him; both physically, as well as mentally. Only now could he appreciate what the elderly experienced.

"Simon, I think it is wonderful that you want to turn such a negative experience into a positive one. Before you leave today, I'll get my diary and let you know who I visit and the days I go, so we can stagger the visits. It will mean so much to them.

"So what is happening on the job front? Are you considering going back to work for Mr Bernstein? I saw him a few weeks ago at the bank. He is looking forward to having you back."

"Not at this moment. I gave him a call recently and we had a chat. Eventually, I will, I guess, but I've not exactly caught the banking bug as they say."

"Well, you're still very young with an excellent education, so there is no need to rush any decision".

"Father, did you ever wonder why Annamae did it?"

Fr. Mark was caught out by the directness of the question. "I have, Simon. When I read that your mother had been killed over at Annamae's home, I could not understand why she went there. It was no secret that she did not want anything to do with her. Have you any thoughts on it?"

"I've lots of thoughts on it... I've over two months worth of thoughts on it! But I haven't figured it out. I'm convinced it is not something she came across, it is more something she figured out and, when she confronted Annamae, either it led to an argument, or it was so serious that Annamae thought she could not let Mom leave alive."

"I must ask you something, Simon. You described seeing the deaths of Julia and Linda perfectly, why do you think you did not see your mother's death?"

"I don't know Father, I have also thought about this. I just don't know."

"Do you still feel Dr Brookman is around?"

"He is never far away and I know he is protecting me."

Fr. Mark paused for thought. "Simon, I'm going to tell you something you are not aware of. Your mom and I spoke about it at length, but she thought it better you did not know at the time. In light of all that has happened, I believe now, perhaps, is the right time to tell you."

Simon was transfixed with curiosity.

"You and I have spoken in the past about Dr Brookman and the fact that you see him as a demon. You were born at home and Dr Brookman was the doctor in attendance. On your first birthday, he visited your mother and gave you a Bible. It was named: "My First Bible." This Bible was wrapped in a brown cloth and your mother noticed it had what looked like writing on the cloth. It was in a very old form of Aramaic, written on two lines and it translated to—" Fr. Mark paused and looked at Simon. "It translates to... 'I have chosen you. The Apocalypse is written in the back.'

"For many years, Simon, many people have tried to understand this message. It could be nothing, or perhaps there is something to it. I'm not saying your mother understood it, but there was a definite connection between Dr Brookman and Annamae, which Annamae tried to deny."

Simon sat wide-eyed staring at the priest.

"You alright, Simon?"

"I'm fine, Father... yes, I'm alright, but why did Mom not tell me this? I saw that Bible and cloth in a drawer just recently."

"As I said, Simon, we spoke about it, but I'm guessing she felt it may be too disturbing for you."

"Did Mom forget what my life has been like? How can she have thought this would be too disturbing? I passed that stage a long time ago. Almost my whole life has been disturbing!"

Fr. Mark struggled to hold eye contact and looked down at the table.

"Yes. It is disturbing, Father if I allow it, but it is also interesting. How do you interpret that message?"

"No one has been able to, Simon, and to answer your next question, when I say no one, I mean no one. That cloth has made its way from here to Rome and back!"

Simon leaned forward, picked up a pen and paper off the desk, wrote out the message and studied it for a few minutes. Fr. Mark took a sip of his coffee and observed Simon closely.

"I'm not getting it, Father I'm not getting either line. I take it from what you are saying, that it is directed at me when it says, 'I have chosen you'. As for the second part, I'm guessing everyone has studied The Book of Revelations closely, as it speaks of the Apocalypse."

"Indeed, Simon. I believe if there is something to the message, it is directed at you, personally, as the one who has been chosen. Also, yes, we have all closely studied The Book of Revelations. Nothing has been added, or removed from it. Your mother did make one excellent point, in that there are no publishing company's details on it. Again, whether that means anything, or not, I don't know but it is peculiar."

"Father, I think either Mom worked out the meaning of this message, or she figured out that Annamae was involved in the death of Linda or Julia. There can't be much else that Annamae would take her life for, is there?"

"I knew your mother quite well and I am fairly certain there weren't any other issues of this magnitude, so I believe, as you say, it is one or perhaps both of these things. But, of course, if it is regarding the cloth, then that can only mean that the message written on it is very real."

★

On the other side of town, Beth Osbourne was looking anxiously out the front window. Robert had left early in the morning to go to visit his sister in hospital and it would soon be getting dark. Finally, she saw the headlights turn into her driveway. She opened the front door and waited for him.

"I was starting to get worried. How's Angela?"

Robert gave Beth a kiss.

"Yes. Sorry I'm late. I should have given you a call from the hospital to say I was on my way home. She is still in a bit of pain from the operation, but she is doing a lot better."

"Oh, that is great news. When does she get out?"

"All going well, by about the end of the month."

"Sounds good. You must be hungry. Supper is ready, I'll just reheat the soup."

"Yes, I'm starving. All I've had since this morning is a horrible sandwich at the hospital."

"Amos came round this afternoon and he was sorry he missed you. The bottom line, as far as he is concerned, is Annamae Jackson is the prime suspect. However, he is not closing the investigation into Julia or Linda, until he has more evidence. I told him that we sent the back up sample out to the DNA lab in California and we are waiting for the results."

"What did he say?"

"He definitely wants us to let him know as soon as we hear back from them. He will use it as part of the evidence he presents to the judge, to have Holman brought in."

★

Simon got home and went straight to the room where he had last seen the Bible and cloth. He sat on the edge of the bed, opened the drawer and held the cloth up to the light. He studied the ancient writing. *What next?* he thought. *Have I not been through enough that now I must live with this shadow over me?* Suddenly, he was overcome by a dark depression. Everything that had gone wrong in his life and all the pain associated with it, descended upon him.

What is my life? I have tried so hard. There is nothing for me in this world. He looked up to the ceiling and screamed out, "What more do you want? I have nothing left... you have taken everyone I love..."

CHAPTER 22

Simon awoke and looked at the clock on the bedside table: eighteen minutes past six. He knew he dreamt a lot but could not recall any of his dreams. He walked into the kitchen to get some dinner and glanced out the window towards the fields. The sun was just above the horizon. Confused, he looked at the clock on the wall above the fridge; it was twenty three minutes past six. *It must be morning,* he thought. He tried to think; he remembered getting home from seeing Fr. Mark just after 2pm, so it must be morning the following day. I must have been asleep for about sixteen hours.

He opened the fridge but there was not much to eat. He put the kettle on and sat with a cup of coffee, recalling the depression he had fallen to sleep with. Looking around the tiny kitchen, he thought, I *can't live my days within these walls. Options, there are always options.* He picked up an unopened envelope and a dull pencil from the kitchen table. *Go back to work at the bank. Perhaps, I can meet one of the girls downstairs. Giselle is cute and there was a new trainee girl that joined recently, but what if I did fall in love again? Oh God no. Perhaps I'm not meant to be with anyone. Not to mention I don't even want to work any longer at the bank.*

The sun light slowly came through the kitchen window and illuminated half the kitchen table. He looked at the envelope under the heading "OPTIONS" It was blank. *Perhaps if I go for a walk, something will come to me. I need to get out of this house, even if it is just for my own sanity. I'll just walk through the fields, or along the road.*

He put on his jacket and headed out the door. No sooner had he gotten out the door, than he heard Martha's words ringing in his ears. *"Put a scarf on... you should be wearing a scarf."* He turned around, came back in and put a scarf on.

★

Sheriff Amos was just leaving his office at the end of the day when Gaby came in and placed the two thick folders on his desk. "Listed by date as you asked. Good luck, Sheriff!"

"Wow!" he exclaimed. "That woman must have lived on the phone."

"Well, sir, you did request everything. They go back nearly two decades."

The sheriff picked up the folders and examined them. They must each have been over two inches thick.

"You're not taking them home tonight, are you, Sheriff?"

"Yes, I may as well start looking them over."

Gaby looked at him and shook her head.

"What now?" he asked.

"And you wonder, sir, why your wife left you..."

"Yeah... yeah, I know. Trust me, I've heard it for years."

Gaby smiled. "Try and get some sleep, Sheriff. I'll see you tomorrow."

For the next two weeks, the lists of phone numbers became an obsession for Sheriff Amos. Every evening he got home, he sat at his living room table and studied them, looking for times and patterns. Initially, he had hoped he would get lucky. He knew before Annamae left her home with Martha's body, she would have to call someone to arrange with them to collect her at Martha's house, but no such call was listed.

He had made extensive notes and built up a network of all Annamae's contacts. There were phone calls to Martha, to the doctor, to business addresses and other calls he would expect her to have made. However, there were dozens of calls to public phone boxes. These he believed, had to have been pre-arranged calls to Dr Brookman. When he checked the date of the first of these calls to public phone numbers, it was the day after Dr Brookman was first reported missing. Therefore, he had to be within the Sidon area and without a home. Someone had to be looking after him.

One of the most frequent numbers Annamae called turned out to be an old woman by the name of Mrs Paulina Balik, who Simon confirmed to him was his godmother. However, he said he had not seen nor heard from her for years until she attended Martha's funeral.

It was just getting dark when Sheriff Amos got home. He looked at his living room table. It was a mess of notes and papers. For the last few days, he had achieved nothing. He had visited the addresses of all the unidentified numbers. His eyes were starting to trouble him. He was getting headaches from spending so much time in his office and at home with so little sleep. He decided he would take a break tonight and, instead of studying the numbers, he would go and visit Simon's godmother, Mrs Balik. Perhaps she could give him some information about Annamae that he was not aware of.

Sheriff Amos headed out into the country. As he neared the area, he came across a number of small houses, they were all concentrated within a quarter mile of each other. It was a foggy night and there were very few lights on. However, he could see there were people looking out at him from slightly drawn blinds. He stopped and asked an old man walking along the track for directions to Mrs Paulina Balik's home, but he did not respond and just stared at the sheriff. Eventually, after an hour of driving around and knocking on doors with no one willing to assist, he noticed a diminutive silhouetted figure waving at him.

Sheriff Amos turned his car and pointed the headlights at the house. He left his engine running, got out of his patrol car, and walked towards the figure standing by the doorway. His eyes were slowly adjusting to the lack of light. As he approached, the features on the face slowly came into view. It was an old lady with white hair and wrinkled skin.

"I am told you are looking for me," said the old woman.

"Are you Mrs Paulina Balik?"

The old woman nodded, more with her eyes, than with her head.

"My name is Sheriff Amos. Do you mind if I ask you a few questions, Ma'am?"

"We keep ourselves to ourselves, Sheriff. We don't like strangers coming around here asking questions."

"I understand that, Ma'am, I am quite a private person myself. However, if you can assist me, I'll be on my way. I wanted to ask you about Annamae Jackson. I believe she was a friend of yours?"

The old woman said nothing and just shook her head.

"Annamae Jackson, Ma'am… you are Simon Holman's Godmother, aren't you?"

Again there was little response. Sheriff Amos could feel his heart rate increasing. "Do you mind if I look around, Ma'am? Is that your car in that shed over there?"

"I think you should leave now, Mr Sheriff. You are not welcome around here."

The old lady looked behind his shoulder.

Sheriff Amos turned around and squinted his eyes from the glare of his patrol car headlights. He could make out the dark silhouettes of a number of people who were standing near his car. Some were clearly holding shotguns.

"You do not have much time. Leave now and don't ever come back."

"Whose car is that under the shed, Mrs Balik?" he snapped back. "Is that the car you collected Annamae in? Tell me, how did you know she needed help that day? Tell me, how did you know?"

Sheriff Amos took a step back and looked up. Going into the side of the house, he could see a telephone line coming from a pole in the field.

"She must have called you! Idiot, what was I thinking? She did call you, but not from her house. She called you from Martha's house, that is how she contacted you."

The old lady reached out and grabbed the sheriff's forearm. He felt an icy chill run through his body. She took a step towards him and tiptoed. She whispered into his ear, "You will not make it home tonight."

Sheriff Amos pulled his forearm away, at the same time undoing the clip on his holster. He turned and walked towards his patrol car. He knew he was at an enormous disadvantage. The car's headlights had him illuminated, he could see at least six figures standing around his car but they remained motionless. He approached the car with confidence, showing no hint of fear. Every sense in his body was tuned to his surroundings. There was a young man about twelve feet from the back of his car, holding a shotgun across his chest.

The sheriff, head unbowed, stared at him. He turned and looked at the others, then got into his patrol car and drove off.

Visibility was terrible, the fog was dense in patches and it had started to rain. He could see only a few feet in front of his car. High beam made it worse and, as much as he wanted to get off the country road and unto the tarmac, he was forced to drive slowly through the fields. Visibility improved somewhat and he could see the junction with the main road up ahead. He turned onto it and headed into town.

The rain grew heavier and he still had to navigate the occasional bank of fog. Suddenly, as he came around a corner, he saw a figure standing in the road directly in front of him. He knew he could not stop in time, he swerved and lost control of his vehicle. Skidding off the road, he hit a fence post, the back of his car spun around and the car careered down an embankment and into the lake.

CHAPTER 23

The accident investigation report stated that Sheriff Amos lost control of his vehicle, skidded sideways on the wet surface and hit a fence post. The side impact resulted in him hitting his head on the upright metal frame housing the car door window. He was likely unconscious when his patrol car entered the water. The coroner's report attributed the cause of death to drowning. Water and plant life from the lake, were found in his lungs, as well as an injury to the left side of his head, consistent with the impact described in the accident investigation report.

Deputy Blaine determined that Sheriff Amos had definitely gotten home safely after work. He had changed his clothes, had something to eat, and left his home. It was clear from his living room table that he had spent many evenings going over Annamae's phone records. However, Deputy Blaine could find nothing that would indicate where Sheriff Amos had visited. Back at the office there was no mention of it in his work diary and he was not responding to a call coming into the station. Whatever made him leave that night, it was on his own initiative.

Sheriff Amos was considered 'on duty' at the time of his death on 28th September 1990. He was buried with full honours. Police from departments, both within and outside the state, came to pay their respects. It was a demonstration of the brotherhood that unites the force. Deputy Blaine stood in until a new sheriff was elected.

Robert and Beth had not only lost a life-long friend but also the main driving force behind keeping the investigation into their daughter's death open and active. The lab in California found the DNA sample of the hair taken from Julia's hand, when compared to Simon Holman, returned a 99.83% match.

Following the death of Sheriff Amos, the police were unwilling to commit any more department resources into investigating Julia's death, despite the DNA evidence. Robert and Beth's requests were completely ignored. The police were convinced that Annamae Jackson not only killed Martha Holman, but also Julia Osbourne and Linda Bernstein. In December 1990, both investigations were officially closed. For Robert and Beth Osbourne, this marked the end of their personal quest for justice. Without the support of law enforcement, they could not move forward. They continued to believe that Simon Holman murdered their daughter.

Simon continued to contemplate what he wanted from life. He enjoyed getting out of the house and made it a priority, every day, to wake at dawn and go walking through the fields at sunrise. There was something magical about this time. Something he could not explain about the inspiration he gained from being outdoors and witnessing the creation of another day. These slow walks inspired a new way of thinking. He was alone outside but without the feeling of loneliness. His thoughts became more positive and these walks to nowhere soon became planned routes with goals and times. Before long, he bought a pair of trainers and started jogging.

He decided, if he could not help himself, he would help

others. He started visiting the elderly in the community and running errands. He made a 'visit schedule' and built a profile of each of them. For the elderly, after years of neglect, suddenly their birthdays had meaning again and holidays were celebrated. Simon introduced many of them to each other. They exchanged telephone numbers and met for lunch in town once a week at a local café. The original table booking was for just two people but, after a few months, the table ended up being reserved for over fifteen and Simon negotiated a senior's discount for them.

One day, Simon met Mr Bernstein and when he heard what Simon was doing, he asked if his elderly mother could join them. Within weeks, Mr Bernstein had hired a mini-van to collect them every Thursday from their homes in the country and bring them all into town. It was the highlight of their week.

Often when he visited, instead of just sitting and having a coffee, he would encourage them to go for a short walk outside with him. Some adopted or bought a pet for companionship, their lives had purpose again and, for Simon, the positive change in their lives somehow transferred to his.

To this point, Simon had lived his life convinced he was the master of his destiny. With God's help and hard work, he could achieve anything and take his life in whatever direction he willed. Slowly, he began to let go of this philosophy and the realisation set in that destiny was a more powerful force. Instead of thinking what he would do with his life, he developed an unshakable belief that things would turn out for the best and it was no longer about what he wanted.

Simon noticed this change that came over him and analysed why it was happening. Martha had always told him about a universal law that was as certain as the law of gravity.

She said, "What you put out in life will come back to you, good or bad." Simon looked at the change he had brought to the lives of the elderly and became convinced that it was an example of what Martha spoke of.

Eleven months after the death of his mother, Simon decided to go to Sunday Mass. He arrived early, there were just a few other people, either sitting quietly with their eyes closed or reading. As the Mass progressed, Simon started looking around the church and, like visiting the elderly, he had a feeling that at this exact moment in his life, this was precisely where he was meant to be. The time came to go up and receive the bread and wine. As he walked up the aisle towards the Altar, a feeling of peace came over him and Fr. Mark held up the bread.

"This is the body of Christ."

Simon looked up and suddenly he had a vision, he had swapped places with Fr. Mark. He was the one holding up the bread. This was the dream he had when he was asleep for sixteen hours… he was a priest.

Simon left the church and drove home with this vision of himself, it was never a career path he had considered but the image was clear and he could not get it out of his head. For the rest of the day, he could think of nothing else and he got little sleep that night. The following morning he called Fr. Mark and was told to come in and they could have a chat in his office.

"Very interesting, Simon. You sound certain."

"I am, Father. I want to attend a Seminary."

"I have little doubt you would be accepted into the Seminary from an academic point of view. However, to study for a degree in Master of Divinity is a minimum four year course, so you must be totally committed."

"What Seminary would you recommend, Father?"

"There is one in St Louis called Kenrick-Glennon. It is highly thought of, with an outstanding history dating back to 1818. The course is expensive and you would need to pay for board as well."

"As you know, Father Mom left me the house and Annamae also left me her home, I can start by selling Annamae's property."

"Simon, you are nearly twenty-four. Now, if you do this degree and find out later it is not something you want, you will be leaving at twenty-eight perhaps thirty years of age depending on your progress and it will be difficult then to start a new career. Are you absolutely certain this is what you want to do?"

"I am, Father."

"Let me make some enquiries for you as to when the next course starts and the cost. I'll get some literature posted to you, so you can see what life is like at a Seminary. When you have read up on that and done your own research, we will discuss it further. In the meantime, I want you to pray for guidance. This is a huge decision you are about to make."

Fr. Mark knew the background checks done by the Seminary would reveal the police investigations into Simon. He immediately contacted the police and was told officially that all three investigations were now closed. The police considered that Annamae Jackson was responsible for the murders of Martha, Linda and Julia.

In February 1991, Fr. Mark accepted the position and became Bishop of St Louis. To the disappointment of many, he left the small church in Sidon, where he served for so many years. Two months later, in April 1991, Simon Holman's application for a Master of Divinity course was accepted by Kenrick-Glennon Seminary. His first semester started on 15th August 1991.

Simon Holman was ordained a Catholic priest on 3rd May 1996. He was twenty eight years of age and was sent to Assumption Church on the outskirts of Dublin, Ireland. It was a small parish, where Fr. Michael Aaron, the current priest, was being reassigned. There was to be a six-week handover period, until Fr. Simon was fully comfortable with all aspects of running the parish.

Fr. Michael was a large man, horribly overweight, with multiple chins. He was only sixty-one years of age but he looked terrible. Fr. Simon wanted to make a good impression and tried his best to learn as quickly as possible from Fr. Michael. The church itself was in a state of disrepair. Many things had been neglected, the register showed a steady decline in attendances and there were no plans to sort out any of the outstanding issues.

After just three weeks, Fr. Simon soon began to wonder why he had been given this daunting assignment. He had visited Fr. Michael and could not help but notice the contrast between the condition of the church and the luxury that Fr. Michael had created for himself. On a number of occasions that he visited, the elder priest had appeared intoxicated.

Fr. Simon soon got to know a few of the young acolytes that assisted Fr. Michael during the Mass and he began to suspect that things were not as they should be. After four weeks, Fr. Michael moved to a nearby hotel in Dublin and Fr. Simon moved into the priest's house. He came across many disturbing items, including discarded bottles of alcohol and pornography.

One of the acolytes related a truly horrifying story to Fr. Simon. It included not just graphic details of abuse but also the type of alcohol he was forced to drink and the pornography he saw. The amount of detail in the acolyte's account meant his story could not be fictitious. This young boy had suffered terrible abuse at the hands of Fr. Michael.

Fr. Mark went to the hotel that Fr. Michael had booked himself into. It was one of the most luxurious in Dublin. Reception gave him Fr. Michael's room number and he made his way up using the lift. Upon entering, he confronted the elder priest with the allegations. Fr. Michael laughed and had little remorse for what he had done. Fr. Simon looked at this unclean, grotesque man before him and imagined what the young boy must have been subjected to. Fr. Simon lost his composure when Fr. Michel advanced towards him and struck out hitting the elder priest with a punch directly to the eye. The older priest fell backwards and Fr. Simon, with the red mist truly descended on him, repeatedly struck the older priest on the ground until he was unconscious.

Fr. Simon stood up, he was shaking. He had never experienced this level of rage before. In fact, he had never even struck anyone before. His knuckles had blood on them. The elder priest lay on the floor, motionless.

Fr. Simon left the hotel and returned to the church. However, within a few hours, the police were at the church door and he was taken down to the station, where he spent the night.

The following day, the newspaper and TV were saturated with coverage of the incident and they quickly named him 'the punching preacher'. The hotel lobby tape had been leaked, showing him leaving with blood on his clothes. There were pictures of Fr. Michael being taken out of the hotel by paramedics. The orbital bone around his eye was fractured and his face was a bloodied mess.

The public was very familiar with the allegations of sexual abuse by priests and many speculated correctly that Fr. Simon had taken matters into his own hands. For an institution that was obsessed with secrecy, this was impossible to cover up. By the evening of the next day, the story had worldwide attention. At the Vatican, an emergency meeting was held to discuss how the matter could be handled but there were no good answers.

Within the walls of the Vatican, little attention was paid to Fr. Michael's conduct. Instead, the official view was that Fr. Simon had brought shame upon the church. The consensus of opinions was that he must be defrocked immediately and thrown out of the clergy. Yet they knew that this would make a bad situation worse. The public viewed Fr. Simon as a hero. Finally, someone had done something to these priests who, for too long, seemed untouchable by criminal or Canon Law. The Vatican was in full crisis management but their media arm did not know how to respond. All they could agree upon was that the young priest must be controlled and the best way to control him was to get him within the walls of the Vatican. With pressure from the Vatican, Fr. Simon was released by the Irish police and ordered not to comment when questioned by reporters. He was escorted to the church to collect a few belongings and taken to the airport where he was put on the first available flight to Rome.

Fr. Simon's arrival at the Vatican divided opinion. Many of the elder priests were outraged by his actions. However, there were some priests that secretly thought it was about time someone did something. Fear meant they kept their opinions to themselves. To speak against the official Vatican position was dangerous and it was better to discuss the matter within small, trusted groups. Fr. Simon quickly noticed this division. No one supported him publicly, but privately many whispered their support to him and wished him well.

To his superiors, Fr. Simon expressed his regret at the incident and stated he would like the opportunity to continue his vocation. The Vatican was well aware that Bishops and other members of the clergy, throughout the world, had received letters of support from their parishioners for the young priest. Being seen to take too hard a disciplinary line could well back-fire and the situation had to be managed carefully. Fr. Simon was given counselling and had to attend anger management courses. After six months he flew out of Rome.

On his arrival at Dublin airport, Fr. Simon was met by a few local journalists. However, he made it clear that the matter was now behind him and he had no comment. From the airport, he was taken straight to see his superior, the Archbishop of Dublin. Archbishop Donahue was a small, soft-spoken man. He had spent years trying to get Fr. Michael Aaron removed from Assumption Church. There had been numerous allegations against him and Archbishop Donahue felt terrible that he had not taken stronger action. However, Fr. Michael was well protected and knew many people in the hierarchy of the church. As soon as Archbishop Donahue heard what happened at the hotel, he knew exactly why Fr. Simon did what he did.

Archbishop Donahue did his homework on the young priest. He contacted Bishop Mark in Sidon who gave Fr. Simon a glowing recommendation. Archbishop Donahue had been initially due to meet with Fr. Simon months ago, when he first arrived in Dublin. However, due to illness he was unable to do so. After everything that had taken place, he insisted that the young priest come to see him immediately on his arrival. The meeting lasted for over an hour and Archbishop Donahue made it clear that another indiscretion, or misjudgement, would mean immediate removal from the parish and a return to Rome. Archbishop Donahue tried his best to come across as strict as possible but everything he had heard from Bishop Mark, he could see in the young priest.

Fr. Simon left Archbishop Donahue's office and drove the short distance to Assumption Church. He entered the parish office and greeted Fr. Thomas, who had filled in for just over six months for him. He could see, in the short time that Fr. Thomas was there, the positive changes he had made. He thanked him and settled down to his work. As he was going through his mail, he instantly recognised Bishop Mark's handwriting on an envelope.

Dear Fr. Simon;

I pray this letter finds you in good health.

I have been following your introduction into the priesthood closely. I guess, like your life, it has been dramatic, to say the least. You have gone overnight from the newest member of our clergy to its most famous. I am in no position to cast judgement on your actions, but I will say they are entirely understandable and you will always have my support.

I would like us to continue to keep in touch. Please understand that there are powerful forces within our church and we must not discuss sensitive matters by telephone. You have my address. Please feel free to write me at any time, destroy this and all future letters you receive from me.

God Bless;

Bishop Mark

Fr. Simon held the letter to a candle. Over the coming years he relied heavily on Bishop Mark's guidance. The young priest settled in quickly. He adopted the same style as Fr. Mark, where he would stand at the door after Mass and see all the parishioners as they left. He got to know many of them personally and, like he did with the elderly in Sidon, he built up profiles and put them in touch with each other. The most dramatic change Assumption Church saw was in its attendance numbers. Fr. Simon ordered additional seating to be installed and many badly needed renovation projects were completed within budget around the church.

It was tiring but rewarding work for the young priest; there were not enough hours in the day. He was up before sunrise and started each day by going for a run. It did not take long for Archbishop Donahue to recognise the potential in him. He possessed all the qualities that make exemplary priests. He had outstanding communication skills and connected with his parishioners. People started writing articles in the local papers, regarding the inspiration they got from his sermons, but most of all, Archbishop Donahue was in awe of his interpretation of the Bible.

Prior to their regular meetings, he chose verses from the Bible that he wanted to discuss with Fr. Simon. He could not understand how a new priest was able to simplify God's message into everyday language that people could relate to. Because of Fr. Simon, Archbishop Donahue and Bishop Mark kept in regular contact over the years, and the two men became quite close. In April 2001, Bishop Mark was appointed Archbishop of St Louis.

The seemingly, never ending allegations against the church continued, both in Ireland and around the world. The Vatican was unable to change the news cycle and it was clear the media coverage had impacted church attendances and the trend seemed irreversible. Fr. Simon, not only had name recognition because of the incident at the hotel but also due to the fact that almost every year he finished in the top twenty for his age group, in the Dublin ten kilometrers run. The local news media loved him and were always there to have a word with him when he crossed the finish line.

July 2006 marked the tenth anniversary for Fr. Simon at Assumption Church. He crossed the finish line of the Dublin 10K run, in what for him, was a disappointing personal time. However, the media was there as always. While he was being interviewed, some members of his congregation presented him with a plaque, in recognition of his ten years of work in the community.

The following morning, at the Archbishop's house in Dublin, a group of senior clergy had gathered to welcome Cardinal Giovanni Bertello who was considered, by age, to be the most senior Cardinal in Rome. While they were having lunch, a short clip of Fr. Simon being presented with the plaque was shown on the local TV station. It caught the eye of Cardinal Bertello straight away. From his point of view, it offered a welcome break from the constantly negative TV coverage of the church. He also recognised Fr. Simon as the priest who had been involved in the hotel fight. He asked about him and Archbishop Donahue put it simply.

"Your Eminence. He is the only priest I am aware of that has increasing attendances at Mass."

Cardinal Bertello raised an eyebrow. "What's his secret?"

"I have often wondered this myself. I believe he possesses a way of simplifying God's message and delivering it in a way that his congregation relate to. He just has this natural way of connecting with people. I have celebrated Mass with him on a number of occasions. His parishioners listen and do not drift off. At the end of Mass he greets each of them by name as they leave. You would not have noticed, but in the news clip you just saw, quite a few of his parishioners took part in that race with him. In fact, there are a few elderly amongst them that entered and walked the entire ten kilometres. Fr. Simon has got the race organisers to cater for them. There are frequent stops along the way, where they can sit and get a drink if they choose."

"Very interesting. I would like to meet Fr. Simon," said Cardinal Bertello.

"Your Eminence," said Bishop O'Reilly from County Armagh. "You are only in town for a short while and we have a full schedule today. Perhaps another time would be more appropriate."

Cardinal Bertello paid no attention to the words of Bishop O'Reilly and waved his hand in a dismissive fashion.

"Archbishop Donahue, you obviously know Fr. Simon very well. I want to meet him this afternoon."

"Yes, Your Eminence. I will call him immediately and ask him to come over. He is not far away."

"No, I want the two of us to visit him. We will leave straight after lunch. I would like to see his church and the job he is doing there."

CHAPTER 24

Fr. Simon was in his office when he heard a knock on the door. He opened it and was shocked to see not just Archbishop Donahue but also recognise Cardinal Bertello.

"Fr. Simon, I would like you to meet Cardinal Bertello. He is on a brief visit from Rome."

"Your Eminence, it is an honour to have you visit Dublin and, even more so, that you have found the time to visit our church. Please come in. I was not expecting you so my office is a little untidy and we are just completing the last of the renovation work outside, but come on through. I have just put the kettle on."

"Thank you, Fr. Simon. It was not in my schedule to visit you. However, we were having lunch earlier on when I saw you on the TV."

"Of course, yes. My legs have not quite recovered yet but I really enjoyed it, even though it was not my best race."

"The reporter obviously follows you closely. He knew you were more than two minutes off your personal best. Do they interview you every year?"

Fr. Simon nodded. "Yes, it's become a bit of a tradition. Last year a local company even offered to sponsor me if I wore a cap with their logo on it."

"I think it is wonderful, Father, to see such positive

coverage of the clergy. Archbishop Donahue said many in your congregation, both young and old, take part with you. It must be a wonderful experience."

Cardinal Bertello stood up and looked around the office. He picked up the black and white wedding photo on the shelf.

"You look a lot like your father," he commented. "And this children's Bible, looks to have been well used."

"Yes, I was given it as a gift for my first birthday. My mom used to read it to me every night so, when I left to come here, I couldn't leave it behind."

Cardinal Bertello picked up the plaque from the desk and examined it. "You must be even more proud to have received this yesterday?"

"Yes, that was such a nice gesture by the parishioners. It more than made up for the disappointing time I ran!"

Cardinal Bertello smiled and looked at Fr. Simon closely; he was fit and healthy looking, with blue eyes and jet-black hair that was broken with a tinge of grey on the sides. He presented the perfect image the Cardinal was looking for.

Over the next hour, Cardinal Bertello asked Fr. Simon many increasingly difficult questions. He wanted to get his views on marriage, contraception, abortion and church history to judge the young priest's response. The questions got more pointed when he asked about the incident in the hotel. All the while, the Cardinal was assessing not just Fr. Simon's answers but the words he chose, the tone of his voice, his body language and the eye contact he maintained. Eventually, he asked Fr. Simon to take him around the church and show him what changes he had made. Archbishop Donahue was silent throughout but wondered why the most senior Cardinal in Rome would spend this much time speaking to someone considered a junior member of the clergy.

One year earlier, in April 2005, Pope John Paul II, who served as the Bishop of Rome for twenty seven years died. Unfortunately, much of the abuse by the clergy had happened under his watch. It was hoped by many, both within the walls of the Vatican and the wider Catholic community, that the election of a new Pope would mark a new beginning for the church.

In 2005, Cardinal Ratzinger succeeded Pope John Paul II and became the new Bishop of Rome. He took the name Pope Benedict XVI. For many who had seen the decline in the church knew he did not represent the change that was needed. At seventy-eight years of age, he lacked both the will and energy to take on the task of reform. He very much represented the conservative old guard.

There was deep division, thousands of the dedicated members of the clergy were left disappointed with his appointment. For them the two pressing issues within the church were number one, to defrock and hand over to the authorities the monsters who were within their midst and secondly, to carry-out the much needed reforms of church doctrine.

It was against this backdrop, after his meeting with Fr. Simon, that Cardinal Bertello returned to the poisoned atmosphere within the walls of the Vatican. Along with Bishop Donahue, they gathered a trusted group of Cardinals. Something had to be done to improve the image of the church.

Cardinal Bertello had longed for reform. From the time he served as a priest to the present day, he had dedicated his life to serving people. He and many of his fellow clergy were powerless as they looked on at the shame that was brought to the institution they loved. As the senior Cardinal, he now had a level of influence that, if used wisely, he could make a positive difference, but he was under no illusion. He knew he was up against powerful forces that wanted to retain the status quo. A year earlier, he had made many enemies when he tried and failed to get a younger, more reform-minded Pope elected. His only option now was to put a fresh face before the public and what better place to start than in Ireland where so many of the clerical abuses had been committed.

Before leaving Dublin, he visited Irish News Television (INTV) and obtained copies of all the interviews they had done with Fr. Simon. Some were just a few words to the effect of 'well done, Father' after crossing the finish line, to brief chats that lasted a couple of minutes. As the years went by, they tended to get a little longer, but in every one he handled the questions with dignity and class.

All of the cardinals at the meeting had heard of Fr. Simon, because of the incident at the hotel, but knew nothing else about him. Cardinal Bertello told the gathering of his meeting with Fr. Simon and Archbishop Donahue. He outlined the work he had done over the last ten years in Dublin.

After a couple of hours of discussion, the agreed plan was to return to Ireland and set up an interview with INTV, which commanded the largest viewing audience in Ireland. The interview was to be aired live. However, the possibility for embarrassment would be removed, as the questions and answers would be entirely scripted. Within a week of visiting Fr. Simon at his parish, Cardinal Bertello and Archbishop Donahue were again in Dublin knocking at his door. They sat in his office and asked his thoughts on doing an arranged interview. Two weeks later INTV had been approached, an interview agenda was set and agreed after numerous changes to the questions. The interview was scheduled for 8pm on Sunday night to maximise TV audiences.

Fr. Simon was initially apprehensive. He had never done anything like this before, but he studied the script given to him closely. As the day of the interview approached, his nerves had subsided somewhat. As requested, he arrived at the INTV studio two hours ahead of schedule. He was given a brief introduction to the layout of the set and the cameras that would be used, after which he was taken to the makeup room where he was given some final advice. About half an hour's drive away, at the Archbishop's house, Cardinal Bertello, Archbishop Donahue, and a few other members of the clergy were glued to the TV.

3...2...1...live!

"Good evening. My name is Eoin O'Connor. My guest tonight is Fr. Simon Holman, who has been the parish priest for over ten years at Assumption Church on the outskirts of Dublin. Welcome to the show Father."

"Thank you for having me."

"Father, you are originally from the small town of Sidon in Mississippi. I'd like to take you back to your roots. I understand you lost your father during the Vietnam war. Please tell us about your childhood."

Fr. Simon did well not to act surprised. This was not in the agreed list of questions.

"Yes. Unfortunately, I never knew my father, I was an only child, I was raised by my mother, Martha, on the outskirts of town."

"Your father was from a military family going back generations. It is a little unusual for you to become a priest – no?"

"From an early age, my mother made me promise that I would not join the military. The death of my father was very difficult for her and she would not have been able to cope if something happened to me."

"Tragedy has been very much a part of your life hasn't it, Father? From what I have been told, a girlfriend, your pregnant fiancé and your mother were all murdered by your aunt, who committed suicide. This would have turned many away from God, how did you keep your faith?"

With this question, Fr. Simon knew the interview agreement was certainly broken and television ratings were more important. A few miles away at the Archbishop's house, they watched in horror. None of them were aware of Fr. Simon's past. Cardinal Bertello held his head in his hands.

"What have I done?" he whispered.

"Keeping my faith was a challenge of course, but that is what life is about for all of us. The Bible is littered with stories of men whose faith was tested by God and each of us have to face, to varying degrees, the things that happen in our lives that test our faith. No one is exempt from this. May I add for people watching, that it is understandable if, due to personal tragedy, your initial reaction is to drift away from God for a period of reflection. However, these things are always easier to overcome if we keep our faith. When we come back to God, we realise there is a higher purpose. If we hold onto our faith, as the years go by, the sadness subsides to an extent. You look back and understand things do happen for a reason."

Eoin O'Connor stared at Fr. Simon. He was not expecting such a comprehensive answer. "Father your introduction to the priesthood was far from normal. You attacked a fellow member of the clergy in a hotel here in Dublin. I'd like to play for our viewers, who have not seen it, the CCTV footage of you leaving the hotel following the attack."

Fr. Simon thought, this is bad, it can't get any worse. He watched, along with millions, the footage of him walking briskly out of the lobby with blood clearly visible on his clothing.

"Fr. Simon, you have never admitted nor denied the reason behind this assault. However, there were numerous allegations in the past about this particular priest. In fact, while we are being honest, let's name him... Fr. Michael Aaron. After this incident, many who are now adults, came forward with very believable accusations against him. One of his acolytes spoke out recently. He said he told you what had been done to him by Fr. Michael and you immediately left and went to the hotel that evening. As you may know, Fr. Michael was taken from his hotel room, his face covered in blood, with a fractured eye socket. More than ten years have passed and I'd like to give you the opportunity to finally confirm what everyone knows happened."

Fr. Simon paused and thought how best to answer the question. "I would just like to say to everyone, it was a moment of weakness on my part. I should not have done what I did. After the incident, I apologised to my superiors for my actions. I let myself down, as well as the institution I represent, there are better ways to deal with things like that and what I did was wrong."

"Father you say there are better ways to deal with what that priest did, but is it not a fact that this is happening in every country throughout the world? Nothing is being done about it and it is putting people off the Catholic faith."

"Those are all encompassing statements you have made, Mr O'Connor. I do not fully agree with them. Of course, there is no excuse for the actions of some members of the clergy. They must be defrocked and dealt with according to the law in whatever country the offence has taken place. Regarding your last point, you are partially correct when you say their actions may have put many people off from going to Mass. However, for others, it is worse, as it may have entirely cost them their faith. We should do everything through the church to encourage them back to God.

"With that being said, the company you represent and many of your peers in the media are always quick to dedicate many column inches to these type of stories. However, you do not cover the tens of thousands of priests, bishops, nuns, deacons and other members of the clergy that truly live their life in the service of others. Anyone reading or watching the news over the last twenty years, based on your company's reporting, would believe that every member of the clergy is corrupted. You fail to mention that we are feeding, clothing, housing and providing education and medicine to millions of people throughout the world. I am fortunate to serve in Dublin. However, many of my fellow clergy live in abject poverty, along with the people they help in some of the most desperate parts of the world.

"You have spent this entire interview trying to embarrass me and the church to which I belong. You care not that you put people off religion. TV ratings and advertising revenue are the Gods you worship. Therefore kindly allow me to ask you a question regarding yourself and your employer. If you can answer me, we will continue this interview, if not I will end it.

Fr. Simon looked at his watch. "I will give you one full minute. Your company's watchwords are reputed to be impartial and unbiased… therefore tell me and your viewers the last time you or your company did a positive story about the good work of the church?"

The host cleared his throat to buy time, hoping desperately that his producer would say something into his earpiece. There was only silence. He looked up at the production box above the studio lights. His eyes were pleading for help. He quickly began to feel his facial expression was giving away his loss for an answer. For the seasoned host, this was without doubt the most awkward moment he had endured in his entire career. There were no words being spoken. In the chair a few feet away, Fr. Simon sat staring at him with an expressionless look.

It was the longest minute of Eoin O'Connor's life… Finally, Fr. Simon turned to the camera and said, "I'd like to wish everyone an enjoyable evening and may God Bless you all."

He slowly unclipped the microphone from his jacket, placed it on the table and walked off the set.

At the Archbishop's house they watched a blank TV screen. Fr. Simon's premature departure from the set meant that the production department had nothing prepared. The station fell silent. Cardinal Bertello looked around the room, he knew when he got back to Rome there would be many questions to answer.

CHAPTER 25

The following day, the interview was covered around the world and it played over and over. There were phone-in discussions on the radio and it seemed everyone had something to say. Some focused on the tragic events of Fr. Simon's life and the faith he showed when everything had been taken from him. Others enjoyed the way he handled the many difficult questions head-on, with poise and dignity, and there were many who admired his courage to walk off the set.

Cardinal Bertello was due to fly back to Rome that afternoon. However, before his departure, he called INTV and expressed his disgust that they had not stuck to the agreed interview format. They blamed their reporter Eoin O'Connor and claimed they had no idea he was going to do this. However, Cardinal Bertello knew this was not the case, as the director had the hotel lobby CCTV prepared. Cardinal Bertello then called Fr. Simon. He thanked him for doing the interview and apologised that INTV had not stuck to the interview agreement.

Fr. Simon got little work done that Monday morning. The phone rang nonstop. Newspaper editors, TV executives, and even a book publishing company asked to see him, with the view of doing a biography. There was huge interest from the public and the media wanted desperately to cash in on it. Fr. Simon politely declined all offers.

Cardinal Bertello boarded the Alitalia flight from Dublin direct to Rome. He took his seat and the stewardess offered him a newspaper. On the front page of La Repubblica, was one word "EXPLOSIVAE", with a picture of Fr. Simon walking off the set. Thankfully, the article was positive. The young priest was given much credit for the way he handled himself and defended the clergy. After a night of little sleep for the Cardinal, perhaps this idea may not have turned out to be so bad after all.

Over the next few years, the damaging allegations against the church continued. For decades, the Vatican had sent the traditional, old balding member of the clergy to do the media rounds in their defence. However, it did not take long for them to realise that Fr. Simon represented the fastest way to change the news agenda. Soon he became the recognised public face of the church.

In 2009, at the age of forty-one, Fr. Simon was appointed Bishop of the Dioceses of Meath and Kildare in Ireland. After thirteen years of service at Assumption Church, he said goodbye and took up his new role. Within two weeks of his appointment, there was a letter from Archbishop Mark congratulating him.

In 2011, now sixty-seven years of age, Archbishop Mark was elevated to become a Cardinal. Upon leaving St Louis, on his way to Rome, he flew to Dublin to surprise Bishop Simon. They had always kept in contact but this was the first time they had actually seen each other for nearly sixteen years. The two men embraced; so much had changed. Bishop Simon suddenly felt like a child again. His eyes filled with tears as he greeted the man who was the closest thing he ever had to a real father.

Within the walls of the Vatican, Cardinal Bertello was monitoring Archbishop Mark's travel closely. Bishop Simon had mentioned the influence that Archbishop Mark had on him and the support he had given his mother. Unknown to Archbishop Mark, Cardinal Bertello had played an important role in his elevation to Cardinal, despite the fact he had never met him. Cardinal Bertello was desperate to change the weighting amongst the hierarchy of the church, in an attempt to one day get a more reform-minded Pope in place.

Archbishop Mark left Dublin the following day and arrived in Rome to attend the Rite of Consistory, where he would officially become a Cardinal. As he exited the arrivals hall at Fiumicino airport, he was surprised to be greeted by Cardinal Bertello, who welcomed him to Rome. The two men went for dinner that night and, to Cardinal Bertello's relief, everything that Bishop Simon had told him was correct, Archbishop Mark had a clear understanding of the change that was needed and the politics, within the Vatican, that would be involved in making it happen.

On 20th July, 2011, Archbishop Mark was elevated to the College of Cardinals. At sixty-seven, he was their youngest member and his appointment was a great success for Cardinal Bertello.

Less than two years after Cardinal Mark's appointment, Pope Benidict unexpectedly resigned on 28th February, 2013. His resignation sent shock waves throughout the Vatican and led to another struggle between the reform and conservative members of the Vatican hierarchy. It was the opportunity Cardinal Bertello had longed for. In the previous years, he had managed to influence the appointment of some senior members of the clergy who shared his view. Unfortunately, at the Conclave to elect a new Pope, the candidate he pushed for was defeated. On 13th March, 2013 Jorge Mario Bergoglio became the 266th head of the Roman Catholic Church. He took the name Pope Francis.

Pope Francis understood change was needed. However, at seventy-six years of age, he was in no position to go against the powerful forces that opposed any change, which would undermine their power or influence.

On the 26th March, 2014, Bishop Simon was summoned to Rome and asked by Pope Francis to become his special envoy to Syria. He landed in Damascus on 12th June, 2014. By this time the Syrian war had entered its forth year. It was a world away from anything he had seen in Sidon, or Dublin.

He witnessed first-hand, the brutality of man and everything his mother had told him about war became apparent. The soldiers and civilians, on all sides, were bleeding and dying and, behind it all, were the politicians "War Pigs" as she used to call them. At this time, more than any in his life, he thought of his father. The man he knew only because his mother had kept his memory alive, and she was right. It was not a soldier that killed him, but a man in a suit who had brainwashed him with words of patriotism, duty and service to country.

Bishop Simon looked around and saw this once peaceful secular country of various Jewish, Orthodox Christian, Catholic, Armenian Christian, Alawite, Sunni and Shia faiths, practiced by a diverse population of Arabs, Druzes Europeans, Kurds and Turkmen, imploding in an orgy of suffering, death and destruction. However, despite all that was happening around him, Bishop Simon found no shortage of like-minded people from all faiths and he reached out to them. Due to his knowledge of Islam, he related easily to many of their leaders, who were surprised to find a non-Muslim with such understanding of the Quran.

Cultural and religious differences were put aside as many shared a common desire for peace. Through their joint efforts, they encouraged children and teenagers to take part in sports, to visit each other and pray together, in the hope that the hatred would not be passed onto the next generation. Together, they established charities that helped everyone without exceptions. Unfortunately, in a country the size of Syria, their efforts represented only a fraction of what was needed. One of the events that left an indelible impression on Bishop Simon occurred in April of 2015, when he went with Imam Hasan to visit one of the multi-faith schools they had set up for orphaned children.

Sid, a local religious teacher, was just about to start a new lesson and they were invited to attend. Both men gladly accepted the invitation. They were interested to see how the teacher would instruct religion to such a diverse class. The children had each taken out their own religious books and Bishop Simon could see the class represented many of Syria's religions. The teacher stood before the class, held up a thick book and said:

"Everyone has to pretend that this book is God." Pointing to one of the children in the front right, he asked: "How do you see God?"

"Sir, God is red and about eleven inches long and five inches wide."

The teacher pointed to another child directly below him. "Tell us, how do you see God?"

Looking up at the book he said, "I see God as white in colour but only five inches long and about two inches wide."

Lastly, he pointed to a girl with a headscarf at the back, on the left side of the class. "Tell us how do you see God?"

"Sir, God is red and black with writing. He is eleven inches long and five inches wide."

"Good," said the teacher. "Each of the books in front of you, will teach you to develop your personal relationship with the Creator. If you die wanting to know more about your Creator, you will be taken to him. Therefore, we can agree on two things. Firstly, there is only one Creator and secondly, we all see the him differently."

The class laughed and agreed. Bishop Simon and Imam Hasan looked at each other. They were both thinking the same thing. This was, without question, one of the best analogies they had heard in understanding the different interpretations we have of God.

On 3rd July 2016, after two years in Damascus, Bishop Simon returned to Rome where he submitted his report on his time in Syria to Pope Francis. Soon after, he returned to Ireland and continued as Bishop of the Dioceses of Meath and Kildare.

In 2023, at the age of eighty-six, Pope Francis died peacefully in his sleep. Cardinals from around the world were summoned to Rome to attend the Conclave to elect the new Pope. Cardinal Bertello was still considered the most senior Cardinal. However, because he was over eighty years of age, he was ineligible to take part in the Conclave, but behind the scenes his influence was huge. He had many powerful friends, the most important of which was Cardinal Mark.

Eight days before the Conclave started, Cardinal Bertello and Cardinal Mark met in secret, along with a considerable gathering of reform-minded Cardinals. They all agreed that the church they loved could not go on like it had been. By their actions and subsequent inactions, they had alienated many of the over one billion Catholics and something had to be done. They got down to discussing who amongst them could bring about this change. A number of names were discussed. At the top of the list was Cardinal Mark. However, at seventy-eight he declined the opportunity on account of his age. He was fully aware that he did not have the health, or energy needed to take on the powerful ultra-conservatives within the Vatican. Other Cardinals amongst them were discussed but, like Cardinal Mark, they too felt they would not be able to achieve the change necessary.

With no agreement reached, Cardinal Mark put forward the name of Bishop Simon. No one had considered him, as it was nearly always a Cardinal that succeeded the Pope. However, there was no rule that prevented a Bishop being elected Pope. It did not take long for the group to agree that, if Bishop Simon accepted the nomination, it would be he they would be voting for. That night Cardinal Mark telephoned Bishop Simon in Ireland.

The world media, as always, were gathered in St Peter's square and a rumour went around that Bishop Simon was possibly being considered. The rumour was reinforced when he was spotted returning to Rome. With this news confirmed, speculation ran wild, especially amongst the US media outlets. Never in history had there been an American-born Pope. The election of a new Pope is always headline news around the world. However, on this occasion, it took on a new dimension and the media had no shortage of content on Bishop Simon. They played everything they had: from the footage of the hotel lobby incident, to interviews with him competing in ten kilometre runs in Dublin as a young priest, to all the media he did when he officially represented the Vatican. Parishioners who knew him from his early years as a priest were interviewed and every one of them, when asked, stated without hesitation that they wanted him to be elected the next Pope.

Following morning Mass at the Vatican, the College of Cardinals, consisting of 118 representatives, entered the Sistine Chapel and, at 11:30am on 12th September, 2023, the Conclave to elect a new Pope began. From this point, until a new Pope was elected, they were not allowed to have any contact with the outside world.

It took four days and twelve votes before the two-thirds majority was attained on 15th September, 2023. As the ballots were burnt, white smoke could be seen emanating from the chimney above the Sistine Chapel, signalling the appointment of the new Bishop of Rome. Below, in St Peter's Square, the crowds cheered as they waited to find out who had been elected Pope.

In a small room next to the Sistine Chapel, known as the 'Room of Tears', the new Pope prayed before changing into his Pontifical Robe. Meanwhile, the Cardinal Protodeacon walked out onto the balcony of St Peter's Basilica to make the announcement the crowd had been waiting for.

"Annuntio vobis gaudium magnum…habemus papam!"

"I announce to you a great joy… we have a pope!"

"Eminentissimum ac Reverendissimum Dominu-Dominum Simon John Sanctae Romanae Ecclesiae Vescovo – Holman."

"The Most Eminent and Most Reverend Lord – Lord Simon, Bishop of the Holy Roman Church – Holman."

The crowds in St Peter's Square below cheered as the news went live around the world. For the first time in history, there was an American-born Pope. It was quickly noted by many that the new Pope had broken with tradition, by keeping his original name and not taken a papal name. Within minutes, fifty-five year old Pope Simon walked onto the balcony and blessed the crowd. A new pontificate had begun.

CHAPTER 26

The following day, Cardinal Mark was in his office when a copy of the official Vatican newspaper L'Osservatore Romano was handed to him. On the front page was a photo of Pope Simon and above it was the word 'CHOSEN'. A chill went through his body. He sat back in his chair. It was over thirty years since he had thought about it, but the words on the cloth came screaming back…

"I HAVE CHOSEN YOU."

"THE APOCALYPSE IS WRITTEN IN THE BACK."

Again, he was overwhelmed by the feeling that he was a part of something much greater, something he was struggling to understand. He recalled all the events of Simon's life, the number of unexplained deaths and all the strange circumstances that came together. They seemed to almost force him in the direction of the priesthood. It was as if anything that stood in the way of him becoming Pope had been eliminated from his life. Even his original application to the priesthood would have been rejected, as he was still the number one suspect in two separate murders. However, the death of Sheriff Amos shortly before meant those cases were closed when his application was reviewed.

From the moment Simon became a priest, events happened and almost immediately he obtained an almost celebrity status. Then there was his rise through the ranks of the clergy. It was almost unprecedented in modern times. Looking back, it was clear everything seemed to conspire towards the destiny of him becoming Pope. Cardinal Mark knew he had played a massively important role in Simon's life. He also knew him better than anyone and there was no question in his mind, that Simon was a man of God.

Many years before, Cardinal Mark had read about the messages given by the Virgin Mary to Sr. Agnes in Akita Japan. He logged into his computer and typed the words "Virgin Mary in Akita third and final message".

"As I told you, if men do not repent and better themselves, the Father will inflict a terrible punishment on all humanity. It will be a punishment greater than the deluge, such as one has never seen before. Fire will fall from the sky and will wipe out a great part of humanity, the good as well as the bad, sparing neither priests nor faithful. The survivors will find themselves so desolate, that they will envy the dead. The only arms, which will remain for you, will be the Rosary and the Sign left by My Son. Each day recite the prayers of the Rosary. With the Rosary, pray for the Pope, the bishops and priests."

"The work of the devil will infiltrate even into the Church, in such a way that one will see cardinals opposing cardinals, bishops against bishops. The priests who venerate me will be scorned and opposed by their confreres... churches and altars sacked; the Church will be full of those who accept compromises and the demon will press many priests and consecrated souls to leave the service of the Lord."

Later that day, Cardinal Mark requested a visit with Pope Simon in his office. Whether it was doubt or paranoia, he wanted the reassurance now he was Pope, as to what his intentions were for the church.

Cardinal Mark entered the Papal office.

"Your Holiness," said Cardinal Mark.

Pope Simon said nothing. He stood up, walked around his desk, and hugged Cardinal Mark. It did not matter that he was the leader of over a billion people, he still saw Cardinal Mark as his father.

"I am pleased you came to see me, Cardinal Mark. I would like you to simply call me Simon. Please have a seat, we have much to discuss."

"I was going to leave it for some time before I asked to see you, as I'm aware you must be very busy getting settled in."

"Quite the opposite, Cardinal Mark. I think everyone thinks that and have left me alone. Other than letters and phone calls from well-wishers, it has been a quite day so far. In fact, one of the phone calls I got was from Fr. Nicholas, after leaving Kenrick-Glennon Seminary we have only seen each other briefly on one occasion, but we have always kept in touch."

"Yes, Simon. Since you told me about him, I've actually met him a number of times. I can see why the two of you got on so well together at the Seminary – he reminds me a lot of you. I was very pleased to hear that he is going to be ordained a Bishop; it is about time, his work had gone unnoticed for far too long."

"Indeed, he mentioned that to me on the phone. He will be in Rome at the end of October, so I'm looking forward to seeing him. However, as I said, other than a few calls, its been a quiet first day, not to mention settling in is always easier when one does not have too many possessions.

Cardinal Mark looked around the Papal office. There was the same black and white wedding photo of his parents on his desk and on the wall was a collection of his favourite books. His eyes were instantly drawn to the small children's Bible on the shelf. He walked over and picked it up.

"My First Bible, you have certainly kept this a long time, Simon."

"I can still hear Mom reading it to me. I'm afraid I've had it too long now to part with it."

"Yes, Simon. I can imagine. Actually, this morning I was thinking about it and, of course, the cloth it was wrapped in."

Pope Simon looked at his friend intently and gathered his thoughts. "Cardinal Mark, for many years I have been greatly disturbed by the message on the cloth. As much as I wanted it to be meaningless, it is not. I am in no doubt that there is a connection between it and the events of my life. Unfortunately, understanding it has been beyond me, so my only option is to constantly evaluate my thoughts and actions, to ensure that they reflect the teachings of our Lord."

"We are living in frightening times, Simon. The signs of the End Times are everywhere and so few see them."

Pope Simon looked at Cardinal Mark. His eyes were filled with the concern and the responsibility of his new vocation, but his words were spoken with absolute certainty. "We are fast approaching the end. Satan is becoming very powerful and, until our Lord returns and defeats him, we must remain vigilant. I am in grave danger. I want you to make a solemn promise that if you see any change in me, that you will not hesitate to take my life by whatever means necessary."

Cardinal Mark was in no doubt as to what Simon was asking of him. "Simon, I give you my word."

Five weeks into his papacy, Pope Simon could not wait to meet his old friend from Syria. They had shared so many sad as well as wonderful memories together. When he called to say "hello" and wish him well, he had no hesitation in inviting him to the Vatican. Imam Hasan was indeed a man of God; in a world consumed by religious hatred and war, the two men respected each other greatly.

The meeting at the Vatican was everything Pope Simon had hoped for. The two shared so many common beliefs and saw the good in each other's religions. Imam Hasan agreed that he would speak with other Muslim leaders and, together, they could hold a meeting of all religions and celebrate in the worship of God. For Pope Simon, he promised to contact Jewish and other religious leaders and invite them to take part. Pope Simon walked Imam Hasan to the door and they said goodbye. There was so much that could be done to bring religions together.

Change in the Catholic Church is measured over centuries. However, relatively recent history had shown that, against much opposition, Protestants were indeed invited to the second Vatican Council in 1962. This had gone a long way towards bringing peace between the two faiths. More recently, Pope Francis held the first meeting between the Orthodox and Catholic faiths in over a thousand years. Apart from the desire to promote peace between religions, there were so many reforms that needed to be undertaken within the church. Pope Simon began to contemplate the need for a third Vatican Council. He sat at his desk excited for the years ahead. There were enough good people in the world to help him forge a new way, a way to finally see all people, regardless of their religion, as God's creations. Political wars may unfortunately go on but wars between religions could certainly be ended.

He stared across the room to the shelf with his favourite

books. They were all large volumes except for the small Bible. He opened the drawer of his desk, removed the brown cloth, unfolded it and looked at the ancient writing. Suddenly, it came to him.

I HAVE CHOSEN YOU
THE APOCALYPSE IS WRITTEN IN THE BACK

He realised he had indeed been chosen and that The Apocalypse is written in the back had nothing to do with something written in back of the Bible, or in The Book of Revelations. Written in the back really meant 'written in the spine' – it was written in the spine of the Bible. Pope Simon walked over to the shelf and removed the small well-worn Bible. He sat at his desk, picked up the brass knife he used to open letters and forcefully cut down the spine of the Bible, hidden inside was a parchment scroll, he unfurled it…

Simon, son of John and Martha;

From the beginning I have enjoyed these games, from the fruit on the tree to the silver I used to tempt Judas, and now today I distract them with the flesh. So easily have I blinded these creatures of dust. All fools, my wisdom is beyond them. The wisest could not interpret the message on the cloth.

I will take down as many as I can, before the Nazarene returns. You have done your part in what is my greatest deception of them all. Now your time is drawing short.

I have lied and deceived them. You have escaped me but the multitudes have not been so fortunate. My greatest achievement has been to convince them that I do not exist, but you know I exist. You have always known it and now you will meet me.

Suddenly, there was a knock at the door…

Pope Simon put the scroll down, made the sign of the cross and walked apprehensively towards the large teak doors. He took a deep breath and slowly turned the brass handle. Startled, he took a step backwards. Standing before him was a figure dressed in black. He tried to compose himself, as he focused on his identical twin brother.

"We meet at last, Simon."

The figure holding a black-handled knife pushed by him and entered the office. "My brother, Simon. How I have longed for this day. Your time is indeed drawing short. Soon I will take your place but first allow me to open your eyes."

"Away from me, Satan!"

EPILOGUE

Annamae spent her life obsessed by jealousy towards her twin sister. It was unmistakable that they were sisters but, by any measure, Martha was always the more attractive of the two.

Annamae met John at a dance and she fell in love with him. The two dated for a short time but it was never going to last. No matter how much Annamae loved John, he did not feel the same and the pain of rejection had devastated her. A few weeks later, she saw John speaking to Martha and she was consumed with rage. Within a year, the two were married. It was as much as Annamae could take. Jealousy and anger made her an easy target for Satan. She was willing to do anything to see Martha and John destroyed.

The young doctor in Louisiana did not stand a chance as his role would be crucial. Satan sent one of his most powerful demons, the attacks were relentless and frightening. It did not take long before Dr Brookman gave up the fight.

In a small wooden house, the young woman had just given birth. After fourteen hours in labour she was drifting in and out of consciousness. Dr Brookman and Annamae exchanged looks, their work was not completed. After a short while, they delivered the second child, the one they had all waited for – the one they worshipped. Annamae handed him over to the small gathering of women who stood in the room.

★

"You see Simon, Martha was carefully chosen. Did you think the long lineage of twins in our family ended with Martha and Annamae? You and I are not just identical but we have a telepathic connection. You saw me kill Julia and Linda and mistakenly thought you had somehow done it. They stood in my way – it had to be done."

★

Martha sat in her living room with a coffee, trying to make sense of it all. A couple of birds landing on the window caught her eye, she looked over to the fire place. On the mantle were: pictures of John and herself, taken on their wedding day; a baby picture of Simon; and a picture of her and her sister, taken when they were children down at the lake. Suddenly, it dawned on her. She must have had twins. It ran in her family. The hair at the murder scene was a perfect match, the footprints were the same size but the fingerprints did not match. Simon saw the murders happen. Annamae and Dr Brookman were working together. Suddenly, everything made sense. Simon had to have a twin brother.

Annamae had deceived her the entire time. She left the house to confront her, Annamae tried to deny it, but Martha had figured it all out.

Annamae had no option, she could not allow Martha to leave her house alive – she had to die. Annamae tried to cover her tracks, but she missed the fact that one of the bullets that exited Martha had lodged in her front door. It was the critical piece of evidence that led to her.

Annamae looked out her window and saw the police cars approaching. She knew it was the end. She could not allow herself to be taken down to the police station. Under pressure, the sheriff would have made her reveal everything. She picked up the gun, placed the cold steal of the barrel into her mouth, closed her eyes and pulled the trigger.

★

"Lastly, Sheriff Amos had to die, he was relentless and had no intention of closing Julia's or Linda's cases. His fate was sealed when he drove into the small settlement of houses where I lived. My brother, Simon, the demon that controls the doctor, not only delivered you but also has protected you throughout your life. Indeed, you would have died during your appendix operation, had he not been there. He has ensured that nothing and no one stood in the way of your destiny. However, your time has now come."

Simon looked up and saw the steel blade descending towards his chest.

REFERENCES

1) As well as being at least thirty-five years old and a priest for at least five years, he should be "outstanding and in strong faith, good morals, piety, zeal for souls, wisdom, prudence and human virtues",
Reference: http://canonlawmadeeasy.com/2010/07/15/how-are-priests-selected-to-be-bishops/

2) As I told you, if men do not repent and better themselves, the Father will inflict a terrible punishment on all humanity. It will be a punishment greater than the deluge, such as one has never seen before. Fire will fall from the sky and will wipe out a great part of humanity, the good as well as the bad, sparing neither priests nor faithful. The survivors will find themselves so desolate, that they will envy the dead. The only arms, which will remain for you, will be the Rosary and the Sign left by My Son. Each day recite the prayers of the Rosary. With the Rosary, pray for the Pope, the bishops and priests."
"The work of the devil will infiltrate even into the Church, in such a way that one will see cardinals opposing cardinals, bishops against bishops. The priests who venerate me will be scorned and opposed by their confreres... churches and altars sacked; the Church will be full of those who accept compromises and the demon will press many priests and consecrated souls to leave the service of the Lord."
Reference: http://www.olrl.org/prophecy/akita.shtml